MVFOL

D0973228

Lizette was too stunned to move.

She'd had no idea a kiss could make her wish that he'd pick her up and carry her somewhere, anywhere, where they could be alone....

Overwhelmed by desire, she ran her hands up Finn's back, pressing her body against his. She recalled how he'd saved her from Lindall and those others. How kind he'd been to Keldra and Garreth, and how marvelous he looked....

Someone cleared a throat, and she abruptly remembered where she was, and that she had a part to play, too, as Finn did—and this kiss must be no more than a part of their ruse.

Her embarrassed blush was real enough as she drew back, and when she saw the smug satisfaction in Finn's eyes, so was her annoyance. "My lord husband, please!"

"I'm sure Lord Wimarc will forgive me," he said lightly as he gave their host a grin.

Yet she'd seen something in Finn's eyes before he spoke—surprise, shock, excitement—that told her he wasn't as unaffected by that kiss as he was pretending to be.

MARGARET MOORE

Knave's Honor

HQN™

ISBN-13: 978-0-373-77245-2
ISBN-10:   0-373-77245-9

KNAVE'S HONOR

www.HQNBooks.com

Printed in U.S.A.

Also by

MARGARET MOORE

The Notorious Knight
My Lord's Desire
Hers To Desire
Hers To Command
The Unwilling Bride
Lord of Dunkeathe
Bride of Lochbarr

With many thanks to Karen Solem and Donna Warren for their calm guidance and sage advice.

Knave's Honor

CHAPTER ONE

The Midlands, 1204

"I FEARED I'D GO MAD if I had to sit in that wagon another moment," Lady Elizabeth of Averette declared as she lifted the skirts of her blue woolen traveling gown and delicately picked her way toward the mossy bank of the swift-moving stream.

"Don't you think we ought to stay with the men?" her maidservant asked, anxiously glancing back toward the escort of mail-clad soldiers who had dismounted nearby.

As such men were wont to do, they joked and cursed among themselves while they led their horses to drink or let them eat the plentiful grass by the side of the road. Some of them took out heels of bread from their packs or downed a sip of ale. The leader of the cortege, Iain Mac Kendren, did neither. He stood with feet planted and arms akimbo as if he were a statue, only his turning head giving any hint that he was alive and keeping watch.

"Last night I heard the innkeeper talking about a thief who sets upon travelers hereabouts," Keldra said, breathless with a fearful excitement. "A huge fellow, fierce and terrible!"

Lizette, as she was known to her sisters and the

people of Averette, gave Keldra a sympathetic smile. Keldra was only fifteen, and not used to travel. It was no wonder every tale of every thief, no matter how bizarre or exaggerated, frightened her. "According to a serving wench, he's a very handsome thief. She also says he won't rob a woman if she'll give him a kiss, which sounds like something out of a minstrel's song to me. Whatever this thief may be like, though, we have fifty men to guard us, and Iain Mac Kendren, too, so I'm sure we'll be quite safe."

"I hope so!" Keldra whispered, as if she feared the thief might be listening.

Smiling and very glad to be out of the stuffy confines of the wagon, Lizette removed her silver coronet and silken veil, then crouched down on the bank of the stream. "As long as he takes a kiss instead of my clothes or jewelry, I might even enjoy meeting this thief."

"Oh, my lady, you wouldn't!" Keldra exclaimed, scandalized—which showed how little she really knew her mistress.

Lizette cupped some clear, cold water in her hands and lifted it to her lips before she answered. "Wouldn't you be willing to kiss a handsome rogue?"

"Not if he's an outlaw!"

"I'd rather kiss a handsome outlaw than some courtier who may then assume I want to marry him," Lizette said as she rose.

Men she might—and did—appreciate. She enjoyed their company and the teasing banter of flirtation. She envied them their easy camaraderie, although not as much as she envied them their freedom.

Marriage, however, was something else entirely. Most women might find those bonds a form of security, but after witnessing what passed for marriage between her parents, Elizabeth of Averette did not.

"I don't have any jewels, my lady," Keldra pointed out as she, too, bent down to drink. "He might *make* me kiss him!"

"Being kissed against one's will *is* rather unpleasant," Lizette conceded, as she had cause to know. More than one eager suitor who'd come to Averette seeking a wealthy bride had been swift to try seduction of the lord's youngest, and presumably most innocent, daughter as a means to that end.

"I wouldn't *really* want to meet a thief, of course," she admitted, listening to the birds sing as if they hadn't a care in the world. "It would be frightening."

Like the time that drunken nobleman had cornered her in the chapel and no amount of gentle admonition would persuade him to let her go, until she'd finally promised to meet him later in a more secluded place. Her older sister had gone in her stead, and while Adelaide never revealed precisely what had transpired, Lord Smurton and his entourage had departed the next day at first light without even a farewell to his host.

"Oh, my lady!"

Lizette raised her eyes at the sound of Keldra's cry and found her maid pointing at the middle of the stream—where her new silk veil was floating away on the water.

With a curse, Lizette hiked up her skirts and immediately gave chase along the slippery bank. She didn't dare run because the rocks were too slick, but she had to get her veil. Iain would no doubt say she deserved to lose it if she was so careless and he'd probably never let her out of his sight for the rest of the journey home.

While she tried to keep her eyes on the veil as well as look for a stick with which to retrieve it, a man suddenly appeared on the opposite side of the stream as if he'd materialized out of thin air.

"Have no fear, my lady!" the stranger called out as she came to a startled halt. He unbuckled his sword belt and put it down on a nearby rock. "I mean you no harm."

If he was taking off his sword and was alone, he likely didn't mean any harm. More importantly, he sounded educated and of high rank—a knight, at least, if not a lord or baron.

Whoever he was, he wore a simple leather tunic with no shirt beneath, dark breeches and plain boots. Standing by the stream with the woods behind him, he was like some sort of god of the forest—or maybe that thought only came to her because of his simple clothing and dark, waving hair.

He began to wade across the deep stream and when he reached her veil, he plucked it from the water as easily as another man might pluck a daisy from its stem, then raised the dripping rectangle of cloth like a victor with his spoils.

"Permit me to introduce myself," he said as he approached her, the water splashing up around his shins, his deep, musical voice again assuring her he was no rough rogue. "I'm Sir Oliver de Leslille, of Ireland."

Sir Oliver—a knight indeed. Ireland explained the slight, delightful lilt to his words that made it seem as if he were singing rather than speaking.

He also possessed a high forehead, denoting intelligence, a remarkably fine, straight nose and a chin that was exactly what a man's chin should be, while his full lips curved up in the most incredibly attractive smile.

Something deep inside her seemed to shift, as if a mild earthquake had moved the ground beneath her feet. Or the very quality of the air had changed.

Or as if something that had been slumbering had awakened.

"I was hunting with some friends and got separated from them," Sir Oliver explained as he reached the bank and stood beside her. Water dripped from her bedraggled veil, and she couldn't help noticing that his wet woolen breeches clung to his muscular thighs.

"Since I had a powerful thirst," he said, "I stopped here, and then I heard your, um, cries of dismay. Very colorful, I must say."

Sweet Mother of God, he'd heard her cursing. She wasn't usually easily embarrassed, but right now, she was—so much so, she almost wished the stream would rise up and wash her away. Almost.

She wasn't usually prone to blushing, either, but she was doing that, too, even as she realized she should say something. Give him thanks, at least. Unfortunately, the words would not come—another oddity—and instead she found herself transfixed by the steady, brown-eyed gaze of this handsome stranger who'd waded through the water toward her as if he did this sort of thing every day, and as if that water wasn't ice-cold. "You must be frozen!"

"I've been colder than this plenty o' times before, my lady," he said as he handed her the sopping veil. "It's worth a little chill to be of service to such a lovely woman."

"I—I thank you, sir," she stammered.

What in the name of the saints was wrong with her? She'd never sounded like such a complete ninny.

Unfortunately, she simply couldn't seem to think clearly, to form coherent words or a thought other than that he was the most breathtakingly good-looking man she'd ever met. "I'm very grateful you retrieved this for me. I paid a great deal for it—too much, my sister will say—and I would have been very upset if I'd lost it. It's fortunate you were nearby, although you're a long way from Ireland."

God help her, now she was babbling.

"Aye, my lady, I am," he said, a twinkle of amusement in his brown eyes. "And who might you be?"

Fool! "I'm Lizette." *Simpleton!* "I mean, I'm Lady Elizabeth, of Averette."

The man nodded over her shoulder. "That's your maid, I presume? I trust you have others with you and aren't traveling alone?"

"Yes, no, that is, yes, that's my maid. And of course, I have an escort. Of…" *Sweet savior, how many?* "Fifty men. They're close by."

"I'm glad to hear it. There are thieves lurking hereabouts and you'd be a very tempting morsel," he said with a look in his eyes that made her throat go dry and her heartbeat quicken as it never had before.

"So I've heard. That is, that there are thieves, not that

I…I don't mean to sound vain…or imply…" She gave up and silently cursed herself for a dolt.

Sir Oliver laughed softly. "Modest as well as pretty. That's a potent combination."

Merciful Mary, she might swoon like some giddy girl if he kept looking at her that way and she might say… anything.

If this man had cornered her in the chapel, who could say what she might have done?

"Averette—that's in Kent, isn't it?" he asked.

"It is indeed! Have you ever been there?"

What a stupid question! Surely if he'd visited Averette she would remember him.

"No, I've never been to Kent. I've met your sister at court, though."

A surge of dismay and disappointment tore through her. If he'd been to court, if he'd met Adelaide, he would be comparing them in looks, if nothing else, and nobody could come out ahead of Adelaide if beauty was the measure. The men who sought her hand had all tried for Adelaide first, and been refused.

His smile grew and she supposed that was because he was thinking about Adelaide. "Actually, I asked her to run off with me, but she wouldn't. There was another man, you see, that she liked better."

All Lizette's anger and envy disappeared. He'd probably felt the sting of Adelaide's rejection—and Adelaide could be very stinging.

"How unfortunate for you," she replied as her confidence returned, and she gave him a smile of her own. "Why don't you ask *me* instead?"

It was an outrageous thing to say, yet surely he would laugh and say something clever in return, as courtiers and handsome noblemen were wont to do.

Instead, the joviality left his face, and he said, in a voice soft and low that acted upon her like a bold and intimate caress, "Would you say yes if I did?"

He must be teasing. He couldn't possibly be serious.

Yet her heart throbbed as if it wanted to break free of her ribs. Her lungs seemed to stop functioning. God in heaven, she'd craved excitement and adventure all her life, and here it was, in the flesh. Handsome, seductive flesh.

"My lady!"

She'd completely forgotten about Keldra. And Iain. And everything else in the entire world except Sir Oliver de Leslille of Ireland.

She looked back over her shoulder to see Iain Mac Kendren marching toward them, his sword drawn and a hostile expression on his sun-browned face. Keldra must have gone to fetch him, for she came scurrying along behind him.

Iain, who was forty-five if he was a day, had spent most of the journey from Lord Delapont's castle ignoring her complaints that the rocking motion of the wagon made her queasy. He'd also made it quite clear that he resented being sent to bring her home to Averette, although he couldn't be any more annoyed than she at being summoned home as if she were a child.

In spite of Iain's belligerent bearing, however, Sir Oliver didn't appear the least disturbed, and he once again regarded her with amusement in his dark eyes.

"Who's this, then?" he inquired, quirking a brow. "I hope not an irate father or husband?"

"No!" She cleared her throat and spoke in a more ladylike tone. "No, he's the garrison commander of Averette, the leader of my escort."

She turned to Iain and spoke with what she hoped sounded like authority. "Iain, put up your blade. This is Sir Oliver de Leslille, and he means us no harm."

Iain came to a halt, one hand on his hip as he ran a measuring gaze over Sir Oliver who was, Lizette suddenly recalled, still soaking wet.

Despite Sir Oliver's title, Iain didn't look impressed—but then, it took risking your life in several battles to impress the Scot.

"Good day to you, my lord," he growled with only the slightest hint of courtesy. "Traveling alone, are you? Bit dangerous, isn't it?"

"As I explained to your lady mistress, I'm with a party of friends, hunting," Sir Oliver replied, still genial despite Iain's brusque and even insolent tone. "I got separated from them. However, since the hour grows late, I should seek them out, lest I be benighted in the wood and forced to eat nuts for my dinner."

"We'll be at the Fox and Hound tonight," Lizette offered. "Perhaps you could send word there in the morning as to how you are. I'll be worried you've fallen ill doing me a service."

Sir Oliver cut his eyes to the scowling, wary Iain. "I'm flattered by your concern, but I think not, my lady."

She pursed her lips and silently wished Iain back at Averette.

"As he says, my lady," Iain declared, "the hour grows late and we've dallied here long enough."

Unless she wanted to stand on the bank of the stream and quarrel with Iain, she had to go. Besides, it couldn't be good for Sir Oliver to be standing there in wet breeches and boots.

"Farewell, Sir Oliver," she said with more regret than she'd ever felt bidding farewell to a young man before.

How she wished she and Sir Oliver had met another time, such as in a hall during a feast, where they could talk. He would surely be a very amusing companion. Perhaps they would dance...and touch...and slip off into a shadowed corner to share a kiss....

The nobleman bowed with courtly elegance before addressing Iain. "I commend you for your care of the lady, Mac Kendren, and you need have no fear that I'll come creeping into the inn under cover of darkness. I'm not that sort of nobleman."

Iain merely grunted in reply.

Such an act would be most improper; nevertheless, Lizette found herself subduing a surge of disappointment. To think she might have met one man who could tempt her to make love without benefit of marriage, and he was more honorable than most.

Despite her secret regret, it was an insult to imply that Sir Oliver would try to sneak into a woman's chamber for any reason, and she should acknowledge that. "You must forgive the garrison commander for his lack of courtesy, Sir Oliver. He takes his duties very seriously."

Sir Oliver bestowed another smile upon her. "For your sake, my lady, I'm glad of it. These are dangerous times, and evil men roam the land." He backed away toward the stream. "Now I must say farewell."

Realizing she had no choice, she inclined her head as Iain held out his arm to escort her back to the wagon. "Adieu, Sir Oliver," she said as she laid her hand upon Iain's chain-mail-encased forearm and let him lead her away.

She glanced back over her shoulder, but Sir Oliver de Leslille was already gone. He'd vanished like a true spirit of the forest, or a magician who'd stayed only long enough to cast his spell upon her.

LIZETTE LAY BACK upon the cushions piled in the back of the wagon as it jostled and jolted its way toward home. She would much rather be riding. However, given her illness a fortnight ago—one whose seriousness she had exaggerated when Iain arrived shortly after the wedding of Lord Delapont's daughter, Marian and, in typical Mac Kendren fashion, simply announced that she was going home at once—she had reluctantly acquiesced to his orders, even if, as she'd told him, the motion of the wagon tended to upset her stomach.

There were certain compensations at the moment, as she closed her eyes and her maidservant dozed off across from her. She could dwell on that delightful meeting with Sir Oliver de Leslille.

To be sure, rescuing a veil wasn't as exciting as saving a maiden from a fire-breathing dragon, but it had been exciting nonetheless, and certainly a welcome respite from this tedious journey home.

She didn't doubt Sir Oliver would be quite capable of defeating a dragon, if he had to, or anyone or anything else that came against him. She'd met many knights who'd come to court her eldest sister, and none had possessed such magnificent shoulders, muscular arms or powerful thighs.

Maybe he'd be going back to court soon, a place she had never, ever wanted to go before because the king would be there. She hated John for the taxes he demanded to pay for the wars he fought to regain his lost holdings in France, and because he was her guardian, with the power to force her to marry if he chose to use it.

What if Sir Oliver was already married or betrothed? Maybe that was why he hadn't told her with whom he was staying, or why he wouldn't send word to her at the inn, although Iain's rudeness and suspicions might explain the latter, too.

If he *wasn't* married…

She remembered some of the things the girls and women at the wedding had whispered about. The younger girls had spoken of the thrill of a kiss, the brush of an arm, the sight of a bare chest.

The older women had spoken of other things, especially when they hadn't realized the curious Lizette was nearby— more intimate things that men and women did in the dark, whether they were married or not.

Things that reminded her of the times she'd been in the woods on May Day, or Midsummer's Eve, and heard murmurs and mutterings and soft cries in the dark. Creeping forward to see what those sounds meant…

seeing couples in passionate embraces, doing much more than kissing…

What would it be like to be in Sir Oliver's arms? After all, she was no novice hoping to be a bride of Christ. When she'd vowed never to marry, she hadn't promised to be celibate.

Nevertheless, that didn't mean she was willing to make love with any handsome man who crossed her path. It would be too great a risk, especially if she got with child. Who could say what King John might do if he realized her value in marriage had been so drastically reduced?

Despite the risk, for once, she was sorely tempted, as well as curious to know about the handsome, chivalrous Sir Oliver, who must be visiting some noble or rich commoner who had a manor in this area. Perhaps Dicken, the wagon's driver who'd been to this part of the country before, would know.

Moving from the cushions, she lifted the heavy canvas flap that separated the bed of the wagon from the driver's seat. Dicken's bulk took up most of the seat, but she could still see Iain, back straight, helmet gleaming, riding at the head of the men as if he were the king.

He was also looking at a parchment he held in his right hand.

In all the years of his service at Averette, she'd never, ever known Iain Mac Kendren to receive any kind of letter or message. Indeed, she was rather surprised to discover he could read.

Maybe that was a message come from Averette—but surely he would have said if he'd had word from Gillian. It could be from Adelaide at court, she supposed, but that seemed even more unlikely. Perhaps it was something personal, although it was difficult to imagine what that would be. Iain had no family that she was aware of.

Maybe it was a list of some kind, for arms or armor or men. Surely it wasn't anything very important, or he would have told her, she thought, dismissing her concern. "Dicken?"

The driver snorted out of a doze. "My lady?"

"Do you know what noblemen have estates hereabouts?"

"No, um, no, my lady, can't say as I do. Iain probably does. Want me to call him back here?"

"No, it's all right. I'll ask him when we get to the inn," Lizette replied.

"My lady?"

Lizette glanced back at her maidservant, who was rubbing her sleepy eyes.

"How much longer do you think it'll be until we reach the inn?"

"I don't know," she replied with a sigh, wondering if she would ever see Sir Oliver de Leslille again. "Not much longer, I hope."

She was about to lower the flap when she saw another armed party approaching on the road ahead.

"Who's that?" Dicken mused, echoing her own thoughts.

Perhaps it was Sir Oliver and the rest of his hunting party, she thought eagerly, until she recognized the man at the front of the group. It was most definitely not the handsome, broad-shouldered Sir Oliver. "Why, that's Lindall!"

The short, stocky second-in-command of the garrison of Averette should be there, not riding toward them.

Had something happened at home?

Keldra joined her at the front of the wagon, looking out the narrow gap. "What's *he* doing here?" she asked, as worried as Lizette.

"He's probably been sent to escort us, too," Lizette replied, trying to set the girl at ease and calm her own fears, as well.

But the fear would not be quelled, for she didn't recognize any of the men riding with him. Worse, they didn't look like soldiers of Averette; in their various bits of armor and leather, they looked like a motley collection of outlaws or mercenaries.

"I don't like the looks o' this," Dicken murmured as he reached for the hilt of the dagger he carried in his belt. "Best go back into the wagon, my lady, until we know what's afoot."

Keldra immediately ducked inside and cowered among the cushions.

Lizette lingered longer, driven by curiosity. She watched as Iain drew his horse to a halt. He addressed Lindall, and his helmeted head turned as if he, too, were surveying the band of men.

And then, so quickly she could scarcely believe it, Lindall drew his sword and struck Iain down.

CHAPTER TWO

THE UNPREPARED SCOT fell from his horse and hit the ground with a sickening thud. Blood poured from the gash in the right shoulder of his mail.

Crying out in dismay, Lizette rose, hitting her head on the frame of the wagon's roof. Dicken cursed and slapped the reins hard on the horses' backs. They lurched forward, sending Lizette tumbling backward into the bed of the wagon, where she landed on top of a shrieking Keldra. Around them, men shouted, horses whinnied and neighed, and in the next instant, they heard the clash of sword on sword.

The wagon jolted backward, then forward, as the cursing Dicken tried to control the team. Holding tight to the back of his seat, Lizette struggled to her knees and attempted to see past the big man's shifting body through the flapping canvas opening.

It was as if they were caught in the heart of a melee, or two clashing armies.

Where was Iain? She couldn't see him. Nor could she tell which side was winning.

Then she spotted Iain on the ground. He wasn't moving.

Sweet Savior, Iain—the best soldier in Averette— wasn't moving.

More of their men were on the ground, some bloody. Several more were fighting, swinging their swords from horseback, or engaging their opponents on the ground. Riderless horses ran from the road, the whites of their eyes showing, frantic from the smell of blood. The team harnessed to the wagon jostled one another, unable to escape.

Her sore head throbbing, Lizette pushed the sobbing Keldra away and grabbed a small wooden chest. She threw open the lid and found the dagger buried beneath her undergarments.

Dicken yelped. The wagon tilted precariously to the left like a ship in a stormy sea, then fell back hard on its right wheels as Dicken tumbled backward into the wagon, his large body catching the canvas partition and ripping it from its supports.

An arrow was lodged in his chest. Blood spread out from the wound and his eyes stared, unseeing, at the now-bare frame of the wagon's roof.

Keldra began to wail. Lizette clutched the dagger and tried to think. They had to get away from here. If the men were all preoccupied by battle, if they were concerned with their own lives, she and Keldra might be able to escape.

Inspired by that hope, she grabbed hold of Keldra's arm and pulled her to the rear of the wagon. "We have a chance, but we've got to run!"

Putting the dagger between her teeth to free her hands, she climbed over the back of the wagon. She hit the ground with a bone-jarring thud, then looked up to see Keldra still sitting where she'd left her, her trembling hands covering her face.

Lizette took the knife out of her mouth. "Keldra, come! We have to run!"

"I can't! I can't!"

"Yes, you can! You *must!*"

A man came around the wagon—Lindall, on foot, smiling like the devil himself, evil intent visible on his familiar, homely features.

"Looks like somebody gave my lady a little toy," he sneered as he ran his gaze over her and her knife.

Gripping the dagger tightly, she backed away from him. "What are you doing here? You're supposed to be home, at Averette."

"If I stayed there, what would I get?" he returned, his voice loud enough to be heard above the din of the fighting men nearby. "Some food, a place to sleep, a little money for sport now and then."

He grinned, exposing his ruined teeth, and his eyes gleamed with hate. "I'm a rich man now—or I will be soon. A hundred marks Lord Wimarc's promised me if I bring you to him."

Confusion joined her fear. "Who's Lord Wimarc? What does he want with me?"

"You'll find out soon enough, my lady," Lindall said as he went to grab her.

She sidestepped him and turned, ready to run—until she remembered Keldra, sobbing in the wagon. Keldra, who was but fifteen, and terrified.

She spun on her heel and lunged at Lindall. He raised his shield, easily avoiding her blow, then grabbed her right wrist, twisting until she cried out and dropped her dagger. He kicked it away with his blood-spattered boot.

"Don't try to fight me, my lady," he snarled as he hauled her close, his stinking breath hot on her face. "I've got your men outnumbered, and mine are vicious brutes, trained killers from all over Europe. Your men are doomed and you're mine now—at least until I hand you over to Wimarc. So don't give me no trouble, or you'll regret it."

Her view of the battle was blocked by the wagon; nevertheless, she wouldn't believe his men would defeat hers. Her men had been trained by Iain Mac Kendren. Outnumbered or not, it would make no difference. They would win.

"You're going to be caught and hanged for what you've done," she charged. "If you've harmed Iain—"

"*Harmed* him?" Lindall replied with a coarse laugh. "I've *killed* him."

No! she silently wailed, her knees nearly buckling, as he tugged on her aching wrist.

"You're caught, my lady, and now I'm going to get my money."

Rage rose up, strengthened by her grief. Gritting her teeth, she planted her feet. Whatever Lindall planned to do, wherever he wanted to take her, he would have to drag her.

Curling his lip, keeping hold of her wrist, still gripping his sword with his right hand, he kicked her left leg hard.

"I said, don't give me no trouble. I'll break your leg if I have to."

She nearly fell as he tugged her toward the wagon, but she managed to stay on her feet. She squirmed and struggled and tried to hit him.

"Stay there, Keldra!" she ordered when they reached it.

Inside, Keldra lay curled up in a little whimpering ball of fear. "Whatever he says or does, don't get down!"

Lindall hauled her close. "Shut your gob, you stupid wench—you with that pretty little nose of yours always in the air, laughing while the rest of us have to work and march and drill, shouted at by that damn Scot."

As she continued to struggle, another sort of look came to Lindall's face, one that threatened to send her into a different sort of panic. "Wimarc never said you had to be a virgin. No, he never said nothing about that, so I'll have you, and maybe your maid, too. Maybe the rest of the men should have a taste of you, too, before I get my money."

Truly terrified, Lizette fought even harder, while Keldra began to wail louder.

"Shut up!" Lindall snarled at the poor girl.

Yet in that moment, while his attention was on Keldra, Lizette saw a chance. She put her hands on his armored chest and shoved him backward with all her might. He collided with the edge of the wagon, then fell forward onto his knees.

"Come on!" she called to Keldra—and this time, her maid didn't hesitate. She clambered over the side of the wagon and started to run down the road.

Yanking up her skirts so she wouldn't trip over them, Lizette ran after her. Her cloak flapped out behind her like a pennant in the breeze; her coronet fell off her head, and then her veil, but she didn't care. Unfortunately, her bodice wasn't laced for running and soon she could hardly breathe—but still she didn't stop.

Until a hand grabbed hold of her cloak and jerked her to a halt.

"Oh, no you don't," Lindall barked as he pulled her back. "Think you're going to get away when Lord Wimarc's offered all that money, and I can have my way with you?"

A sob of fear and helplessness broke from Lizette's throat as Keldra kept running, not looking back. Leaving her.

"Let go o' the lady and drop yer sword, boyo, or I'll be runnin' you through and sendin' you straight to hell."

Lizette's breath caught. She knew that voice. Dear God, she knew that voice! Sir Oliver, come like a hero to save her!

With a sound between a sob and a cry of joy, she turned to see Sir Oliver with the point of his sword pressing against Lindall's back as the former second-in-command of Averette raised his arms in surrender.

"Go after your maid, my lady," Sir Oliver said. "Now, before this blackguard's men realize you're getting away."

She nodded once and gathered up her skirts, then hesitated. "And you?"

Sir Oliver gave her a smile that had no mirth or joy in it. "I'll join you soon, my lady."

Pleased, relieved, but far from feeling safe, she did as he told her, and ran.

THE IRISHMAN, who was sometimes known as Sir Oliver de Leslille, waited until Lady Elizabeth was out of sight, then ordered the lout at the end of his sword to go into the woods.

He hadn't planned to interfere. He hadn't even been

following Lady Elizabeth's cortege. Yet he'd been close by and heard the sounds of fighting, and when he'd seen the hard-nosed Scot lying dead on the ground, he'd known there was only one thing to do: find the lady and her maid and keep them safe.

Thank God he'd gotten to them in time...although he might not be such a hero as he wanted to believe. As she'd faced her enemy, her bountiful fair hair disheveled, her clothing rumpled and muddy, Lady Elizabeth had been no meek and terrified victim; he had seen the fierce courage in her eyes and knew she would have fought to the death to protect herself and, even more impressively, her maidservant.

"Hurry up," he commanded the varlet who'd led the attack against the lady's cortege, shoving the tip of his sword against the man's mail-clad back to make his point.

As they entered the shelter of the trees, the lout turned around, wary, but not afraid. "You don't want to kill me. I can get you money—lots of money. Lizette—Lady Elizabeth, the woman you let run off—Lord Wimarc de Werre's offered me a reward if I bring her to his castle."

These men belonged to Wimarc? They were no band of outlaws and thieves, but that man's mercenaries?

Then this attack had been on his orders. But why?

It could be to force a marriage—except that Wimarc already had a wife.

Rape?

To be sure, Lady Elizabeth was lovely and spirited, and he certainly wouldn't put rape past Wimarc, but abducting a ward of the king—which she must be, since her sister Adelaide was—was a far different crime from raping a servant or peasant, or even another nobleman's daughter or wife. Wimarc wouldn't dare do something like that unless he thought he could get away with it, or didn't care if he roused the king's ire. "What does he want with her?"

"Who knows?" the lout retorted as sweat dripped down his wide face. "What have men like us to do with the likes o' them? It's enough to watch out for ourselves, and he's willing to pay if we take her to him."

Giving Lady Elizabeth to Wimarc would get him inside the man's fortress, but getting in was never the problem.

The problem would be rescuing his imprisoned half brother and getting out again.

Besides, he wouldn't use a woman that way. Not any woman, and especially not any relative of Adelaide d'Averette.

But he wasn't about to let this blackguard know that. "If she's so important, maybe he'll pay even more. That's not so large a sum when split between so many."

"Wimarc only offered the reward to me. Those others are Wimarc's mercenaries. I'm not."

The lout licked his dry lips. "And I wouldn't try to haggle with him, not unless I wanted to wind up in his dungeon. Do you know what happens to his prisoners?"

"I've heard." Slow starvation. A little food in the beginning, gradually diminishing to nothing.

Was Ryder still getting something to eat? Or had his time run out?

The lout took a step forward, only to halt abruptly as the Irishman raised the tip of his sword level with the man's eye.

"A fellow's got to look out for himself," the black-guard said, desperation in his voice and sweat dripping from his brow. "Come, man, it's fifty marks he's offered! That's twenty-five marks for you, and all you have to do is help me get hold of a woman."

"You seemed to be having a little trouble with that woman."

"That's because she's a hellion, but the two of us should have no trouble taming her. And Wimarc doesn't care if she's a virgin. Leastways, he never said she had to be, so add that to your payment. Twenty-five marks and a pretty virgin—that ought to be worth my life."

The Irishman lowered his blade.

"I knew you were a smart fellow," the lout said with relief. "Come on. She can't run far. There's her maid, too. We'll have fine sport tonight!"

He went to go past the Irishman, but in the blink of an eye, the Irishman shoved his blade beneath the lout's arm with a thrust so powerful, it went right through his mail.

As the Irishman held the former second-in-command of Averette in a deadly embrace, Lindall's eyes widened with shock. Blood trickled from his lips and he tried, uselessly, to talk.

"Rape holds no appeal for me," the Irishman said. He shoved the sword in farther. "This is for the other women you've raped, the men who died today, and especially the lady."

TRYING TO DRAW IN a deep breath, perspiration pouring down her back and sides, Lizette rounded a bend in the road and saw Keldra hiding—ineffectually—behind a chestnut tree.

The girl let out a cry of relief and ran toward her.

"Oh, my lady," she sobbed as she threw her arms around her mistress, "what are we going to do?"

Lizette gently disengaged herself from the girl's fierce grasp. "We can't stay here," she said. "We have to hide and wait for Sir Oliver."

"Where?"

"The safest place I can find."

"How will he find us if we're hiding?" Keldra wondered aloud as she trotted after Lizette.

"He knows which way we went, and we'll watch for him," Lizette replied.

As she plunged into the shadowy undergrowth, branches and brambles caught her cloak and hair. Fatigue and the stress of all they'd been through began to creep over her. She wanted to cry, too—to weep and wail and mourn for Iain, a good man dead because she had been reluctant to hurry home.

She swiped at her tear-filled eyes. Mourning and re-criminations could wait. Now they had to find a safe hiding place not too far from the road so they could watch for Sir Oliver.

She came upon a thicket of beech saplings around what must have been a boar's wallow. There was no boar using it now, or the muddy bottom and sides would be churned up. And it would smell of such a beast, too. They should be safe here.

She pushed her way through the natural fence, pulling Keldra along behind her, then knelt on the leaf-covered ground and peered through the slender branches, making sure she could see the road and anyone who came along it.

Keldra sat beside her, covered her tear-streaked face with her hands, and wept.

As they waited for what seemed hours, Lizette tried not to let despair and dismay overtake her, even though she was haunted by the memory of Iain's death, and racked with guilt.

If she hadn't been so annoyed at being summoned home like a child, if she hadn't dawdled on the road, or fallen sick and then claimed she was still unwell and so must travel slowly, they would all be safely back at Averette by now.

Perhaps Iain wasn't dead, but only wounded. Lindall might be lying, or he could have been wrong. Maybe if they went back, she would find Iain seriously wounded, but alive.

Yet she didn't dare return to the site of the attack, at least not yet. Not until Sir Oliver arrived and told her it was safe.

Perhaps he would also know what this Lord Wimarc might want with her. All *she* could think of was ransom.

She finally heard something that prompted her to inch forward, moving more branches out of the way. Relief melted her fear as Sir Oliver, scanning the trees, jogged down the road toward their hiding place, his sword in his hand.

He was alone. Where was the rest of his hunting party? Where were her men?

She pushed her way out of the thicket, followed by the weeping Keldra. "Sir Oliver!"

He came to a halt and gestured for them to join him. "Stay with me and be as quiet as you can."

"Where's the rest of your hunting party?"

"I'll take you to them now."

"What about the rest of my men?"

"Dead or dying, my lady."

"That can't be true!" she protested, fear rising again. "Iain's the best soldier in England and the best commander. My men are the best garrison in England. Surely no motley crew of outlaws or mercenaries could defeat them *all*."

"They were outnumbered three to one, and now the blackguards who attacked you are going to be coming after you. We've got to get away from here as quickly as we can."

It seemed her choice was simple: stay and risk capture, or go with Sir Oliver.

Without another word, Lizette put her arm around Keldra to support her, and went with Sir Oliver.

CHAPTER THREE

"THANK YOU for coming to our aid," Lizette panted some time later as she and Keldra continued down the road with Sir Oliver. It had been morning when they'd been attacked; judging by the sun, it was now past noon.

"No matter," he brusquely replied.

No matter to him perhaps, but if he hadn't appeared, if he hadn't stopped Lindall… She tried not to think of what could have happened to her and Keldra then.

Sir Oliver suddenly stopped and held up his hand. At nearly the same time, a youth of about sixteen slithered down a nearby tree, a bow slung over his back and a quiver of arrows hanging at his side. Like Sir Oliver, he wore a leather tunic with no shirt beneath, woolen breeches and boots, and his hair likewise brushed shoulders that were nearly as broad as the Irish nobleman's.

He must be one of the hunting party, a servant probably, although she had no idea why he'd be up in a tree.

"Ah, Garreth, here you are," Sir Oliver said as the young man walked toward them, his questioning gaze sweeping over them before coming to rest on Sir Oliver.

"Lady Elizabeth, this is Garreth," Sir Oliver said. "Garreth, this is Lady Elizabeth and her maidservant."

"Keldra," Lizette supplied as the young man regarded them with furrowed brow and wary eyes.

"I got separated from the rest of our party," Sir Oliver explained. "I assume you did, too, and were up there searching for me, or one of the others. I have no idea where the rest of the hunting party's got to, but thankfully I was able to come to this lady's aid when her cortege was attacked, although I couldn't do much more."

Nodding, Garreth tugged his forelock. "A pleasure, my lady," he replied, in an accent quite different from Sir Oliver's. If she had to guess, she'd say he was from London, not Ireland. "And as you say, my lord, I was looking for the others. No sign of 'em, I'm afraid. That gamekeeper's going to have some explaining to do— and that dog boy, too," he added with righteous indignation. "Telling me to go north and then disappearin' with the dogs. I'd like to get my hands on him, I would, and teach him a thing or two about—"

"In good time," Sir Oliver interrupted. "For now, we'd best get this lady and her maid to safety, to the convent."

"The convent?" the young man repeated, although he wasn't nearly as surprised as Lizette.

"Will your host not give us sanctuary?" Lizette asked.

"The convent would be better," Sir Oliver said shortly, with no more explanation. "Now come."

Lizette made no move to follow. Perhaps she'd been a fool to trust this nobleman after all. What did she really know about him except what he himself had told her?

She began to back away. "Where are you taking us?"

"To safety," Sir Oliver impatiently answered.

"Not Wimarc?"

"Wimarc?" Garreth cried as if her suggestion wasn't just ludicrous, but sinful.

"Apparently he's offering a reward for this lady, but he's not going to get her," Sir Oliver replied.

Get her? He made her sound like a bone two dogs were fighting over.

This was not good. Not good at all.

Taking hold of Keldra's trembling arm, she moved back more, ready to run again even if they died of exhaustion.

Sir Oliver realized what she was doing and frowned with frustration. "I'm not going to hurt you and I'm not taking you to Wimarc. I give you my word that I'll not give you, or any woman, into his keeping, whether there's a reward or not."

That promise didn't assuage her dread. "I don't know you. I've never met you before, never heard your name. How can I be sure your word's worth anything?"

His handsome features hardened to a stony mask. "Unless you want to be taken by Wimarc's men, my lady, I don't think you have much choice except to trust me."

Garreth nodded as he plucked the string of his bow against his chest. "You can trust him, my lady. Finn never hurts women."

Finn?

"Nor robs them, either, if they give him a kiss."

God help them! "You're the thief!" she gasped while Keldra moaned softly.

The thief apparently named Finn both scowled and—surprisingly—*blushed* as he darted an annoyed glance at his young confederate. "As I said, I don't hurt women, so I'm not going to hurt you, or take you to Wimarc, who does. He's a bad, wicked man and whatever he wants with you, it can't be anything good. There's a convent a few miles from here. I'll take you there and you can write to your sisters and tell them what's happened."

"How do you know my family?" she demanded warily.

"He's been to court," Garreth supplied, as if insulted by her question. "He's even met the king."

She had believed this thief an Irish nobleman; perhaps he'd been able to fool the courtiers, too, as impossible as it seemed—but that didn't mean she and Keldra were safe.

Not even when a sparkle of amusement appeared in the Irishman's eyes. "Your sister wears a gold-and-emerald crucifix that was your mother's."

Merciful heavens—that was true.

"And because I *have* met her and she's a good woman, I'll do my best to keep you safe."

He reached into his belt and drew out her dagger, presenting it to her by the handle. "Here. If I wanted to do you harm, I wouldn't give you this, would I?"

She grabbed it, gripping it tightly. "This doesn't mean much. You're stronger than I am and could probably get this away from me in a moment."

"Aye, I probably could," he conceded, "but if I wanted to rape you, my lady, I'd have done it by now, and if I was going to hand you over to Wimarc, I wouldn't have let you run away from his mercenaries. Now, unless you want to meet up with some of Wimarc's men who *will* take you to him, I suggest we get moving."

He was a liar, a thief, an outlaw—and yet he expected her to trust him?

Right now, what other choice did she have, except to try to get back to Averette on her own, on foot, with the distraught Keldra and without a coin to her name?

And she did have the dagger if he tried to touch her. "Very well," she said at last. "Take us to the convent—but I'm a ward of the king, so if you think to—"

"I assure you, my lady, you'll be perfectly safe with me. I'd sooner touch an adder than a ward of the king's. Or Lady Adelaide's sister."

IAIN MAC KENDREN groaned softly. Pain racked his body. His head throbbed as if he'd been drunk for a week. His back was sore, and his chest ached with every breath.

He was dying. Dying, here in a ditch. In the darkness. In the cold. He'd let that bastard Lindall kill him.

Where was Lizette—merry, frustrating, aggravating Lizette? Was she alive, or dead? Had she died quickly, or was she still alive and suffering?

He was still alive, at least for now, and while he lived, he was the garrison commander of Averette, charged with keeping Lizette safe. As long as he had breath in his body, there was a chance…a hope…he could do his duty.

Iain moved his fingers, then his feet and legs.

His back wasn't broken. He tried to move his right arm and blinding pain nearly rendered him unconscious again. He remembered the blow from Lindall's sword and the man's grunt as he made it. Lindall had cut deep. It was a wonder or a miracle that he hadn't bled to death already.

A wonder or a miracle. Maybe God wasn't ready for him to die.

Iain licked his dry, chapped lips. He was so thirsty.

With a groan, he rolled onto his side. There was a trickle of muddy water in the bottom of the ditch. He tried to cup it with his right hand, but the pain was too much, and the effort useless. He tried with his left and succeeded, greedily slurping the gritty water that tasted of his leather glove, and blood.

He struggled to his feet and looked around. His men lay dead nearby, some killed in the fight, others who'd been wounded had obviously had their throats slit later. He could see the signs of looting, the thievery of cowards.

His right arm useless at his side, he reached for his own throat with his left. His ventail was still closed. Either they'd not taken the time to finish him off, or they'd thought him already dead.

A horse, he thought vaguely as his eyesight blurred and he started to sway. He needed a horse.

"God help me, a horse," he whispered hoarsely. "God, please, a horse."

ELSEWHERE IN THE DARKNESS, two fires burned in the shelter of a small, tree-encircled clearing. The Irishman and his companion were seated at one, Lady Elizabeth and her maid lay by the other, sleeping, or trying to, Finn supposed. No doubt the lady wasn't used to sleeping on the ground.

His sword lay across his knees and his dagger was within easy reach in his belt. He was tired, but not about to sleep, not with that scum of Wimarc's after them. And with Lady Elizabeth's vibrant presence to distract him.

"Is there any more bread?" Garreth asked, shifting to

a cross-legged position after swallowing the last of the loaf of coarse brown bread they'd bought in the last town they'd passed through.

Finn shoved another stick into the fire before answering. They'd been careful to use only dry wood to ensure there was as little smoke as possible. He would have preferred not to have any fire at all, but the women would be too cold and Garreth liable to spend most of the night complaining without one.

Unfortunately, it seemed the day's events had not wearied Garreth at all, but only served to energize him. The youth showed no signs of wanting to lie down and rest any time soon, and he was a bottomless pit for food. Too bad for him, most of their meagre provisions had been given to the women. "No, it's all gone."

Garreth shrugged and scratched and then nodded at the other fire. "So, that's a lady."

"Aye, that's a lady," Finn replied, careful not to so much as glance at the women.

It had been difficult to ignore them as they'd prepared to sleep on the rough beds he and Garreth had made of branches and leaves, with only their cloaks for coverings. Even in a stained and wrinkled gown, its hem inches deep in mud, with her hair a tangled, riotous mess that she'd tried to comb with her fingers, he'd found himself fascinated by the lady as she moved with brisk, yet graceful, movements, and never once complained.

"Are all the ladies at court like her?"

"She's not like any noblewoman I've ever met," Finn truthfully replied.

Lady Elizabeth wasn't even like her sister. Lady Adelaide was cool and dignified, aloof, like an angel sent down from heaven to be admired by mere mortals below.

Lady Elizabeth was something else entirely—spirited and fiery and defiant. Even from the first, her flustered, honest manner by the bank of that stream had been very different from the attitude of the haughty ladies of the court. Later she'd gotten an intriguing spark of mischief in her eyes.

Even so, he could just imagine the look on her face if he'd told her who he really was and what he'd really been thinking by the banks of that stream. *My name is Fingal, my mother was a whore, I've been a thief since I was five years old, and I'm thinking it'd surely be a grand thing to lie you down right here in the grass and make love with you, my lady.*

Despite the impossibility, his mind persisted in imagining taking that lithe, shapely body in his arms and capturing those full lips with his own, kissing her until she was breathless while his hand moved slowly along the curve of her hip, her waist, her full, rounded breasts....

He mentally gave his head a shake.

"So what's she doing traveling about the countryside?" Garreth asked. "If she's a ward of the king, shouldn't she be with the court?"

"I suspect she was on her way home to Kent when they were attacked. The king and his court are at Salisbury, and that's the other way."

"Maybe her family will give us a reward for helping her," Garreth suggested.

"Maybe they will," Finn agreed, although he wasn't

planning to find out. He didn't want to see Lady Adelaide, or her husband, again. "We've no time to go to Kent and find out. If we don't get Ryder out of Wimarc's dungeon soon, he'll be dead."

Slowly starved to death, like all Wimarc's prisoners.

Garreth tossed another stick into the fire, sending up a small shower of sparks. "So we're really taking them to St. Mary's-in-the-Meadow?"

"Aye." He caught the look of displeasure in his companion's eyes. "We can't leave them to get there on their own."

"Her maidservant looks at me as if I smell bad."

"She's afraid."

"Why? We helped them, didn't we? Lady Elizabeth doesn't look at us that way, and she was frightened, too."

"I daresay she was," Finn replied, "but she's older, and I think she's learned to hide her feelings. Keldra's only a girl and a servant. She can't count on her rank to protect her, the way a lady can."

Unfortunately, from what he knew about Wimarc, rank wouldn't necessarily protect Lady Elizabeth, either.

"Why do you suppose Wimarc sent his men for her?"

"Politics. She's allied by marriage to men loyal to the king, and Wimarc is not. He probably hopes to use her against them." He slid Garreth a glance. "Sometimes being a noblewoman has its shortcomings."

"All right, so we've got to take them to the convent—but I hope that stupid girl doesn't keep sniveling tomorrow. It's enough to set my teeth on edge."

"She's not stupid, she's frightened," Finn explained again. "And you should rest. We've a long way to walk

tomorrow, and the sooner we can get to the convent, the
sooner we can go back and get Ryder."

Garreth nodded and after a moment's hesitation, he
quietly asked, "You think he's still alive then?"

"I have to," Finn replied as he reached for another stick.

Or it would be his fault his half brother was dead.

THE NEXT MORNING, Lizette put her hands on the small
of her back and arched to relieve the ache as she followed the silent Irishman along the narrow path that had
probably been made by deer or some other creature
through the wood of alder, beech, oak and chestnut.
Finn had a leather pouch containing food and a few
meagre articles of clothes slung over his back, and he
seemed to have a knack for finding such paths.

Garreth was just as quiet and, mercifully, Keldra
wasn't crying as they both struggled to keep up with the
Irishman's brisk pace.

Was he really taking them to a convent? They could
be anywhere as they marched through trees and the
small valleys made by streams and brooks.

How could she trust this man? How could she have
any faith in anything he said, or be sure he would help
them? He was a thief, outside the law, perhaps even a
murderer…yet he'd been true to his word and not
touched her, or Keldra. She'd even been able to sleep a
little, dozing off, then waking with a start to find him
still sitting by the fire.

Most of the time he'd been motionless, as still as a
stone, but every so often he'd lean forward to add more
wood or stir the ashes. Then the flames would flare up,

and she could see his handsome visage as he stared into the fire as if trying to foretell the future. Or maybe he'd merely been trying to stay awake.

At dawn he'd risen and told her they had to start moving, and so they had, with the thief in front and the youth behind.

Now, her feet felt as heavy as millstones, and her stomach growled with hunger. Every impulse urged her to ask the Irishman to stop and let them rest and eat whatever he had in that leather pouch he carried. But her pride was stronger than both her fatigue and her hunger, so instead, she quickened her pace until she was near enough to talk to him.

Since she didn't want to anger him, she started with something relatively unimportant. "Is Garreth your son?"

The Irishman checked his steps. "Jaysus, no."

He started forward again, pushing a low branch out of their way, and slid her an aggrieved look. "I'm not that old."

"I thought perhaps he was because he so obviously admires you," she replied, worried she'd offended him as she likewise moved the branch back, not above a little flattery if it would encourage him to talk.

"If he admires me, it's because I treat him decently. Garreth was born in the gutter, my lady, same as me, so being treated with respect's a rare thing."

Could this Irishman who passed for a nobleman really be of such humble origin? "Are you truly of low birth? You sounded exactly like a courtier."

"Because I took the time and trouble to learn."

"Why?" she blurted, her curiosity overcoming her desire to be subtle.

"Why else but to make thieving easier? If you can talk like a noble, you can get yourself invited into a hall or manor with no trouble at all."

She realized she'd been hoping he wasn't really an outlaw—a hope now dashed.

He laughed with sarcastic mockery. "Ruined your little fantasy, have I? Want to think me some bold, brave fellow who's only fallen on hard times temporarily? Well, I'm not. I've been thieving since boyhood, because it was that, or die of cold or starvation."

His expression changed to one of aggravating condescension. "I don't expect you'd know much about suffering."

"Perhaps not in the way you mean," she replied, her temper flaring, "but it wasn't easy living with a father who drank too much, cursed you for being born a girl and sometimes used his fists when he was angry, which he often was."

The Irishman's brown eyes darted to her face. "On you?"

"No, not me. My poor mother and sometimes Adelaide when she tried to protect us. But we could never be sure he wouldn't hit us, too, Gillian and me. I was always afraid when my father was at home. I confess I was relieved when he died last year, even though that means the king now has the right to decide my fate. At least John doesn't live at Averette."

"I was glad when my mother died, too," he quietly

replied. "She made my life a living hell during her last years."

Surprised by that revelation, Lizette wasn't as careful as she should have been and tripped over her muddy hem. He immediately reached out to steady her. Taken aback, she tried to ignore his touch, and the strength apparent even in that simple act, and pulled away the moment she was steady on her feet.

"I didn't have any motive other than to keep you from falling flat on your face," the Irishman coolly observed, "so I hope you're not thinking of killing me for daring to touch you."

Was he trying to be funny? "Not now," she tartly replied. "Garreth called you Finn yesterday. Is that your real name?"

The man's frown deepened as he stepped over a rock that she had to walk around. "Aye. It's short for Fingal."

"So you're really from Ireland?"

"My mother was."

The mother who had made his life a hell. "Did *she* teach you to speak like a courtier?"

"God, no—and that's all you need to know about me or my mother, my lady."

There could be no mistaking the finality of his tone.

"Tell me about this Lord Wimarc," she said, starting to pant as the path went uphill. "I've never even heard his name."

The way was muddy and slick, the ground damp and covered with dead leaves, and she had to keep her eyes on the ground so she wouldn't fall. Behind her, she could hear Keldra likewise struggling to stay on her feet.

"Garreth, give the girl a hand," Finn ordered as he looked back. He was finally starting to sound a bit winded, too.

"Wimarc's rich, he's recently wed the daughter of a minor but wealthy earl, he hates the king and he's an evil brute."

Merciful Mary! "Is that all?"

Finn reached the top of the rise and, holding on to a slender branch, put out his hand to help her. "He's dangerous and you don't want to get anywhere near him."

"Have you any idea why he'd want to abduct me?" she asked as she clasped his offered hand and let him pull her forward, his grip sure and strong and warm.

Keldra, huffing and puffing, reached the top of the hill, an obviously disgusted Garreth supporting her, and Finn let go of Lizette.

"It could be because of your older sister's husband," the Irishman proposed as he started walking again.

She gasped with surprise, then ran after him and grabbed his arm to make him stop. "Adelaide isn't married!"

He regarded her with obvious confusion as he folded his arms over his broad chest. "Yes, she is. She recently married Lord Armand de Boisbaston."

It couldn't be true. It couldn't be. "That's a lie!"

The Irishman's well-cut lips turned down for a moment, then he shrugged and started walking again. "If it's a lie, it was told to me as truth—and that marriage would give Wimarc a reason to want you in his power. The man loathes John and rumor has it there's a conspiracy afoot against the king. Armand de Boisbaston's the sort of loyal idiot who'll protect John because of his oath of fealty and his faith in the Earl of Pembroke, no matter what he might think of the king himself. If Wimarc thinks Armand's in his way, how better to get at him than through his family? If your sister's his wife, that makes you family. Could be Wimarc plans to hold you hostage to force de Boisbaston to do what he wants."

"But my sister *can't* be married to this Lord Armand de Boisbaston!" Lizette persisted as she hurried after him.

Adelaide would surely sooner lose a limb than break her word. To be sure, she hadn't actually seen Adelaide in months, not since Adelaide had gone to court after their father's death, and she had gone to stay first with Sir Merton's family and then to Lord Delapont's estate. But surely her sister couldn't have changed that much—and after all, their solemn promise had been Adelaide's idea.

Even if the impossible had happened and it was true… "She would have told me in her letter, or had Iain tell me when he came to fetch me home."

"Unless she was waiting to tell you in person," he suggested, sliding her an enigmatic glance.

No, she wouldn't believe it. She couldn't. Adelaide had been too certain, too adamant, that marriage would only bring pain and heartache. This man must be lying, or misinformed.

They came upon the massive trunk of a downed oak. "We'll rest here awhile," he said.

Still stunned and suspicious, Lizette sat heavily, while Keldra sank down upon the trunk and sighed with relief.

"If what you say is true, as ludicrous as it seems, and

Adelaide *is* married," she said, "and there's a conspiracy against the king led by this Wimarc, my sisters could be in grave danger."

"They may be," he agreed. "From all I've heard—and I've heard a lot this past fortnight—Wimarc is a very cunning, dangerous and ambitious man. He may stop at nothing to gain his ends, and if he thinks your family might be a hindrance—"

Suddenly terrified for her sisters, Lizette jumped to her feet. "Then we have to send word to Adelaide at court and Gillian at Averette immediately!"

"You can do that from the convent," the Irishman replied with aggravating calm. "I'm going to go back a bit and make sure we aren't being followed. Your men may all be dead, but Wimarc's aren't. Garreth, give them what we have left to eat, and have something yourself."

With that, he turned and headed back down the path.

CHAPTER FOUR

LIZETTE WATCHED the Irishman disappear through the trees. Could Adelaide really be married? Why would he lie if she wasn't?

As she tried to convince herself that he must be mistaken if he wasn't lying, Garreth rummaged in the pouch. With the flare of a magician producing a bag of gold coins, he brought forth an apple that looked rather the worse for having been battered about in the pouch.

"It's not as fine as you're used to, I'm sure, my lady," he said, offering it to her with a sheepish grin, "but apples are all we've got."

"I'm sure it'll be delicious," she replied, giving it to Keldra.

"You have it, my lady," she demurred. "I'm not hungry."

"I'm ordering you to eat it," Lizette said. "You need to regain your strength."

"That was the best one," Garreth muttered as Keldra reluctantly took it. "I meant it for you."

"I'll gladly take the second-best one."

Although still obviously displeased, the young man dived back into the pouch and this time, he produced a smaller apple. He polished it on his sleeve, which didn't look overly clean, before handing it to her with a shrug.

"Thank you, Garreth," she said, hoping to assuage his wounded feelings with a warm smile. Ignoring her qualms about the dirty sleeve, she bit into it.

It was indeed not as fine a fruit as she was used to; however, she was very hungry and they needed to keep up their strength. They had to get to that convent as quickly as possible.

Looking slightly mollified, Garreth brought forth another apple, slightly smaller than hers. He removed his bow from his back, settled himself on the ground at Lizette's feet and started to eat, gobbling it up as if he hadn't eaten for days.

Perhaps he hadn't, or didn't get many good meals, which was often the lot of peasants and poor folk, she knew. Iain and Gillian would believe she did not, or that she chose to ignore such unpleasant facts of life. Yet if she rarely mentioned such things, it wasn't from ignorance or because she thought them unimportant. She didn't speak of them because such things always made her feel helpless, and guilty.

"Have you been…traveling with Sir Oliver…Finn… a long time?" she asked, trying not to think of Iain, or home.

"Since last Christmastide," Garreth replied.

That took her aback. "I assumed you'd known him for years!"

Still chewing his apple, Garreth said, "He saved my life. This candle maker thought I'd stolen from him and he came up behind me and hit me with one of his molds.

Finn saw and grabbed the man's arm before he could hit me again. I'd be deader than that tree you're sitting on if it weren't for him. The candle maker threatened to call the reeve, and Finn told him to go ahead, but he'd be sorry. It wasn't exactly a threat, my lady, but the candle maker let go quick enough."

Tossing away her apple core, Lizette wiped her fingers on a part of her cloak that wasn't spattered with mud or bits of leaves from pushing through bushes. "No wonder you admire him."

"Lots of people do—although he's not as good with a bow as me."

Keldra sniffed scornfully.

"What, you don't think I'm good?" Garreth demanded, rising. He grabbed his bow and drew an arrow from the quiver at his side. "Pick a target, my lady."

She saw no reason to stop him from proving his mettle. "How about that rowan branch there?"

"Too close and too easy."

He was certainly a confident young man. "Then that low branch on the chestnut there," she said, pointing at a branch about twenty yards away.

Garreth took his stance, nocked his arrow, drew his bow, took aim and let fly. The arrow zipped through the air and struck the branch, making them both quiver.

Lizette was impressed, and said so, after Garreth had trotted to the tree and retrieved the arrow.

Garreth gave Keldra a smug glance while he loosened the string again. Her maidservant ignored him, apparently more absorbed in picking bits of greenery off the skirt of her gown than watching Garreth show off his skill.

"I thought perhaps you were Finn's son," Lizette said as Garreth plopped down again.

"I wish to God I was."

"Does he have any family living? His mother? A father?"

"His mother's dead. He doesn't like to talk about her, and he's never mentioned a father. He's got a half brother, though, named Ryder." Garreth frowned and shook his head. "I don't think I should tell you about Ryder. Finn probably wouldn't like it."

The man himself was a thief; how much more shame could his half brother bring to the family? But she didn't think prying on that subject would yield any answers from Garreth—at least not at present.

"Finn's certainly a clever fellow. He can sound just like a nobleman," she remarked instead, noting that Keldra had found a place to lean back against a branch. Her eyes were closed, and her mouth gaped a little. If she could sleep, that would do her good.

"He fooled all the nobles at court the same way he fooled you," Garreth replied, clearly not caring if he woke Keldra up or not. "He said they're thieves and beggars, too, only dress better and ask for more. The king's the worst of them for lying and cheating, Finn says."

She couldn't disagree. "What do *you* suppose Lord Wimarc wants with me?"

Garreth flushed and looked away. "Well, my lady, you're pretty and Lord Wimarc likes pretty women."

If she were not a lady, she might give that explanation more credence. As it was, she doubted ravishment would be his goal and worth so much effort. "I'm also a ward of the king, so surely Wimarc wouldn't dare to assault me."

"If you say so, my lady," the young man replied with a shrug—and skeptical expression. "But that's not what we've heard."

And this man was after her? God help her, and her sisters, too.

Too agitated to sit, wondering where Finn was and why he hadn't returned, she jumped to her feet.

The sudden motion of the tree trunk woke Keldra, who looked about her with confusion until she remembered.

"You don't need to worry about Finn, my lady," Garreth said, again ignoring Keldra. "Wimarc's men won't catch him. He's like an eel in water if he's chased. The only time he came close... But I shouldn't talk about that, either, I suppose."

Why not? Why shouldn't she know more about the man who claimed to want to see her safely to some alleged convent? "He got away, I assume. By himself, or did you help him?"

Garreth shot a proud glance at Keldra. "Aye, I helped him. I shot him."

"You *shot* him?" Lizette repeated incredulously.

"Put an arrow in his foot, or he would have run after Wimarc's men and got caught himself instead of just Ryder."

Garreth plucked his bowstring like a minstrel about to start playing a tune. "Don't tell him I told you about that, eh, my lady? I don't think he'd like it, and you don't want to see him in a temper."

No, she didn't believe she would. "I won't."

He glared at Keldra. "Nor you, neither."

"I don't want to talk to him, and I certainly don't care to repeat anything *you* might say!" Keldra retorted.

Wanting to lessen the tension between them, Lizette turned the subject to Garreth himself. "What about you, Garreth? Where are you from?"

The young man shrugged his shoulders. "I don't know where exactly I was born. London, I suppose. The first thing I remember is running through the streets with a hot loaf of bread and being chased and called a thief."

His jaw clenched as he regarded her. "No need to pity me, my lady. I wasn't the only lad living rough in the alleys. We was like a family, most of the time. And we had some jolly times."

With youthful bravado, he proceeded to regale her with a few adventures, clearly proud of the narrow escapes and illegal adventures that, Lizette knew, could have ended with his death at the end of a rope. But there were a few other stories, too, of camaraderie and friendship and loyalty that made it easy to see why Finn would take him under his wing and consider him a trustworthy friend and ally, despite his lack of years.

Even Keldra's expression held a dollop of admiration by the time he came to his rescue by Finn. "And I've already told you about that," he finished.

"I hope you're not talking the lady's ear off."

Lizette nearly jumped out of her skin.

Finn had come up right behind her. Blushing, although she'd done nothing wrong, she got to her feet and smoothed down her skirts to give herself a moment to regain her composure.

"I trust you've eaten and rested enough," he said, starting down the path. "Even if you haven't, we can't stay here any longer. Wimarc's men aren't close yet, but they've got horses and we don't."

Garreth grabbed the pouch and hurried after him, leaving the women to follow.

"I didn't tell them anything important," he said as he reached Finn.

"I didn't think you did," the Irishman replied. "But be careful of beautiful women, Garreth. They can weave a spell around a man and make him tell all his secrets."

As he had recent cause to know.

LADY JANE DE SHEDDLESBY knelt in front of her mother's memorial plaque in the small church. It was an expensive thing, finely carved, the name and dates deeply etched, just as her mother had directed before her death.

"I want it to be legible forever!" she'd decreed, as if that would somehow ensure she would live on in people's memories.

She would anyway, at least in her daughter's, although perhaps not in quite the way she'd hoped. Lady Ethel de Sheddlesby had not been a font of gentle kindness to her daughter, or anyone else, during her long life.

In spite of that, however, her death had left a void in Lady Jane's existence. She had her small household to oversee, of course, and since it was unlikely she would ever marry, given her age and lack of beauty, she must find her joy in that. Or become a nun, and that she didn't want to do.

No, she would maintain the estate until she died and

it passed to a distant male relative, and she would go to the church to pray for her mother's immortal soul, although she rather expected her mother was not in heaven and never would be, no matter how many prayers and masses were said in her behalf.

Still, the building, made of stones that came pale from the earth, then turned to a warm brown, was not an uncomfortable place to spend some time, and the lingering scent of incense and damp wood and stone was a comfort in its own way.

"My lady! My lady!"

At her maidservant's panicked cry, Jane glanced at the double doors, where Hortensa pointed a shaking finger into the yard. "There's a…a man!"

Despite her maid's agitation, Jane saw no need to be frightened or rush to the door. Hortensa was prone to hysterics, so this man could be a peasant, a tinker, a soldier or even a priest passing by. Instead she rose, made the sign of the cross and then, wrapping her cloak more tightly about her, started toward the door.

"I think…I think he's *dead,* my lady!" Hortensa cried with ghoulish relish.

That made Jane quicken her steps. When she reached the door, she peered into the churchyard.

There was indeed a man lying prone among the gravestones. He wore chain mail and a surcoat, and his arms were at his side as if he'd been crawling toward the church when he'd collapsed on the ground. He had no sword in his scabbard, or helmet on his head, and his gray-and-black hair looked damp, no doubt from the dew. He'd probably been there at least a portion of the night.

Most disturbing of all was the dried blood on his surcoat. He'd obviously been attacked—but by whom and how had he come there? Was he alive, or dead?

Jane opened the door wider, intending to go to him, until Hortensa stuck her arm across the opening to bar her way. "If he's alive, he might be dangerous!"

"If he's alive, he's unconscious," Jane replied, certain of that if nothing else. "Look at his surcoat—that's no thief or outlaw's."

"He could be one of them mercenaries riding about the countryside! Terrible men they are, robbing and raping and God knows what else!"

There was a chance Hortensa was right, yet Jane didn't think she was. "I've seen the sort of mercenaries Lord Wimarc commands, and they don't dress like that."

"That fellow could have robbed a knight. I wouldn't put nothing past those blackguards Lord Wimarc hires."

Hortensa was right about that, too, and yet…"I can't leave a man in such a state," Jane declared as she pushed away Hortensa's none-too-slender arm. "He might die before our very eyes."

"What if he's a thievin', rapin' murderer?" Hortensa protested as she reluctantly followed her mistress, trotting to keep up with Jane's brisk pace. "What would your poor sainted mother say?"

Her mother had never been *poor*, and she would never be a saint. "Probably exactly what you're saying."

Despite what Hortensa might want to believe, her mother's postmortem censure had no power to influence Jane. She'd lived too long under her mother's thumb while she was alive not to enjoy her freedom now that she was dead.

Jane knelt beside the man and gingerly parted the torn surcoat of thick black wool where a blade had cut through both surcoat and mail into the right shoulder; the mail, cloth and flesh beneath were now crusted with dried blood.

How long had it been since he'd been wounded? How had he managed to live despite that grave injury? He must have lost a quantity of blood.

He groaned.

Startled, she sat back swiftly.

"Careful, my lady!" Hortensa unnecessarily warned.

Jane looked up at her anxiously hovering maid. "He's too seriously injured to do us any harm," she said before she gently rolled the stranger onto his back.

He moaned piteously and his arms flopped as if they had no muscles. More blood trickled from his full lips and matted his grizzled beard and hair. His nose arched like one of the Roman emperors whose busts she'd seen in London, and his skin was brown from hours in the sun. A soldier, surely, and perhaps a knight.

"Sir?" she ventured as she looked for more wounds. She couldn't see any more, thank God. "Sir?"

When he didn't answer or open his eyes, she laid a hand on his forehead.

"God's wounds, he's burning. Hortensa, run back to the manor and fetch two men with a wagon. We've got to get him home and in a bed. Then go for Brother Wilbur. This man's wounds and fever are too severe for my skills."

"But my lady, we don't know nothing about him—who he is nor how he come here. Your mother would never do such a thing."

Jane pressed her lips together. No, her selfish, querulous mother would never bring a wounded stranger into her household—but she was not her mother.

"My mother is dead," she said firmly, "and I'm chatelaine of Sheddlesby, so if I order you to fetch my men to take this poor Samaritan back to my hall, you will do it."

"Yes, my lady," Hortensa replied, suitably chastised by Jane's forceful words.

As Hortensa ran off toward Sheddlesby, Jane took the stranger's callused hand in hers.

"You're going to be all right," she softly vowed. "I'll take care of you, whoever you may be."

CHAPTER FIVE

NORMALLY, LIZETTE enjoyed being in the cool, quiet
woods. Many a time she'd fled to the forest outside
Averette to get away from the conflict in the household:
her tyrannical father raging at her poor, sick mother;
Adelaide doing her best to come between them and
make peace; in more recent years, Adelaide's unwanted
suitors, who could be amusing or interesting, but just as
often a lascivious nuisance; Gillian gravely looking on
or going to the kitchen to be with the servants, endear-
ing herself to them with her quiet, competent ways.

Alone in the forest, Lizette could pretend to live the
exciting adventures she craved. Sometimes she was a
poacher sneaking up on a mighty stag; sometimes she
was a 'Gyptian girl, telling fortunes or dancing for
money. Other times, she was a bold knight tilting at trees
with a long stick, guiding her imaginary trusty steed. Or
else she was simply Lizette, singing with the birds—ex-
hibiting her one true talent to them alone.

Unfortunately, this forced march through trees and
undergrowth, over a barely visible path, fleeing men
who wanted to do her harm, led by an outlaw who'd pretended to be a knight, was something else entirely.

Finn abruptly held up his hand to halt them.

They had come to a road, Lizette realized. Keldra sat on the ground and tried to catch her breath, while Garreth trotted up beside Finn.

After looking up and down the road, Finn glanced at the panting Keldra, then addressed Lizette. "I think it's safe enough to use the road a ways."

Thank God—but if he was expecting her to thank *him*, he was going to be disappointed. He'd been silent and sullen, brooding and grim since his return, although it was his own fault if he was annoyed that she'd spoken to Garreth. If he'd been less mysterious and more forthcoming, she wouldn't have had to ask questions of his friend.

"It can't be so very far now," she said to Keldra to encourage the girl.

"I hope not, my lady, or my legs are going to give out entirely."

"Mine aren't much better," Lizette confessed as she helped her maid to stand, and that wasn't a lie.

If they had to keep walking at such a brisk pace for much longer, she'd have to ask Finn to let them rest again, and she didn't want to do that. She would hate to imply that she couldn't keep up with him.

As they started for the road, Finn ordered young Garreth to help Keldra. He looked as if he'd like to refuse; however, she could tell from the set of Finn's shoulders that he wouldn't welcome a refusal and so, obviously, could Garreth.

Then the Irishman said, "My lady, I would have a word with you."

It was a command, not a request, which did nothing to assuage her ill humor. "So, you deign to speak to me now?"

He gave her a sour look as he started down the road, expecting her to follow as if she were his trained hound. Unfortunately, since she had absolutely no idea where she was, she had no choice but to follow him.

"During the rest of the remaining time together we may share, if you have questions, ask them of *me*," he said. "Leave Garreth in peace."

"I didn't think I was upsetting him," she countered, "and your secretive manner left me no choice. Is it really so surprising that I'd want to know about you? I've put our lives in your hands."

Scowling, Finn stepped over a puddle in the rutted road. "Very well, my lady. Ask me what questions you will, and I'll do my best to answer."

Now that he was willing to respond, she wasn't sure what to say. She would start, she decided, with his half brother. "What has your half brother done that's more shameful than stealing?"

The Irishman's jaw clenched and his strides lengthened a little, as if he'd like to hurry away from her. She wasn't about to let that happen, so she quickened her pace. "You said you would answer my questions," she reminded him.

Before he could, a pheasant, roused from the verge of the road, flew up into the sky in a flurry of wings, and they both checked their steps. In the next moment, an arrow caught the bird, sending it plummeting into the bushes ahead of them.

"Good shot, Garreth!" the Irishman exclaimed. "No need to worry about our supper tonight."

"Aye!" Garreth replied as he jogged down the road toward his fallen catch, leaving Keldra and the others behind.

"While Garreth's getting the bird, we'll rest a bit," Finn said. He gestured at a nearby stump. "Keldra, you sit here. Garreth won't be long."

He turned an inscrutable gaze onto Lizette. "If you'll walk over there with me, my lady, I'll answer your questions in private."

Lizette told herself it was proper that he speak so formally. That denoted respect, and a necessary change from his casual insolence. After all, he was an outlaw and a thief. She was a lady and the king's ward.

The Irishman led her a little farther down the road and pointed at another stump for her to sit upon, out of earshot of Keldra, although not out of sight.

Finn leaned his weight on one leg, crossed his arms over his broad chest, fixed his steadfast brown eyes on her and said, "Ryder and I had the same bitter, broken mother, but different fathers. For the past ten years, Ryder's been in a monastery in the north, studying, or so the plan was, to be a priest.

"Lately he decided against the priesthood. Celibacy, apparently, was not for him."

If Ryder looked anything like Finn, Lizette thought, celibacy would be a waste.

Embarrassed by that thought, she immediately lowered her head so Finn wouldn't see her blushing, even as she tried to stifle her wayward imagination and the vision of Finn in a bed, smiling and waiting for…some woman.

"So Ryder left the monastery and came looking for me. He thought being an outlaw an exciting life. He managed, by a miracle, to find me and when he did, he quickly learned the folly of his notions. Life as an outlaw is not adventurous, or even comfortable—sleeping rough, eating when and where you can, hiding, always on the move, never at home, never at peace, wondering every day if your luck's going to run out and you'll be caught and hanged."

Although she'd always craved an adventurous life, at least she'd had a home—a place to lay her head, and where she could always be sure of food and a certain respect, if not happiness. "I'm not surprised you wanted something else for your brother. Yet surely there were alternatives other than the priesthood and thievery."

"Aye, and so I told him," Finn replied. "But he's young, like Garreth, and he resented my advice and my refusals to let him try his hand at robbery. He took to finding solace in drink and picking fights to prove he could defend himself, that he was as tough as his brother and worthy of respect. One night, he laid into some of Wimarc's men—too many, as any man of sense could have told him, but Ryder was drunk and I was with a woman."

Lizette swallowed hard and stared at the toes of her boots. Of course he must go with women. Between his handsome face, magnificent body and the romance of being outside the law, he probably had to beat them off with a stick. She shouldn't think the less of him for that. He was a very masculine man, after all, and men had their needs....

"Disgusted you, have I?"

Disgusted? No. Rendered envious of the women who enjoyed his nocturnal company, yes—although she wouldn't say so. "It's a little disconcerting to hear a man admit he was with a woman."

"I'm no priest," Finn replied. His gaze seemed to grow even more penetrating. "How do you know I wasn't with my wife?"

Wife? Lizette thought, stunned. "I didn't think outlaws married."

"Oh, they do—common law, same as peasants." He smiled as if enjoying her discomfort. "Not that I have."

"But you said—"

"I said, how do you know I wasn't with my wife? You assumed I was with a whore, didn't you?"

He was right, so she didn't reply.

"I may not be married, but I don't use whores. I know what that life did to my mother."

It had clearly affected him, too. "Yet you'll make love with a woman outside of wedlock?"

"Aye, if she's willing, and I am." He regarded her with cool deliberation. "Would you hold a peasant to a higher standard than the nobles of the court? Even the courtiers who are wed take their pleasure wherever they can get it."

She had heard that from Adelaide, too. Nevertheless, she had no intention of commenting on the morality of the court, or thinking about his conquests, so she returned to the original subject of their discussion. "And while you were with this woman, your brother was captured by Wimarc's men."

"Aye," Finn said grimly, "and by the time I heard

what was afoot, three of them had him pinned, and when I went to help him, Garreth stopped me."

Remembering that she'd assured Garreth she wouldn't reveal what he'd told her about that, Lizette didn't let on she already knew how.

Finn gave her a wry little self-deprecating smile. "He shot me in the foot. Well, my boot. He thought he was doing the right thing, so I don't fault the lad. I blame myself for Ryder's capture. I should have taken better care, but I did not. Fortunately, Garreth did more harm to my boot than he did to me."

She could see and hear his remorse and guilt for not saving Ryder. But whose fault had it really been? His, for being with a woman, or his brother's, for starting the fight?

She, who'd dawdled and left her cortege open to attack, knew—and it was not the older brother's. "Garreth probably thought you'd have been imprisoned, too, and then where would you be? Now at least you can try to rescue your brother—although that won't be easy if Wimarc's men are like the ones who attacked my cortege. How do you plan to do it?"

"If I had a plan, I'd be acting on it already."

"You impersonate a nobleman very well. Could you not use that to your advantage?"

"Aye, if getting into Wimarc's castle was all I needed to do. Unfortunately, it's finding Ryder and getting out again without being caught that's the trouble."

Garreth burst out of the trees as if he'd been flushed like the pheasant he carried by its feet. "Somebody's coming!" he panted. "Just round the bend. Men and horses, and I heard a woman, too."

Finn stiffened as if he'd seen Medusa. "Into the trees," he ordered.

Garreth obeyed at once, while Keldra jumped to her feet, panic in her face. She was about to follow Garreth, until Lizette ordered her to wait.

"I don't want us to get separated," Lizette lied when she saw Finn's brows contract in consternation.

Paying him no more heed, she hurried to her maid.

"What are you up to, my lady?" he demanded.

Since he'd guessed she wasn't simply going to Keldra to ensure they stayed together, she decided to be honest, or at least partly, and if he were truly taking them to the convent as he claimed, he should agree with her plan.

"If there are women in the group approaching, it must not be Wimarc's mercenaries," she said, meeting his querying gaze steadily. "These must be other people—farmers, perhaps, or merchants, or maybe even nobles. I'll ask them for assistance, and surely they'll give it when they find out I'm a noblewoman."

Then she wouldn't have to worry about trusting an Irish outlaw, or be troubled by her attraction for him, which was risky and unwise, no matter how handsome he was.

Surprise, and something that looked rather like dismay flashed in Finn's eyes, although it was quickly quelled. "You don't know who these people might be. I can tell you, my lady, that there are bands of outlaws who have women among them. There's no guarantee the people approaching will be any more likely to treat you honorably than Wimarc's men."

"I'm grateful for your assistance, but Keldra is exhausted, and so am I. We can't keep going at such a pace, and it's just as likely these people will help us as the nuns at the convent—which you've never named," she noted.

"St. Mary's-in-the-Meadow," he shot back. "And I didn't risk my life to have you put yourself—and your maidservant—in danger again."

She'd obviously wounded his pride as surely as if he were a knight of the realm and she had called him dishonorable, but that could not be helped. "I don't think that's likely, so unless you want to be seen, you should hide."

"Oh, now *you* will protect *me?* How generous, my lady," he replied, making a mocking imitation of his formerly elegant bow.

"Will you linger to disparage me and get caught?" she demanded, more worried about his safety than upset by his sarcasm. "It would be poor recompense for you if I let that happen."

She would never see him again; what harm to say more if it encouraged him to leave? "Indeed, I would regret it very much if you were to suffer because you helped me."

He didn't reply. He simply continued to look at her with those intense brown eyes of his.

"What will happen to your brother if you're taken?" she demanded at last, determined to have her way in this and prevent his possible capture.

Finally she had said something that would make him go, and he turned on his heel.

She was relieved. She had to be.

"Godspeed!" she called out as he strode into the woods with Garreth quickly following. "And thank you." Finn didn't even look back.

CHAPTER SIX

LIZETTE WAITED by the side of the road with a trembling Keldra and tried to convince herself she was doing the right thing.

After all, could she really be sure that Finn and Garreth were helping them? He *could* be taking her to Wimarc, or some other place where he could hold her for ransom, since he knew who she was and to whom she was related. She was surely right to get away from him as soon as she could.

Brushing her tousled hair back from her face, she realized she must look more like a peasant than a noblewoman with her disheveled, matted hair and dirty face. Hopefully her accent and demeanor would mark her for the noblewoman she was. Nevertheless, she smoothed down her mud-stained skirts and pulled her cloak more tightly about her over her soiled gown.

Two soldiers rounded the corner—proper soldiers, not mercenaries in motley armor probably stolen. Their helmets gleamed in the morning light, no spots of rust marred their mail, and they wore matching woolen surcoats of scarlet and green. There was something vaguely familiar about those surcoats and the arms upon them, and the banners flapping from the pikes they carried.

Before she could remember to whom those soldiers belonged, a knight in gleaming chain mail seated on a marvelous destrier, with a woman dressed in a cloak of green-and-gold damask trimmed with fox fur, rode around the bend. The man had pushed back his coif and wore no helmet, so his fair hair, smoothed and cut in the bowl shape the Normans favored, shone in the sunlight.

She knew that hair, and she knew that face, and now she remembered whose standard it was: Lord Gilbert of Fairbourne, who had once visited Averette in the hopes of winning Adelaide's hand in marriage. Or Gillian's, if Adelaide said no. Or even hers, if he were desperate, although that's not the way he'd put it when he'd cornered her in the stairwell.

She'd heard Gilbert had got himself a bride from Lincoln, the daughter of an earl who had no sons, so her dowry was considerable. Helewyse was the girl's name; Lizette remembered because Gillian had commented she must not be a very wise woman to accept Gilbert.

One of the soldiers at the front of the cortege nodded at Lizette and Keldra and said something to his companion, who grinned and made a disgusting gesture.

Perhaps this was a mistake, after all, and they should run for the trees—except that Gilbert's men had spotted them and if they gave chase, they might also find Garreth and Finn. No doubt Finn could come up with some kind of explanation, speaking with that noble accent he managed with such ease, but these soldiers might simply assume they were poachers or outlaws and kill them before Finn could say a word.

And despite her personal dislike of Gilbert, he *was* noble. He should help a noblewoman in distress, even if she'd slapped his face.

"Here, you, out of the way!" one of the lead soldiers shouted at them before he addressed Lord Gilbert over his shoulder. "There's a couple of beggar women in the road, my lord!"

"Beggars?" the lady said, loud enough for Lizette and Keldra to hear her as she spoke to Gilbert. "You assured me Wimarc's lands would be free of such troublesome creatures."

Wimarc's lands? Gilbert and his lady were headed for Lord Wimarc's estate?

She'd thought Gilbert arrogant and greedy, but not evil. Perhaps she'd been wrong—and if he was in league with Wimarc, she would much rather take her chances with Finn.

Throwing the hood of her cloak over her head, she moved to the side of the road. "We can't go with these people after all," she whispered to Keldra. "Say nothing, not even if one of them speaks to you."

Keldra must have also heard them speak of Wimarc, for she immediately did as she was told and sat abruptly on the ground, pulling her hood over her head, too.

The first soldiers were only about twenty feet away when Lizette rounded her shoulders, clutched her cloak about her throat with her left hand and held out her right hand in a begging gesture.

"Alms, noble lord!" she called out in a hoarse voice, imitating the sickly mother of the alewife at Averette. "Alms for a poor woman and her dumb daughter!"

"Out of the way, hag!" one of the first soldiers growled, raising his foot as if he meant to kick her.

Lizette scurried out of range and stayed there as the cortege passed.

"We should be at Castle de Werre before nightfall tomorrow," Gilbert said, giving his wife a slightly peeved glance. "You didn't have to come. I told you this was no courtesy visit."

"And you said you'd never met the man."

"I haven't, which was why I was surprised by the invitation."

"Which was to both of us," his wife reminded him with a pout. "So of course I ought to come."

Her husband didn't respond, but rode on in sulky silence.

In addition to the soldiers, the knight and his lady, there was a wagon full of baggage, no doubt bearing all the items the lord and his lady considered necessary for their comfort, regardless of who their host might be.

Keeping her head down, Lizette waited until the last of the soldiers were out of sight before she straightened, her back aching. Then a frowning Finn emerged from the trees, his scabbard slapping his thigh as he marched toward them.

She couldn't blame him for being angry; she'd as good as admitted she didn't trust him, and then not done what she'd said she'd do.

Garreth, however, rushed past him, grinning with delight. "Damn, my lady, you're good!" he cried. "Not as good as Finn, mind, but you could have fooled me! You

MARGARET MOORE 77

sounded just like an old crone." He gave Keldra a condescending smile. "And you make a good simpleton."

"You look like one," her maid snapped back.

Finn ignored them both. "So, my lady, may I ask what prompted your change o' mind? Didn't like the looks of him, after all?"

"As a matter of fact, I know him. That was Lord Gilbert de Fairbourne, who once came courting my sister. I'm quite sure he would have helped us if I'd chosen to ask."

Finn cocked a brow and waited expectantly.

"He's on his way to Lord Wimarc's castle."

That removed the contempt from Finn's features. "What for?"

She lifted her chin with haughty disdain as she swept past him. "I didn't inquire."

As he hurried after her, Finn cursed himself for a fool. He'd been as peeved as a child who loses a friend when she'd told him what she was planning, silently condemning her for an ungrateful wench when he'd given up time and trouble to help her. God save him, he'd even been tempted to pick her up and throw her over his shoulder and carry her into the woods.

Because unlike the lady, and even though she had the bearing, speech and manner of a noblewoman, he couldn't believe anybody would simply take her word that she was Lady Elizabeth of Averette. They'd more likely think her a peasant who was trying to trick them, or perhaps a courtesan who'd fallen on hard times. Either way, they would treat her with disdain and disrespect.

Or worse. Once, when he was ten years old, he'd seen what soldiers might do to a peasant woman alone and unprotected on the road. A pack of wolves would be more merciful.

So in spite of knowing what a brave, spirited woman she was and that she could probably hold her own with any nobleman and get the respect and aid she deserved, he'd hidden and watched, ready to rush out to her defense again if necessary. He simply couldn't abandon her to her fate, any more than he could leave Ryder to die in a dungeon.

And even if that made him a fool. "My lady, you're going the wrong way!"

She halted and turned abruptly. Without a word, she marched past him, going back the way she'd come.

He hurried after her, leaving Garreth and the girl to follow. "So this Gilbert was going to Castle de Werre?" he asked, hoping to achieve some kind of truce.

"That's what he said."

"What sort of fellow is he?"

"Greedy. Arrogant. Like most men."

"Then he might be allied with Wimarc if the man's up to no good."

"Perhaps. He's ambitious, too." She cut her eyes to Finn. "Gilbert came to Averette to court Adelaide—or Gillian, if Adelaide refused him, or me, if they didn't want him, which they didn't. He had the audacity to kiss me, too."

She hadn't enjoyed it, obviously. He was fairly certain *he* could kiss her in a way that would make her remember it with something other than contempt.

"He's a pompous, arrogant *fool*," she continued, yanking Finn back to the here and now. "I can believe he would turn traitor if he felt slighted or exploited. Perhaps Adelaide and Gillian were right to worry that John's the sort of king who forces men to rebel because of his greed and lust."

Finn had seen and heard enough at court to know how deep the hatred of John ran among the nobles. "Lots o' the barons hate him. He's not just taxed them for his wars, they've lost sons in his quest to get back his lands in France and he's seduced their wives and daughters, too."

"He may be a terrible man, but he *is* the king," she replied, "and rebellion will only lead to more death and destruction."

"You'll get no argument from me there, my lady," he said. "It's always the poor who suffer most when the nobles go to war."

Lady Elizabeth suddenly came to a dead halt and turned to him with the fire of resolve in her lovely eyes. "I'm not going to that convent. I'm going to help you get into Lord Wimarc's castle."

She couldn't be serious—or else she didn't appreciate the danger there.

"No, you're not," he replied with equal conviction, while her maid turned as white as washed fleece and Garreth's mouth fell open. "I'm not going to let—"

"I'm not asking your permission," the lady interrupted. "To protect my family and prevent war, I've *got* to find out what Wimarc's up to. I'll need some proof of his plans, too. He must have powerful allies if he thinks he can overthrow the king, so my word may not be enough to convict him or even have him arrested."

She fixed Finn with her steadfast gaze. "*You* need to

get into Wimarc's castle to rescue your brother. Together, we can do both."

He felt a surge of hope, until reality intruded. "Just
like that, eh, my lady? We'll just walk up to the gates
and ask to be allowed to pass? You'll demand to know
what Wimarc's planning, and I'll go to the dungeon and
order my brother freed. Then we'll all saunter out the
gates as easy as you please."

Lizette drew herself up, not the least dissuaded by his
mockery. "We won't walk up to the gates. We'll ride—
if you can steal some horses. I hardly think Lord Gilbert
and his wife would arrive on foot."

As Finn stared at her, she continued, clearly growing
more enamored of her harebrained notion. "Gilbert's
wife said they haven't actually met Wimarc, so he doesn't
know what they look like. I know enough about Gilbert
and Helewyse that we should be able to fool him."

"It's still daft and far too dangerous," Finn declared.
"Even if we could fool Wimarc, what about Gilbert's
escort? They'll likely notice the difference."

"Aye," Garreth reluctantly agreed. "If it was just you
and Finn—"

"Oh, my lady, you mustn't! You'll be killed!"
Keldra wailed.

"You've no better plan, have you?" the lady countered,
ignoring both Garreth and her maid. "As for their escort…"

She fell silent and as she puzzled over that problem
and her plan, Finn was sure she would reconsider—until
her eyes lit up like a torch bursting to life in the dark.

"You and Garreth can pretend to be a new escort
sent from Wimarc. Tell Gilbert Wimarc doesn't like

any soldiers but his own on his estate. He should send his men home."

"As if Gilbert would believe that!"

"If he's on Wimarc's land, why would he need his own soldiers? And we could say that Wimarc's a suspicious fellow who doesn't like unknown soldiers in his fortress. That would make sense, wouldn't it?"

Finn blinked, amazed at the rapidity with which her mind worked, and the way she dealt with his rational objections…a way that just might be viable.

A nobleman and his wife. Without an escort… They could claim they'd been set upon by thieves and their escort…fled. The louts. He'd deal with them when he got home!

"If you aren't willing to take the chance," she said, interrupting his ruminations, her expression fiercely determined, "I shall find a way inside that castle by myself. No doubt Wimarc would welcome a pretty serving wench."

"Aye, he would," Finn retorted, horrified by that suggestion. "And when he's done with you, he'll pass you around to his men."

Her gaze faltered for a moment, but then that stubborn, determined gleam returned to her beautiful eyes. "With or without your help, I must do whatever I can to find evidence of Wimarc's treachery. My family's safety, and the welfare of the entire kingdom, could depend upon it. And would you let your brother die in that man's dungeon although I offer you a way to prevent it?"

"Oh, my lady, you mustn't try such a thing!" Keldra pleaded, her hands clasped like a supplicant before a shrine. "It's too dangerous! You could be killed! And what would your sisters say if you were?"

"I would hope they would be proud of me," she answered without hesitation, and with the merest hint of wistfulness that suggested she didn't believe her family had much cause to be proud of her now.

He understood how painful wounded pride could be; he'd had his own pride injured many times by the taunts of village children when he was a boy. He knew how much a person would want to heal those wounds by proving himself. He'd done that every time he tricked someone into believing he was a nobleman, and never more than when he was at the king's court.

Why else had Ryder picked those fights, except to assuage his wounded pride?

So she must prove her worth by exposing Wimarc for an evil, plotting traitor. Yet her need would be putting her in danger…although her rank would surely offer her some protection, whereas if he were caught…

"Finn, we could do it," she persisted. "I know you can act the noble. I've seen you do it, and I can tell you things about Gilbert to avert any suspicion. As for playing the man's wife, it won't be very difficult. I *am* a lady, and this marriage is recent, so any ignorance or awkwardness between us can be easily explained—and most important of all, *Wimarc has never met them.*"

"That isn't the only problem," Finn said, still hesitant to put her life at risk. "It may take time to find out where Ryder is as well as get the evidence of Wimarc's treachery. We'd have to keep Lord Gilbert and his wife imprisoned all that time, which would be risky—or kill them,"

Finn concluded, loath to murder. He was a thief, not a cold-blooded killer.

"I know where we could keep 'em," Garreth eagerly offered. "That deserted charcoal burner's hut we stayed in a few days ago. It's in a lonely spot and nobody's likely to come near it."

"Yes, we can keep them imprisoned until we've succeeded," the lady agreed with obvious relief, if no appreciation for the additional risks that would entail.

"And if they escape?"

"They must be watched."

Finn's gaze instinctively went to Garreth, who frowned and shook his tousled head. "Not me! You need me, Finn. How can you rescue Ryder and get out of there without me?"

"We were never going to be able to fight our way out," he replied, which was true. That had been one of the reasons he'd not been able to come up with a plan of rescue. "Who else can I trust with such a responsibility? All will be lost if Gilbert or his lady escapes and reveals us to Wimarc. It's you or no one, Garreth."

The young man reluctantly nodded.

"Keldra can help guard them, too," Lizette suggested.

Finn didn't disagree. If they did attempt this, it would be best to keep the girl away from Wimarc, and not just because of Wimarc's reputation. Finn was unfortunately sure Keldra would betray the ruse by a slip of the tongue or other mistake.

"I don't need some sniveling *girl's* help," Garreth protested, a mountain of scorn in the word *girl*.

Keldra ignored him and looked beseechingly at

Lizette. "You'll need me, my lady. A lady always has a maid. Who will dress your hair? Who will help you with your clothes?"

"I daresay Wimarc will have women servants who can do such things," Lizette replied. "Besides, Garreth can't watch Lord Gilbert and his wife all by himself. He'll have to sleep sometimes. And then there's Lady Helewyse. She'll suffer with no maidservant to help her."

Lizette put her hands on the girl's shoulders and regarded her with confidence and respect, as if they were equals. "Keldra, I need you to do this for me, and for Adelaide and Gillian, too."

The girl's shoulders slumped, but she nodded her agreement nonetheless. "Yes, my lady, for your sake and your sisters', I'll do what you ask, even to putting up with that stupid boy."

"Boy? I'm not a *boy*, you…you *girl!* Finn, tell her I'm in charge!"

It seemed the plan had been agreed upon, with or without his consent. Yet what plan had he come up with since Ryder had been captured that had any less risk, or more chance of success?

It was this, or…what?

He walked over to the maidservant and gave her a companionable smile. It was troubling to think of their fate in the hands of these bickering young people, but if they were to have any chance at all, they had no choice.

"Keldra," he said, "it'll be an ease to my mind if you stay with Garreth. As Lady Elizabeth says, he can't keep watch all the time. He must sleep.

"However," he grimly continued, "in any battle, there

must be a general, and in this case, it has to be Garreth. He's been through tricky situations before, so if trouble comes, I ask that you defer to him."

The girl blushed as red as cherries. "Well, if you think I should…"

"I do." He turned to the triumphant Garreth, who had a lot to learn about women. "I trust that *you* will treat Keldra with respect."

The youth's smug satisfaction left his face and a frown took its place. "I'll try."

CHAPTER SEVEN

EARLY THE NEXT MORNING, Keldra chewed her lip as Lizette pulled some clothing from Finn's leather pouch and handed it to the girl, who looked as if she feared they'd fall apart.

"Oh, my lady, I don't like this!" she said, glancing toward the leaves of the bushes that shielded them from Garreth, clearly believing he was eavesdropping.

"This is necessary for our plan," Lizette replied, hoping Keldra wasn't going to make things difficult, and that she and Garreth could cooperate enough to keep Lord Gilbert and his wife from escaping after they were captured.

"How can anybody believe we're men even if we dress like them?" Keldra protested.

"Finn says people don't look much beyond a poor fellow's clothes," Lizette said as she drew off her soiled gown. "And Wimarc's men don't wear proper armor anyway. It's not as if we'll have to fight, either. We simply have to look like a small escort."

Sitting by the fire last night, after she'd told Finn all she'd ever heard or remembered about Gilbert and his wife, they'd discussed their plans, trying to think of anything that might go wrong. Finn had also suggested making it look as if there were four men come from Lord Wimarc, not two. She and Keldra could wear Finn's and Garreth's clothes and sit a horse some distance behind him.

Seeing the merit of this addition to their plan, she'd eagerly agreed, and asked him where he intended to get the horses.

"Best not to ask, best not to know," he replied.

"I hope you won't get caught," she said, acutely aware of the danger he would face before they even got to Wimarc's castle.

"I've done it plenty enough times before," he'd assured her.

And then his smile had drifted away in the flickering light of the small fire. A different kind of light had kindled in his eyes, one that made her heart race, her breathing quicken and her eyes wander to his full lips, then to his broad shoulders, muscular arms and strong, slender hands.

Wary of the powerful feeling rushing over her like a strong wind, knowing it for lustful desire, she'd stood hastily, nearly tripping on the hem of her gown. He had half risen to help her, catching hold of her arm to steady her.

His touch was like fire, sending thrilling, invigorating heat along her arm, to her heart and every other part of her body. She knew desire; she'd felt it a few times before when some of Adelaide's more attractive suitors had looked at her with speculation. She'd imagined their kisses and even wondered what it would be like to be in their arms—but never had she felt anything as powerful as the need and longing that Finn inspired, even with a glance.

Whatever she had felt, he quickly let go and sat back down on the ground. When she'd bidden him goodnight, he'd not replied. He'd simply nodded as he stared into the flames.

Trying not to remember those feelings, and keeping on her shift for the moment, she pulled on the only other pair of breeches Finn owned. They felt strange on her legs as she tied the drawstring at the waist. They were also much baggier on her than they were on Finn's muscular limbs.

Nor could she quite ignore the fact that these had been on his body, covering his nakedness.

She took a few steps. "I believe I could get used to wearing breeches," she mused aloud, giving Keldra a smile before she quickly took off her shift and donned a loose-fitting shirt that had been washed to softness and mended several times.

The sleeves dangled a good six inches past her fingertips, and the opening at the neck went down nearly to her navel. She pulled the laces tight, but the neck still gaped.

I just won't bend over, she told herself as she put a moth-eaten gambeson on over the shirt and buckled it closed. She sat on the ground and put her boots back on, glad she'd been wearing them in the wagon and not thin shoes.

Standing, she spun slowly in a circle. "How do I look?"

"Like a mummer, and not a good one," Finn said.

With a gasp, she turned and saw him standing in a gap in the bushes, holding the reins of four horses. "How long have you been standing there?"

"Sadly, I just arrived," he replied, devilish amusement in his brown eyes.

She raised her chin and gave him a saucy, defiant smile as she walked toward him, once again struck by the difference between the freedom of her skirts and the sensation of the fabric of his breeches rubbing between her limbs.

"Tuck your hair in this," Finn said, tossing her a leather cap that, when she put it on, went down over her eyes.

When she shoved it back, she realized he was trying not to laugh.

"Very amusing, I'm sure," she retorted. "I won't be much help if I can't see."

"It'll sit higher on your head with all your hair tucked under it."

She shoved her unbound hair under the cap and discovered he was right.

Then Keldra sidled out from behind the bush, her head down and sniffling as if going to her execution. She wore patched breeches and a heavy wool tunic that was clearly too large for her narrow frame.

Garreth burst out laughing and leaned against the trunk of an oak tree for support. "You look like a scarecrow!"

"I'd like to see how good you'd look in my clothes!" the girl retorted, wiping her nose with the back of her hand.

Lizette hurried to take the pouch from her and try to

restore a little peace. "This is necessary, Keldra, and when we're home, I'll have some new dresses made for you."

Keldra managed a little smile as she wiped her nose with the back of her hand. Stifling a sigh, hoping their plan would succeed, Lizette turned and started toward the horses.

Finn stepped in front of her, and his steady gaze held hers. "When we reach the cortege, you'll do exactly as we planned, won't you, my lady? There will be no unforeseen changes?"

She gave him a simpering smile. "Aye, my lord husband-to-be. I shall do exactly as I'm told, as a dutiful wife should."

His only answer to that was a skeptical grunt.

A SHORT WHILE LATER, Lord Gilbert rode closer to the soldiers at the front of his cortege to see why they had stopped.

A mounted man waited in the middle of the road, blocking their progress. A short distance behind him, three more mounted men were lined up across the road.

If these were thieves, Gilbert thought, they were incredibly stupid ones, for he had thirty soldiers...unless this was but part of a band of outlaws.

"What is it, Gilbert?" Helewyse asked anxiously behind him.

"Probably nothing," he replied as he started to draw his sword.

The fellow in the middle of the road held out his arms. "I mean you no harm, my lord," he called out with an Irish accent.

It was said Wimarc hired mercenaries from everywhere and anywhere, as long as they could fight well. This fellow certainly looked as if he could wield a sword.

"It *is* Lord Gilbert, isn't it?" the Irishman inquired. "Lord Wimarc's sent us to meet you. We're to escort you and your lovely wife the rest of the way to his castle."

"I have my own escort, as you can see," Gilbert replied as his wife rode a little closer to him.

"Aye, but Lord Wimarc's fussy about having soldiers he hasn't hired himself in his castle. He's a suspicious fellow, you see. O' course, he trusts you and your lady—which is a great honor—but he won't take any chances on your men, so before you enter Castle de Werre, he requests that you dismiss your guards and send 'em back home. When your visit's over, me and me men will see you safe back to Fairbourne."

This was definitely unusual. "He only sent the four of you?"

"To see you to his castle, aye," the Irishman replied. "You're on his land now, so no need for more. The peasants and any scoundrels hereabouts know better than to do mischief to any nobles on *his* land. A fierce fellow for the punishment, Lord Wimarc. There'll be more to see you back to Fairbourne, o' course."

"This is most irregular."

Indeed, it had all the makings of a trap, Gilbert realized.

"Aye, odd it may be," the Irishman cheerfully agreed, "but it's Lord Wimarc's way, you see. And sadly, my lord, if you don't agree, you won't be admitted to Castle de Werre, which would be a pity after you come all this long way."

"How can we be sure you're from Lord Wimarc? I'm not about to take the word of some...some..."

"Irish bloke? O' course not, which is why I've got a letter from his lordship."

Finn reached into his belt and drew out the message Lizette had written on a piece of parchment torn from one of Ryder's precious books that Finn had in his pack. They'd also used some of his equally precious ink and a duck's feather for a quill.

His brother would be furious that they'd used his things, but that didn't bother Finn a bit, as long as they got Ryder out of Wimarc's castle alive. He was also silently thankful Lizette had thought of this contingency last night, or what would he have done now?

Remembering their discussion by the fire brought back the memory of the end of it, when she'd looked at him...that way.

Despite his past, she seemed to respect him and—most exhilarating of all—he was sure she wanted him.

He'd seen desire often enough in other women's eyes to recognize it. Indeed, no man of his age with a comely face and robust build could pass unnoticed and ignored by women, including those of the king's court. But those noblewomen hadn't known the truth about him, and he'd been sure their passion would turn to disgust if they did.

Not so Lady Elizabeth. For once, a noblewoman *did* know the truth and she wanted him anyway, perhaps even as much as he wanted her.

That realization had been so incredible and over-whelming, her subsequent slight touch had been like fire on his skin, and all he could think to do was pretend she wasn't there, lest he sweep her into his arms and do what he so much yearned to do.

What he'd believed she wanted him to do.

Lord Gilbert's voice broke into his thoughts. "Dismount and bring that document to me."

Finn gave the man and his wife another genial smile before he obeyed, walking past the guards at the front of the cortege with every appearance of calm. In reality, sweat trickled down his back and he was ready to draw his sword to save himself as he approached the knight wearing some of the finest, most intricately linked chain mail Finn had ever seen. Gilbert's surcoat was of well-woven wool, and his helmet fairly glowed like the sun in summer.

As for his wife, she was a pretty enough woman in that pale, Norman way, with dark hair and pink lips. Her hazel eyes held a bit of spirit, but nothing like the vitality and resolve that sparkled in those of Lady Elizabeth of Averette.

"Here you are, my lord," he said, handing Lord Gilbert the parchment.

Lord Gilbert took the scroll and swiftly perused it. The writing was as fine as any he'd ever seen, neat and tidy and masculine.

"Greetings, my lord Gilbert," it began in the educated French of the nobility, and continued just the same. No uneducated Irish outlaw could have written such a letter.

Gilbert also studied the signature at the end. It was signed in Wimarc's name by his steward.

An ignorant outlaw would no doubt have tried to forge Lord Wimarc's signature.

Satisfied, he rolled it up again. "This looks in order."

He dismissed his men, sending them back to Fairbourne. They didn't look pleased; nevertheless, they turned around and started back the way they'd come.

"Garreth!" the Irishman called out as he returned to his horse. "Give the wagon driver your mount and take the reins."

"What, even the driver is to go home?" Gilbert asked with surprise.

"Aye, even your driver," the Irishman replied. "Lord Wimarc's orders."

"But, Gilbert—" Helewyse started to protest.

"All is well," he assured her, stifling any doubt. "Lord Wimarc is wise to be cautious in these troubled times."

"GILBERT, can this possibly be the right way?" Helewyse asked after they left the main road and started along a narrower track.

The road was barely wide enough for two to ride abreast, or the wagon to pass. It was so shaded by overhanging oak, elm and the occasional pine that there were still puddles from the rain three nights before.

Ahead, the whistling Irishman led the way, seemingly without a care in the world, while behind came their wagon driven by a mere stripling, and the two other silent riders. One had a cap pulled down low upon his head, the other wore a hood.

"Perhaps it's a shortcut," Gilbert replied, even though he was beginning to wonder if he shouldn't have insisted their own men accompany them, at least to the gates of Castle de Werre.

Yet they must be on Wimarc's land by now. They

would soon see Castle de Werre. And surely if these men were thieves or cutthroats, they would have acted by now...although if this road got any narrower, he'd draw his sword and be prepared to fight.

Gilbert was so busy reassuring himself and thinking of what he'd do if they were attacked, he didn't immediately notice that one of the four men had ridden close behind him. "Well, Gilbert, how long has it been? Two years? Three?"

He gasped and twisted to look behind him, and found himself staring at a familiar face—a familiar *female* face. Not as lovely as Adelaide d'Averette, but just as memorable, albeit for a different reason. *"Lizette?"*

The impertinent shrew grinned like a gargoyle. "In the very flesh, my lord."

"What in God's name are you doing here with these men?" he demanded, running a shocked gaze over her as she maneuvered her horse beside his.

She had on old, baggy breeches and a shirt with sleeves that fell past her delicate wrists, covered by a decrepit gambeson. Her curling, thick blond hair must be tucked up in that ridiculous cap.

"I'm on the king's business," she replied, just as impertinent as she'd been at Averette.

He'd been relieved when she'd rejected his advances, or so he'd told himself. "The king's...? I don't believe it! Is this some prank of yours, some jest?"

"No jest," she replied, and indeed, neither her face nor her voice held any amusement now. "I'm also planning to pay a visit to Lord Wimarc."

"Dressed like that?"

Her blue eyes flashed with a look he remembered, one that heralded a rise in her temper, and he felt again the sharp sting of her slap on his cheek.

"Who is this woman, Gilbert?" Helewyse demanded. Her eyes went from the top of Lizette's capped head to her booted feet. "How do you know my husband, you hussy?"

"Your gallant husband once sought my hand in marriage," Lizette replied. "To be honest, it was my eldest sister he really wanted—or at least her inheritance. However, I believe he told my father he'd take Gillian or me if she wasn't willing. Hardly the sort of wooing to win a maiden's heart, eh, my lady? No doubt he wooed you with better grace."

"He did!" Helewyse vehemently replied.

Lizette's shapely brows rose with maddening skepticism. "Did he now? Perhaps he learned a thing or two about how *not* to woo a lady at Averette, although—to his credit—I seem to recall his kisses weren't entirely without merit."

"Kisses?" Helewyse hissed, her angry gaze darting from Lizette to her husband and back again.

"One or two in the stairwell when he thought he'd get away with it. Isn't that right, Gilbert?"

God's wounds, he'd like to strangle Lizette. He was also somewhat taken aback to discover his wife possessed such a temper. She'd never shown such a fiery spirit before. "I must have been drunk."

"Were you drunk when you accepted Lord Wimarc's invitation?" she asked.

"I see time has not made you any less insolent," he replied. "Why should I not visit whomever I choose?"

"Because the king might not approve."

Gilbert's lip curled with disgust. "As long as I pay my taxes and send the men he requires, what business is it of his?"

"It could be very important, if what I suspect is true."

"Who is this...this *creature* to speak to you this way?" Helewyse demanded of her husband.

"Lady Elizabeth of Averette," Lizette announced as the Irishman wheeled his mount to face them.

He slipped from the saddle and sauntered toward them, his hand on the hilt of his sword. "Now, my lord, if you'll give me your blade and any other weapons on your person."

"What?" Gilbert gasped, going for his own sword.

Before he could, an arrow zipped past his face and the Irishman had put the tip of his sword not at Gilbert's breast, but at Helewyse, who looked about to swoon. A swift glance proved that the driver of the wagon had drawn the bow.

And Lizette? She was looking nearly as surprised.

"There's no need to panic, my lord and lady," the Irishman genially remarked. "We just want to borrow you both for a little while and when we're done, you'll be free to go back home, or to Lord Wimarc, if you'd prefer."

"Borrow?" Gilbert repeated as his wife clutched her reins with trembling hands, her face as white as fresh snow.

"It's like this, my lord," the Irishman explained. "We need to get inside Wimarc's castle, but we don't have an invitation. You and your lovely wife do."

Gilbert looked from him to Lizette as understanding slowly dawned. "You're going to pretend to be me and my wife?"

"Yes," Lizette said through tightened lips that had lost their rosy hue. "It's necessary, Gilbert."

"Aye, very necessary, so if you're clever, my lord, you'll do as you're told and not give us any trouble," the Irishman warned. "But if not...well, I'm a terrible wicked fellow, my lord, and there's your lady wife to think of."

Helewyse gave a little shriek of dismay, while Lizette swallowed hard. Finn had never told her they would try to enforce Gilbert's cooperation by threatening his wife, and she'd nearly cried out when he'd raised his sword to her.

Perhaps she'd made a terrible mistake. She hadn't fully considered what Finn might be willing to do to get his brother back—and now it was too late.

"Your sword, please, my lord," Finn said. "Take it off and drop it on the ground. Garreth, put it in the wagon when he does."

As Garreth clambered down and did as he was directed, Finn grabbed the reins of Lady Helewyse's dainty mare that snorted and refooted nervously. "We've got a fine place for you to stay, my lord. Not what you're used to, I'm sure, but better than many a place I've had to lay my head."

CHAPTER EIGHT

"YOU EXPECT US TO SLEEP in this…this…*hovel?*" Gilbert demanded as he balked in the doorway of the small hut.

The building was old and weathered, and hidden by a stand of trees, which made it extremely difficult to see if you didn't know it was there. It was also extremely small and full of cobwebs. Nearby, a clear stream ran over some rocks, its burbling the only sound, save their voices and the jingle of the horse's accoutrements, to break the silence.

After Lizette and Keldra had changed back into their own clothes, Finn had ordered both the nobleman and his wife to dismount and go inside the hut. He'd kept his sword unsheathed, and Garreth had his bow at the ready. It was obvious Keldra was upset by the sight of these weapons, as was Lizette, and she almost wished she'd never proposed this plan—except that she had to find out about Wimarc somehow. And she could hope Finn wasn't really going to hurt their captives unless he was provoked.

Although who could say what might do that? Not she.

A slight poke from the tip of Finn's sword sent Gilbert and his weeping wife farther inside. "Aye, my lord, I do expect you to sleep here and even you must admit, it's better than a grave."

"We don't want to kill you," Lizette hastened to assure them as she followed them inside.

She remembered all too well the terror she'd felt when Lindall had threatened her and was determined to make certain both they and Finn understood that she didn't intend any harm to come to them. "You only have to stay here a little while, and Garreth will bring you whatever you want or need from your baggage. You'll be as cozy and comfortable as can be."

Lady Helewyse wiped her eyes as she glared at Lizette. "Cozy? Comfortable? Imprisoned here? What kind of cruel, unnatural woman are you?"

Lizette knew that to many men and women, she would be unnatural. That would be the only answer they would accept for her reluctance to noose herself with marriage vows. But she also knew that wasn't what Helewyse meant. "The sort that will do whatever she must to protect her family."

Finn went to the door and gestured for her to leave with him. "Come, my lady. We'd best get on our way, or it'll be too dark to see the road."

As Lizette followed him to the door, Helewyse threw herself into her husband's arms and burst into tears.

Once Lizette was outside, Finn closed the door and placed a thick branch against it, shoving the bottom deep into the dirt.

"You weren't really going to hurt her, were you?" Lizette asked as they went toward the fire, where Keldra was stirring something in a pot Garreth had scrounged from the wagon.

"I never hurt women," Finn replied so firmly, she

believed him. "I was only trying to encourage the fellow to cooperate. Women's tears and fears tend to do that. O' course, there are some brave, bold women not prone to either."

He slid her a glance that made her wonder if he thought her one such woman. She hoped so, although nobody had ever called her brave before. She had always been Lizette the heedless, Lizette the merry gadabout. Lizette, the girl who fled conflict and pain and trouble.

Until now.

Near the wagon, Garreth was making a lean-to out of branches, with dry, dead leaves for a floor. He was going to sleep there; Keldra would have the bed of the wagon.

Keldra was also busily offering Garreth unwanted advice about how to build his shelter, while Garreth muttered about bossy girls who ought to keep their mouths shut.

Seeing them squabble like little children, Lizette put her hand on Finn's forearm to detain him, trying not to notice that it was as firm as the stones of Averette. "Perhaps it's a mistake to leave Garreth and—"

Finn glanced at her hand, which she swiftly removed. "Don't underestimate the lad, my lady," he said. "In some ways, he's more mature than men twice his age and he knows how important this duty is."

She hoped Finn was right as they continued toward the tethered horses. They would share one for this part of their journey, to make their story of an attack upon their cortege more believable.

"Did that lout really kiss you?"

Finn's abrupt question caught her off guard. "Yes, he did. Twice. I slapped him."

The corners of the Irishman's lips turned up in a grin. Remembering the look on Gilbert's face that night, she smiled, too, and relaxed a little, until they reached the horses and she remembered what they were about to do.

Finn mounted first and held out his hand to help her up behind him. She clasped his hand, and in the next moment, was seated on the rump of the gelding, her arms around Finn's waist.

Keldra looked up from the pot she was putting on the fire. Realizing they were about to leave, she immediately ran toward them. Garreth saw her and came loping from his lean-to like a young buck, a small ax in his hand.

"You're off then," Garreth said. "Good luck, Finn—not that you'll need it. I'll be seeing you and Ryder soon, I'm sure."

"God keep you, my lady!" Keldra said fervently. "I'll be worried sick until you're back."

That, Lizette was fairly certain, was true. "We'll be as quick as we can," she promised.

"You should kill that Wimarc if you get the chance," Garreth suggested to Finn.

"I'll bear that in mind," he replied, ruffling the lad's hair and giving him a smile. "Now you take care, Garreth. That man could be a tricky devil, and don't underestimate his wife. Keep a careful watch—the pair o' you."

"I will!" Garreth vowed.

"And I!" Keldra seconded.

Finn twisted to look at Lizette over his broad shoulder. "Shall we, my lady?"

She wasn't going to change her mind now. "Yes!"

AS THEIR GELDING GALLOPED through the quickening dusk, Lizette held on to Finn for all she was worth, terrified that the horse was going to stumble and she would be thrown to her death. To be sure, there was still light to see by and Finn was warm and solid, but she was no bold horsewoman.

She was also afraid she'd not fully comprehended the risk they were taking when she saw the massive bulk of Castle de Werre looming ahead.

All castles could be frightening in the dusk, with their imposing walls and fortifications and torches flaming in their sconces like harbingers of hell. This time, however, given what she'd learned of Wimarc, the comparison to hell seemed more apt.

Even as they neared and she realized that Castle de Werre was smaller than many others, that feeling of riding up to a cursed place held her as tightly as she gripped Finn.

Finn swore softly, his words barely audible above the pounding of their horse's hooves. "You're squeezing the breath out of me!"

"I don't like the looks of this place!"

"Neither do I."

He reined in when they were still some distance from the barbican, in the shadow of a stand of trees. Unlike most castles, there was no village clustered around the base of the fortress. That area was barren save for grass, up to and into the deep, dry moat. Above, they could see sentries pacing on the battlements, illuminated by the setting sun.

There were a lot of sentries.

Their horse pranced impatiently, as if sensing their anxiety, but Finn managed to keep it under control.

"You don't have to come, my lady," he said quietly, and with conviction. "I can go by myself. I'll tell Wimarc my wife was killed in the attack."

Looking at that grim, forbidding fortress, Lizette was sorely tempted to flee, yet there was really only one answer to give. "No. You need me if we're to both free your brother and find evidence of Wimarc's treachery."

"Bold and brave," Finn replied, and she could hear respect and admiration in his voice.

Not only was she thrilled to hear his praise, she had greater confidence they would succeed—and she needed that confidence. This was her plan, and if it failed…

They must not fail.

Finn patted her arm. It was the way he might console a child, yet whatever his intention, the feelings he aroused with his touch were anything but childish. Warmth and need, longing and desire, seemed to spread along her skin.

Her lustful reaction reminded her of a part of her plan she hadn't shared with Finn. With a few sharp tugs, she tore her right sleeve from her bodice. She undid the knot in the laces at the back, so that it gaped slightly.

Finn twisted around to see what she was doing. "What's that for?" he asked, his eyes on her bodice and his voice low and husky in a way that made her suddenly yearn to cover herself. "Jaysus, you'll have every man in the place trying to get a look at your breasts."

As long as Lord Wimarc was one of them. "That's what I'm hoping. And that they'll be too distracted to ask a lot of questions."

"Oh, they'll be distracted, all right."

"I also want to make it look as if we really were attacked."

"Maybe I should knock myself on the head."

"If you think it would help the ruse," she countered. She'd been right to think he wouldn't agree with this part of her plan, so she was glad she'd kept it to herself.

He didn't reply and, with an exasperated sigh, urged the horse into a trot.

When they entered the grassy area in front of the barbican of Castle de Werre, two sentries came charging out of the gate. It was still light enough that they didn't need torches to see, and one drew his sword while the other tilted his spear toward them in warning.

They weren't dressed like most garrison soldiers. It looked as if they'd put on any bit of armor and leather they could find, or steal. Both were large men, and their faces were scarred, one above the eye, the other on the jaw.

"Hold!" the taller of the two cried. "Who are you and what do you want?"

Finn answered, sounding exactly like a distressed nobleman. "I'm Lord Gilbert of Fairbourne. We were attacked. My wife and I barely escaped with our lives!"

Two more soldiers trotted out of the shadows of the massive portcullis, their spears leveled. As they approached, Lizette started wailing. "Oh, let us in! Let us in!"

"Let us pass!" Finn ordered. "Can't you see Lady Helewyse is distraught?"

The soldiers exchanged wary glances.

"Fools! If I meant to attack you, would I come alone and with a woman? For God's sake, let us enter! We're guests of Lord Wimarc!"

A good-looking man in a long, dark tunic embroidered in silver about the neck and hem came striding out of the gate, his clothing, his face and his attitude a sharp contrast to the soldiers'. He wore a sword belt around his slender waist, and his shoulders were nearly as broad as Finn's, but there was nothing at all belligerent about him. He had the lithe grace of a courtier, and his face was unlined. Black hair curled about his ears and she was sure she could smell some kind of perfume emanating from him—not a feminine odor, but certainly better than sweat and leather.

The sentries fell back before him, and she realized who he must be.

Her expectations had been utterly wrong. She'd been expecting Lord Wimarc to be a middle-aged man, gray haired and sly as an old miser, not a much younger man nearly as good-looking as Finn.

"Lord Gilbert? Lady Helewyse?" he cried in dismay as he quickened his pace. "Good God, of course you may enter. What's happened?"

"Lord Wimarc?" Finn inquired.

"The very same," the man replied with a bow. "I was

on the wall walk giving the sentries the watchword for the night when I saw you approaching. I'm very sorry this has happened, and on my lands, too. You're most welcome to my castle, and my home."

Wimarc certainly looked upset, and sounded it, too. That could be feigned, of course. He could be as clever as Finn when it came to pretence.

Lord Wimarc took hold of the reins of their horse and started to lead it inside his castle himself. "I shall speak to my patrols and have the brigands who dared to attack you apprehended."

Although Lizette was glad their plan had succeeded so far, she couldn't suppress a shudder as they rode beneath the portcullis, then the murder hole. It was through such a gap that defenders would rain down stones or boiling water, or even burning pitch, to prevent their enemies from entering the castle.

She had seen a person burned by flaming pitch once, when a servant had dropped a lit torch on his leg. She'd never forget that gruesome sight, or his screams, or the smell of his burned flesh.

They continued through the massive gates to the outer bailey, which wasn't as large as she'd expected, either. Perhaps this Wimarc wasn't as rich or powerful as people said, or Finn believed.

Wimarc led them through an equally well-guarded, massive oaken gate in the three-foot-thick inner wall and into the courtyard. That cobblestoned area, with several buildings around the walls, was larger than she'd expected and well lit with torches and braziers.

She guessed that the long, tall building opposite the

gates with stairs leading inside was the hall. Abutting it at a right angle was another stone building, with wide, arched windows on what must be a second floor, and smaller, narrower openings below. Family apartments and bedchambers, she suspected. Attached to the hall on the other side by a covered wooden walkway was what must be the kitchen, judging by the quantity of smoke rising from two louvered openings in the slate roof.

There was another building attached to the hall, tall and narrow, with only loopholes for windows. It looked older than the rest, and she suspected it must have been the original keep. Perhaps the entrance to the dungeon was there; it usually was in such a building, although that looked too small to house as many prisoners as Finn thought they had here.

In addition to these stone edifices, there were half-timber stables and other outbuildings, and some of wattle and daub that were probably storehouses or barracks for the many soldiers milling about the yard.

Every one of them looked big and tough and battle hardened. She doubted there was a one of them younger than twenty, and many of them had terrible scars, or were missing pieces of noses, or ears. If their ruse was discovered by such men...

She wouldn't think about that. She'd study the walls, the gates, the position of the sentries, trying to figure out a way to escape undetected once she'd found her proof and they'd rescued Finn's brother.

Finn put his hand over hers. Once again, his touch was unexpected, yet undeniably welcome, and she felt her courage return. After all, she wasn't alone, and if this man could make the king and all his court believe he was a nobleman, he could surely convince Wimarc.

"It's all right, my love," Finn softly said. "We're safe now."

He was only playing a part. She knew that, yet she was grateful nonetheless.

Now a little less anxious, she realized not every person in the yard was a soldier or mercenary. Several were servants, men as well as a few women who'd come out to see what was happening.

Wimarc halted and Finn dismounted, then reached up to help her down, his hands strong and firm about her waist. As she slid from the horse, her bodice gaped and fell off her shoulder.

Finn's gaze flashed to that bare flesh and he immediately pulled her into his arms before shoving it back into place.

"Oh, my poor darling!" he cried.

Then he captured her mouth with his and kissed her with unbridled passion.

CHAPTER NINE

FOR A MOMENT, Lizette was too stunned to move. She'd had no idea a kiss could feel so…could render her so…could make her wish he'd never stop…that he'd pick her up and carry her somewhere, anywhere, where they could be alone….

Overwhelmed by desire, she ran her hands up Finn's back, pressing her body against his. She remembered him sitting by the fire, with that remote, grim expression, as if he were the last man on earth and haunted by what he remembered. She recalled how he'd saved her from Lindall and those others. How kind he'd been to Keldra and Garreth, and how marvelous he looked….

Someone cleared a throat, and she abruptly remembered where she was, and why.

And that she had a part to play, too, as Finn did—and this kiss must be no more than a part of their ruse.

Her embarrassed blush was real enough as she drew back, and when she saw the smug satisfaction in Finn's eyes, so was her annoyance. "My lord husband, please! How inappropriate!"

"I'm sure Lord Wimarc will forgive me," he said lightly as he gave their host a grin.

Yet she'd seen something in his eyes before he spoke—surprise, shock, excitement—that told her he wasn't as unaffected by that kiss as he was pretending to be.

Nevertheless, she tried not to assign any importance to his reaction.

Lord Wimarc laughed in an oddly noiseless way. "Indeed, I do. It's delightful to see such passion between a married couple. It is so rare."

He turned to Lizette, his gaze on her face and not her torn bodice. "I shall have one of my servants take you to a chamber where you may refresh yourself," he said before he addressed Finn again. "If you don't mind, my lord, I would speak to you about this attack—where, and of the men—while the memory is still fresh."

"Of course," Finn agreed with a gentlemanly inclination of his head.

Since Lizette was supposed to be the dutiful wife, she gave Wimarc one of her very best smiles and bowed slightly, giving him a glimpse of her cleavage. "My lord, I thank you for your generous hospitality and kind concern."

Wimarc's gaze finally flicked where she intended. She knew she was commencing an even more dangerous game, but it was no more risky than the one she was already playing, and if it helped their cause to play the flirt, she would.

"You are most welcome, my lady," Wimarc said, "and you must avail yourself of my wife's wardrobe. She's visiting friends not far from here, and I'm sure she won't mind, especially under these circumstances. You, my lord Gilbert, must avail yourself of mine."

"Thank you, my lord, I will," Finn replied.

Wimarc turned toward the building that looked like the hall.

"Greseld!" he called, and a wizened old woman came tottering from the doorway. "Lord Gilbert and his wife shall have the north chamber. See that it's prepared, and that Lady Helewyse has everything she desires, including whatever gowns of my wife's she finds to her taste. Have wine and bread and cheese brought to the hall for Lord Gilbert and me."

The old woman nodded, then pointed at a younger female servant loitering nearby. She was pretty, with nut-brown hair and a pointed chin and slender nose— and Lizette surmised she knew it, judging by the slightly insolent curl of her upper lip.

"Ellie, take my lady to the chamber," Greseld ordered before gesturing to two other women who were likewise in the yard, both young and rather slovenly attired. "Water and linen," she snapped at them before she turned and tottered back into the hall.

"Greseld was my nurse when I was a boy and runs my household in my wife's absence," Lord Wimarc explained as Ellie walked toward them, hips swaying.

Lizette silently vowed she would *not* look to see if Finn was watching the buxom young woman.

"If you'll come with me, my lady," Ellie said softly, sliding a glance first at Lord Wimarc, then at Finn—a coy and flirtatious glance that told Lizette that if Greseld sometimes took the place of Lord Wimarc's wife running the hall, Ellie no doubt sometimes took his wife's place in his bed. She'd probably gladly share Finn's bed, too, if she got the chance.

Before Lizette left with Ellie, Finn pulled his supposed wife into another embrace. "I'll see you soon, my dear."

He was playing his part a bit *too* well. As Wimarc had implied, noble marriages weren't made for love, but politics and gain. If Finn acted too much the smitten lover, that might raise suspicions—and Wimarc might keep his distance from her, which she most certainly did not want if she was to find out his secrets.

So she pulled away and gave Lord Wimarc another smile. "I look forward to speaking with you again when I'm more presentable, my lord."

The man made a sweeping bow. "You are so lovely, you are always presentable, my lady."

"Such delightful flattery," she said with a giggle before she turned to follow the maidservant toward the two-story stone building attached to the hall. "You must try and teach that skill to my husband."

"YOU'RE A LUCKY MAN," Lord Wimarc remarked after Lizette had disappeared inside the building and he and Finn had started toward the hall.

"Luck had little to do with it. Her father wanted a courtier for his daughter and was willing to pay a great deal," Finn replied, settling once more into the role of nobleman even as he tried to calm his shattered composure.

They'd definitely ridden into a hornet's nest. There had to be a sentry every ten feet or less on the wall walk, and the men here were obviously battle-hardened mer-

cenaries, just as he'd been told. There was a bevy of
servants, too, and aside from the crone, they were all
young, both men and women. Another form of "payment" for Wimarc's mercenaries, Finn supposed, and
likely used to satisfy Wimarc's own lustful appetites, as
well, at least when his wife was away from home.

He'd been prepared for those dangers. What he hadn't
been prepared for was how he'd felt when he kissed Lady
Elizabeth. He'd thought only to make their ruse more believable, even if, deep in his heart, he knew he'd been
wanting to kiss her since he'd seen her by that stream.

The moment his lips touched hers, though, it was as
if any desire or passion he'd ever felt before had been
but mere shadows of the true feelings. He'd never experienced such desire for a woman. It was a hunger so
strong, he'd nearly forgotten where he was, and his
purpose here. Nor had he anticipated that she'd kiss
him back with such ardor.

"You did well to get her," Wimarc said as he pushed
open the double door to his hall.

Of course Finn had noticed the way Wimarc looked
at Elizabeth and her torn bodice. That kiss had also
been intended to tell Wimarc that she was *his*, even
though she really wasn't, and never would be. She was
a lady, he was an outlaw, and after they succeeded
here—if they succeeded here—they would part and go
their own ways, back to the lives they knew.

But he'd be damned before he'd let Wimarc think he
was like too many men at court, willing to trade his wife
for friendship or favor.

Still, he had to be polite, so he put a smile on his face

as he surveyed the high, beamed ceiling, the corbels holding the foot-square beams carved to resemble animal heads. The floor, made of stone and not packed earth, was covered with rushes, and the pleasant odor of rosemary and other herbs arose as they crossed it. The furnishings—narrow benches and trestle tables now leaning against the wall—shone dully, evidence of much waxing. Three great iron rings hung from the roof by thick chains that were attached to the wall so they could be raised and lowered, and each had to contain fifty candles at least. For now, only the one hanging over the dais was lit; the other illumination in the hall came from torches in iron sconces on the pillars and walls.

If all the candles and torches were lit, this place would be nearly as bright as day, even at night.

Two huge hearths, their mantels also finely carved, had been built into the walls, one in the main part, the other to warm the dais. This was something only the most modern halls possessed, and bespoke a concern for comfort over cost. A tapestry, huge and finely woven, depicting a royal court, hung over the outside wall to shield the occupants from drafts.

An interesting choice of subject for a tapestry, Finn thought. And the hall would have been much more pleasant if it hadn't also housed several of Wimarc's mercenaries, who watched them pass.

God help him, pretending to be a noble at the king's court seemed like child's play now!

Upon reaching the dais, Wimarc gestured for Finn to sit in a wooden chair bearing a blue silk cushion. Finn did, accepting the silver goblet of wine Wimarc handed him from a pair resting on a small, ornate table near the hearth. A silver carafe held more wine, and there was also a silver platter bearing cheese, bread and sweetmeats.

Since Finn was hungry, and because eating would delay talking, he eagerly availed himself of the food, wondering if Lizette was likewise getting something to eat. Wimarc sat nearby, smiling and twisting a ruby ring around his slender finger as he watched his guest.

Wimarc was as smooth and polished as any of the nobles Finn had met at court. He was handsome, too, in an oily sort of way, and very well dressed—the sort of nobleman who made Finn feel every inch the peasant and son of a whore he was.

Unfortunately, the food didn't last forever and when Finn had eaten his fill, Wimarc said, "How large was the band of outlaws that attacked you?"

Taking another sip of the excellent wine, Finn leaned back in his chair. "We were attacked by at least fifty."

"Where?"

Finn described a location some miles from where they'd actually encountered Lord Gilbert and his wife, and then told Wimarc the outlaws had fled in a direction away from Wimarc's castle, and the hut in the wood.

"They might have been soldiers no longer employed by a lord or other nobleman," Finn suggested. "Ever since John has taken to having so many hired soldiers in his service, England's been overrun with such louts."

Despite his reference to the king, Wimarc's attention was no longer on Finn, or what he was saying, and when Finn followed the baron's gaze, he saw why not.

Lady Elizabeth stood on the threshold of the hall at the bottom of a curved staircase leading to the building abutting it. Her hair had been combed, braided and wound around her head like a gleaming coronet. She wore a gown of rich burgundy shot through with gold threads that shimmered in the candlelight, and the long sleeves were lined with golden silk. The high-waisted, square bodice was likewise bordered with gold embroidery and the gored skirt flared over her slim hips.

But that was not what made Finn's mouth go dry, nor likely what caused Wimarc to stare so boldly.

The gown was too small and thus slightly too tight in the bodice—not enough to render it unwearable, but enough to push her breasts together and up, so that they seemed about to spill right over the binding fabric altogether.

"A lucky man indeed," Wimarc murmured as he rose. "I envy you, my lord."

Finn likewise got to his feet and told himself to remember this was just a ruse. Lizette was not his wife, or his mistress, or his lover. She never would be. Never could be, given the difference in their rank and what he'd done to survive. And the lie he'd told to her sister and Armand de Boisbaston.

"You are truly a lovely sight for a man's eyes, my lady," Lord Wimarc said as he handed her into the chair he'd vacated. "I hope you found the bedchamber to your liking?"

"I did. So large and comfortable." She slid him a coy look. "I was surprised to learn that your wife doesn't share your chamber, my lord."

"She prefers to sleep alone," Wimarc answered easily. He gave them both a genial smile. "It seems, my lady, I kick."

Lizette giggled—*giggled!*—at that. "Gilbert snores."

He did not, and said so.

She gave him a smug smile. "Oh, yes, you do!"

"I'm glad to hear I'm not the only man whose wife finds fault with his nocturnal habits," Wimarc said, refilling his goblet and handing it to her, effectively ending their disagreement. "You must be sure to tell me if there's anything more you require."

Lizette sipped her wine before answering. "I shall, my lord. You are most kind." She sipped some more. "And your wine is very good."

"Have you had anything to eat?" Finn asked, fearing the wine would go quickly to her head if she hadn't.

"I have, thank you. That girl—Ellie, is it?—brought me some bread and cheese. Very fine bread and cheese, too. I must speak to your cheese maker, Lord Wimarc, for I've never tasted better."

She lowered her goblet, and Wimarc—damn him—was quick to fill it again, stealing a look down her bodice, too, the cur.

Lizette giggled again, and it was obvious the wine was taking effect. "This really is very good wine. From France?"

"Burgundy," Wimarc answered, standing back and setting the carafe on the table.

"You must sit, too, my lord!" she declared, giving him a slightly lopsided grin. "Gilbert, fetch that chair for our host."

He might be an outlaw, but he was supposed to be her husband, as well as a nobleman, not a servant.

Fortunately, Wimarc called for one of his men to fetch the chair, and when he sat, he gave them both a magnanimous smile. "I trust the rest of your journey was better than the end?"

"We—" Finn began.

"Well, to be honest, my lord, it was a nightmare," Lizette interrupted, leaning so far forward, Finn feared her breasts were going to pop right out of her gown. "The roads were terrible, the weather worse, and my lord husband was loath to rest. I had to practically beg him to stop for the night, he seemed so anxious to get here."

She reached out to pat Wimarc on the arm. "Of course, now that I'm here, I understand his urge for haste. Such a fine castle and hall, my lord! If I were your wife, I would never leave it."

"I'm delighted it meets with your approval, my lady," Wimarc replied. "I'm sure Roslynn will be most distressed she missed you." He picked up the carafe again. "More wine?"

The last thing Lizette needed, Finn thought, was more wine. If she got any drunker, who knew what she might say? Or do.

If he'd had any doubts that he was right to have such concerns, she dispelled them when she declared, with another giggle, "I do believe he's trying to get me drunk, Gilbert!"

Finn got to his feet. "You don't appear to require much assistance, my lady," he said. "I suggest it's time you retired."

"Retire? Nonsense!" she retorted, holding out her goblet as if she hadn't already drained it twice.

Jesus, Mary and all the saints, she was like some of the women he'd seen at the king's court when they were in their cups. She was acting just as silly and coy, batting her eyes at Wimarc, and ignoring *him* except to say deprecating things. "I think not, since what you want apparently includes making a fool of yourself in front of our host."

He grabbed her hand to pull her out of her chair. "If you'll excuse us, my lord."

Lord Wimarc rose, and wisely didn't urge them to stay. "Of course. Good night, my lady. My lord."

"I don't want to go!" Lizette protested, tugging her arm free and nearly falling over with the effort. "I want to stay *here* and talk to our handsome host! He must know everybody at court, and I want to hear all about the queen and—"

"Not tonight," Finn snapped. "It's late and we've had a very trying day—or have you forgotten how we were attacked?"

"No, I haven't—or that you didn't lift a finger to save me! You went charging off after one of the outlaws and left me to fend for myself!"

"I did not!" he returned, wondering what else might come out of her mouth before he got her out of there. "You had plenty of guards."

"Who all ran off when you did!"

"I came back." He glanced at the rest of the hall, to see that all the men and servants were watching, and listening, too. "My lady, if you please, you are making a spectacle of yourself!"

She gave him a sour look. "If you're unhappy, you can retire—by yourself!"

She took a step toward Wimarc and practically fell into his arms. Tapping his chest and looking up at him, her body pressed against his, she said, "He thinks he's irrest…irriti…irre*sis*tible to the ladies, you see. Ha! I could resist him—I do resist him! My father *made* me marry him. Locked me in my room and threatened to starve me if I didn't!"

With a wary glance at Finn, Lord Wimarc put his hands on her upper arms and moved her toward her supposed husband. "Gilbert's a fine fellow."

"You don't have to make love with him."

"That's enough!" Finn declared. He grabbed her arm, spun her around, picked her up and threw her over his shoulder as if she were a sack of grain.

She emitted a shriek of protest, which Finn ignored. If she said anything more, so help him, he'd smack her on her shapely bottom.

"I hope you can forgive this shocking behavior, my lord," he said to their host while Lizette struggled in vain. "I assure you, it will not be repeated!"

Carrying Lizette like a sack of wiggling grain, Finn marched toward the steps and upward to their chamber.

CHAPTER TEN

"WHICH CHAMBER IS OURS?" Finn demanded when they reached the top of the stairs.

"The...last...one," Lizette gasped. "Put...me... down!"

Ignoring her, Finn kicked open the door and strode into the room lit with a single candle on a table beside the large bed.

He paused, scanning the chamber and the fine furnishings—a far cry from most of the rooms he'd slept in, even when pretending to be a courtier. There was a washstand with plenty of linens, and a bronze basin and ewer. A chest stood in a corner, painted the same bright colors as the table beside the bed. A tapestry depicting women in a garden covered the wall opposite the bed, behind two chairs carved with vines and flowers, with another small table in between.

There was a hole in the tapestry—something definitely unusual in such a well-kept chamber.

"And just what, my lady, was the reason for that performance?" he demanded as he dumped Lizette on the enormous curtained bed.

She scrambled to sit up without tearing the gown that

was laced so tight, she could scarcely breathe, while he crossed his arms over his chest and regarded her with scorn. "I was only doing—"

"What you always do," Finn sneered. "Flirt with every man you meet."

"How dare you take that tone with me?" she said breathlessly as she got to her feet. There was no need for him to play his husbandly role here. "I was merely—"

"You're my wife, by God, and so help me, you'll behave with honor or I'll send you back to your family in disgrace!"

This was ridiculous. There was no need to maintain the ruse when they were alone. "Need I remind you—?"

He grabbed her shoulders and tugged her into a crushing embrace, his lips taking hers with force as well as fervor.

Sweet savior! she cried inwardly as she struggled, twisting and turning in his powerful arms. Had he gone mad? Or had she been wrong to trust him after all? He was an outlaw, and he had her at his mercy here as much as if they were in the wood—more so, if he was allegedly her husband. He could rape her, beat her, insult and demean her, and no man would try to stop him, because his wife was, by law, his chattel.

"Stop fighting me!" he commanded as he swept her up in his arms and carried her to the bed.

True panic set in. She hit and slapped him, cursed and reviled him with every terrible epithet she could think of as he threw her down onto the bed.

"You're dressed like a whore and you curse like one,

too!" he shouted. "Dowry or not, I never should have married you!"

She saw a chance to escape and took it—but he lunged for her over the bed, grabbed her arm and pulled her back. Then he was atop her, his hands holding her wrists, the rest of his body covering hers. She flailed helplessly, desperately, as he leaned down to kiss her.

"Stop struggling!" he hissed as he slid his lips toward her ear. "This is for show. We're being watched."

He had to repeat it before she understood what he was saying. She did at last, and as relief swept over her, she stopped fighting and lay still.

He kissed her, and this time, his kiss was gentle, almost tender, as if he intended only to calm and comfort her, not arouse her.

Although he did. Whether he meant to or not, he did.

"That's better," he said, not whispering. "Never forget you're my wife, Helewyse. If you do, you'll regret it."

She nodded as he got off her, and the bed.

Uncertain what he meant to do next, wondering where a spy could be hidden and sincerely hoping it wasn't under the bed, she lay still and waited.

"That gown is a disgrace," he said as he went to the washstand and splashed cold water over his face. "You were flaunting your breasts like a cheap harlot."

"I can't help it if Lord Wimarc's wife is smaller than I," she said as she sat up. "None of the gowns in that chest are any larger. It was choose one, or go down in my soiled dress. I didn't think I could wear my shift beneath, either."

He slowly turned around to look at her, the linen forgotten in his hand. "You aren't wearing a shift?" he asked, his voice a little strained.

"Of course I am!" she answered, suddenly wondering what he would do if she weren't. "I borrowed one of Lady Roslynn's. Fortunately, it fit better. Still, I hope I haven't torn it, for the linen is quite fine and thin."

Without a word, he poured more cold water from the ewer into the basin, then washed his face again.

She rose from the bed and, wanting to breathe normally, decided to unlace the gown while he was otherwise occupied, which she did rapidly, glad that the knot was loosely tied.

If somebody was watching, Finn could hardly sleep on the floor as they'd planned. He wouldn't try to get into the bed with her, would he? No, he wouldn't. He mustn't touch her.

What would she do if he did? Or tried to…

She'd stop him. Of course she would. She had to, because this was only a ruse. He was an outlaw and she was Lady Elizabeth of Averette.

That seemed rather difficult to remember, or believe so very important, when he removed his shirt and sat on the end of the bed to remove his boots, the muscles and skin of his naked back moving with fluid, manly grace.

She should take advantage of this time while his back was turned. Wondering where the spy might be hiding, she nevertheless swiftly took off her gown and laid it on the chest, then scrambled into the bed, still clad in the thin shift.

She found it even more difficult to remember that they were not lovers when he rose and turned toward her, his bare chest gleaming in the dim candlelight, his breeches tight about his hips, his eyes unreadable in the shadows as he stood at the foot of the bed. Then he yanked the bed curtains closed.

Like a specter, he appeared at the left side of the bed and closed those curtains, too. And then, when it seemed she might swoon from anticipation and uncertainty, he came to the right side, knelt upon the bed and closed those curtains from the inside, plunging them into darkness. Alone. Together.

She felt the bed move and knew he was close to her. She held her breath until he spoke softly, but sounding completely, utterly matter-of-fact. "I think we should be able to speak freely now, as long as we're quiet."

"Why do you think someone's watching us here?" she asked in a whisper. "Where are they hiding?"

"When we first entered the chamber, I saw a hole in the tapestry on the far wall. Given the state of the hall and this chamber, why would a tapestry with such a flaw be hanging there unless that hole served a purpose—and what more likely purpose than spying on the people in this chamber? Wimarc may simply not trust his wife, but I'm not taking any chances. For now, we must behave as if we're being watched, so we must act as if we're really married. Which reminds me—what exactly were you trying to do below?"

"I was being friendly to our host, as a guest should be," she said with a hint of defiance to hide the shame she'd felt at playing the fool.

"Why did you pretend to be drunk?"

"I want Wimarc to believe he'll be able to seduce me without much effort."

She could easily imagine the glare that went with Finn's next whispered exclamation. "Are you mad? I told you, he's a dangerous man."

She wasn't willing to abandon that part of her plan, not on his say-so. She was already in danger; what more risk if she could play on Wimarc's vanity? "If he thinks he can seduce me, he'll surely try to impress me, and in doing so, tell me things he shouldn't, such as who his friends and allies are, or who's visited here recently."

"So you hope," Finn sarcastically replied as he lay down.

"Yes, I do. Surely you didn't think I was flirting with a possible traitor simply for the excitement?"

"Obviously I didn't know what the hell you were doing, since you didn't deign to tell me of this plan of yours until just now. I'm no mind reader, my lady, and you're supposed to be my wife."

"Is that why you kissed me?"

"Of course."

"It wasn't your manly attempt to assert your authority and possession of me, to tell Wimarc that I belong to you?"

When Finn didn't answer, she knew she was right. "Fortunately, your jealousy works in our favor."

"I'm playing a part, my lady," he reminded her, annoyed.

"As am I. Now Wimarc will believe there's trouble between us and it will be easier to seduce me."

"And if he gets you alone? What will you do then?"

She answered without hesitation. "Fend him off until we find out what we need to know."

"And if he wearies of your teasing? Lord Wimarc is a selfish, greedy man, my lady. You're playing with fire."

"I'm not a child, Finn. We both need to gain Wimarc's trust, albeit in different ways. You must make him believe you're ripe for treason and I must make him believe I'm ripe for something else."

"I don't want you alone with him."

"I don't want you alone with him, either. You weren't raised a nobleman, so you might make a mistake and cause him to doubt our story."

"If you had such doubts, you shouldn't have come here."

"Too late now, my lord," she replied. "We're here and we're married."

"Aye," he answered, his voice soft and low. "And sharing a bed."

"Except not really," she retorted, shifting to the far edge of her side of it.

"If we have an audience tonight, we must make him believe we're married," he said, beginning to bounce like a child playing, making the ropes holding the straw mattress creak.

"Moan as if we're making love," he prompted. "Hopefully if we are being watched, the spy will realize he—or she—is not likely to hear anything important tonight and go away."

Praying he was right, although she felt ridiculous, she did as he proposed.

"Not like that. You sound like you're about to be sick. Moan like a woman making love."

"I wouldn't know how," she replied in a tense whisper. "I'm a virgin."

There was a moment of silence, and the bouncing ceased until Finn groaned softly and started to bounce again. "So whimper. Can you whimper?"

She tried.

"Good enough," he said before groaning again.

"You sound as if you're dying."

"I sound as if I'm making love, which you claim you don't know anything about."

"Just because I'm a virgin doesn't mean I'm completely ignorant," she retorted. "I wasn't raised in a convent. And I was on my way home from a wedding when we were attacked. What do you think women talk about at such celebrations? It's more than the dowry or her gown, or the feasts, I can assure you. And I've seen—"

"What, you've *watched?*"

She was sorry she'd said that, but there was an explanation, which she hastened to supply. "By accident."

"So make some of those sounds, and when I tap your arm, cry out as if I'd pinched you."

She could guess what that was supposed to indicate, and if that was what was required…

He tapped her lightly, she duly cried out—and then he let out a groan as if she'd stabbed him in the stomach.

Did a man really sound like that when he…when he…?

She wasn't going to ask and mercifully, he finally stopped bouncing. She was beginning to feel as she had in the wagon.

His chuckle came out of the darkness. "That was perfect, my lady. If I didn't know any better, I'd swear your husband has just brought you to the heights of ecstasy."

The heights of ecstasy? That sounded…fascinating. And yet… "I assume that will be enough such activity for tonight."

"Oh, aye, that's enough. Any more and I'd be giving myself an injury. I'll stay right where I am, on the edge of the bed, on top of the covers and sincerely hoping I don't fall off."

He might think this was amusing, but she didn't. "Do you promise?"

"Aye, you have my word." His voice seemed like the soft brush of fur against her skin. "What of you, my lady? Will you promise not to touch *me?* I need my sleep if I'm to be on my toes tomorrow."

"Of course," she hissed as she rolled onto her side so that her back was to him. "You're the one who's always kissing *me!*"

"And you're the one always kissing me back."

"I am not!"

The ropes creaked again as he moved. Was he coming closer?

"Are you telling me that when I go to kiss you, somebody else slips in at the last moment and takes your place, then slips out again before I open my eyes?" he asked, his voice low in her ear, his breath warm on her cheek, as if he were mere inches away.

"I do not enjoy your embraces or your kisses."

"No?"

In the next instant, she was on her back, and he was

above her and kissing her passionately, with all the ardor of before, and more. Taken aback, she squirmed and wiggled, but he kept kissing her, his mouth gentling her, then soothing, until she gave up the struggle and surrendered to the pleasure of his lips, and then his supple tongue.

She moaned softly and her arms slid around to hold him, reveling in the feel of his powerful warrior's body against her own, delighting in his kiss that made her feel so cherished and desired.

She almost whimpered with dismay when he drew back, then moved over to the other side of the bed. "That's the sort of moan I meant," he said as if discussing the state of his saddle. "Good night, my lady. Sleep well—and never lie to a man who lies for his living."

She tried to think of some clever retort, something that would make him feel ashamed or embarrassed. Unfortunately, nothing came to her, so she wrapped the covers tightly about her, rolled onto her side and ordered herself to sleep.

AFTER REMOVING HIS CLOTHES and slipping into his bed robe, Wimarc drained his goblet and shifted in the chair in his well-appointed bedchamber, still aroused by what he'd just seen and heard while hidden in the small passageway.

He'd had that spy hole made so that he could ensure his wife never took a lover; it was proving to have some additional benefits now, and as his lust continued to warm him, he was contemplating how he could use these two guests, and their apparent enmity, to his own ends. Not that they were completely acrimonious. Not to judge by the sounds from that curtained bed.

Nevertheless the woman was clearly ripe for adultery. Her husband annoyed her, and she was unappreciated. He would certainly appreciate her—at least for one night in his bed. And then, fearing what could happen if that become known to her husband, she would be in his power.

That would be pleasant, too, in its own way. Desperate women were willing to do almost anything, in bed or out of it.

At the sound of a knock on his door, he rose and went to open it, taking his sword or dagger. As expected, Ellie stood on the threshold, swaying those seductive hips of hers, a coy look on her pretty face.

Did she, even now, think he was some lovesick lad to care about such games? It might have been amusing, if he wasn't impatient to satisfy his needs.

He grabbed her arm and pulled her into the room, shutting the door behind him. Before she could speak, he hauled her close and took her mouth with swift and brutal desire. His arousal rising to feverish heights, he hauled her to the bed and pushed her down. Shoving up her skirts, he parted his bed robe and shoved inside, taking her with primitive force, regardless of the sounds she made or the look of anguish on her face.

As always when he took his pleasure, the only woman's face he saw was that of Ephegenia, the woman who'd spurned his youthful advances and made a mockery of his affection. It was a selfish world, she'd said, and he hadn't enough to give.

He'd given her something to remember him by that day. As always, the memories of her cries and pleas took him over the edge to release.

Satisfied, Wimarc withdrew. Without a word, ignoring his servant, he closed his bed robe and walked toward the table bearing the silver carafe of wine and a single goblet.

Meanwhile, Ellie pushed down her skirts, straightened her bodice and sat up. If there were tears in her eyes, she blinked them away, and spoke with that same coy seduction. "Something's got you in a fever, my lord."

He poured himself another goblet of wine and drank it. Then he walked over to the small embossed chest on the side of the bed and took out a small purse. He removed a single silver coin and tossed it on the bed beside her. "Go."

She took the coin and shoved it in her bodice. As always, her eyes gleamed with avarice, but this time, there was something else there, too: speculation, and perhaps a tinge of dread. "If I was the jealous sort, I'd think it was Lady Helewyse and you hope to seduce her."

He strode to the bed and grabbed Ellie by the throat, glaring into her frightened eyes. "Never presume to guess my plans."

He let go and she fell back, panting, her hand on her throat. "Yes, m-my lord. I won't. Not never again."

"Good." He ran a coolly measuring gaze over her, studying her as he would any other piece of property that could be useful.

He thought of a use. "Lord Gilbert is a handsome man, is he not?"

Ellie smiled, her lips trembling, trying to appease him—as if he cared a whit about her—as she slid off the bed and came to him.

"Not so handsome as you, my lord," she murmured, insinuating herself against him, trying to regain what she thought she'd lost.

Pathetic creature. But he would play her game, if that would make her eager to obey.

So he gave her a smile and caressed her cheek. "I'm sorry if I was a little harsh with you, Ellie. We live in dangerous times, and a man must be careful with his plans."

"You can trust me, my lord," she said, leaning against him and slipping her hand into his bedrobe to caress his chest.

His lust was sated for now, so that didn't distract him. As for trusting her…he'd sooner trust his weak, stupid whore of a mother. Ellie would sell information for anything she could get, unless she thought she'd be more amply rewarded by remaining silent. "I'd like you to do something for me, Ellie, for which you'll be well paid."

Just as he thought, the gleam of avarice came to her brown eyes as she moved her hand lower. "Anything you like, my lord."

He lifted her searching fingers away. "Not that— well, not me. I want you to seduce Lord Gilbert."

CHAPTER ELEVEN

"THIS WAS THE KEEP," Wimarc said to Finn as he opened the door to the lower level of the building attached to the hall on the north side of his castle the next day. "This level was for storage and for keeping prisoners. It had only one cell, though, which is now the guardroom."

Wimarc nodded a greeting at the two men currently in the small, dark guardroom that had no window, so it could be night or day outside, and one would never know.

They were two of the ugliest men Finn had ever seen. Only two, though.

The room smelled of sweat and urine and blood, and chains hung on the far wall. There was also a battered wooden table and a bench, and light came from a stinking oil lamp suspended on a chain from the ceiling, as well as a torch in the sconce in the wall outside another door.

"Uldun, we're going below," Wimarc said as he lifted the torch from the sconce.

The biggest and ugliest of the men moved to the door, taking the ring of heavy iron keys from his belt to unlock it.

As he did, Finn surreptitiously studied the keys and

then the lock into which Uldun fit one of them. A large lock, but a simple one, easily picked by someone who knew how.

The door swung open and Wimarc brushed past Uldun to lead the way down the slick, damp steps lit with more spluttering, stinking pitch torches.

Hell itself could hardly be worse, Finn thought with dismay as he followed, and to think Ryder was somewhere below....

"I had this lower level dug," Wimarc said, obviously proud of his idea. "I can have up to fifty men down here, more if they stand."

Crammed into cells like cattle awaiting slaughter.

"Alas, too many brigands and outlaws roam the highways and byways these days, as you and your charming wife unfortunately found out. I do my best to keep my lands safe, but by God, it's not easy."

"Yes, there are villains everywhere," Finn agreed, clenching his hands to still their angry trembling. "I'm surprised, my lord, you don't simply hang the louts and be done with it."

"But then they wouldn't suffer," the nobleman replied with a calmness that turned Finn's stomach.

He'd seen men hanged, and there was nothing merciful about that awful death, especially if the hangman was a stupid one who miscalculated the length of rope.

They reached the lower level. Water dripped down the stone walls, and the chill seemed to penetrate Finn's very bones. "Impressive," he lied as a rat scurried along the edge of the wall.

Wimarc saw the creature and laughed noiselessly.

"Sometimes the prisoners try to catch the rats, but they rarely succeed. I imagine raw rat only appeals to the most desperate."

"Yes, I suppose one would have to be truly starving," Finn replied, raising his voice, hoping it would carry to the far reaches of the door-lined corridor so that Ryder would hear him, if he was still alive.

Lifting out another torch, he went ahead of Wimarc and strolled past the cells. "Quite an accomplishment," he said, surveying the ceiling of the corridor. "You must have had a master mason."

"I did. The man didn't come cheap, but he was worth it."

"You must give me his name. I need some repairs done on Fairbourne, and I'm thinking I could use a bigger dungeon, too."

"Gally? Sweet Jesus, is that you?"

The voice came feebly through the thick door to his right. Only Ryder had ever called Finn "Gally."

Ryder was alive. Thank God and all his saints and angels, his brother was alive.

He wanted to call out to him. He wanted to get the keys and free his brother. He wanted to kill Wimarc and anybody who tried to stop him…except they would never get out of this castle alive if he did. He couldn't risk Lizette's life, too.

Instead, he turned on his heel and started back toward Wimarc. "Very impressive indeed, but I confess the stench is rather overpowering."

"Yes, it is," Wimarc agreed, starting back up the steps. "Unfortunately, there's nothing to be done about that."

As Wimarc continued upward, Finn paused on the bottom step and looked back over his shoulder. He didn't dare do more, but it wasn't easy leaving Ryder there.

Soon, he silently promised. *Soon I'll have you out of here.*

INSIDE HIS FETID CELL, Ryder pressed his ear against the door. Had that been Fingal's voice, or was his mind playing tricks on him?

It had sounded so much like Fingal...

"Gally?" he called again, listening intently for that familiar voice, speaking like a nobleman. *"Gally!"*

Silence, except for the trickle of water down the walls, and the scratching of rats nearby.

"Oh, God, am I going mad?" Ryder whispered as he slid down to the ground and covered his filthy face with his even more filthy hands. "God help me, I think I'm going mad!"

"THEN LORD WIMARC doesn't often have guests?" Lizette asked Ellie as the maidservant threaded a needle.

Although Lizette hated sewing, she had little choice unless she wanted to have every dress so tight that she found it difficult to breathe and exposing so much of her, every man in the hall stared at her.

Wimarc's attention was necessary, Finn's couldn't be helped, but she didn't enjoy being the object of Wimarc's mercenaries' lust.

"Not often, no, my lady. Your invitation was a great honor. He must hold you and your husband in high esteem."

"How could he, since he's never met us?"

"Oh, he hears things, my lady, and he's got lots of friends. There's messengers coming and going all the time."

"Oh?" she prompted, but Ellie's attention was elsewhere.

"Here's your husband and my lord now," she said, nodding at the entrance to the hall.

Lizette put aside her sewing, while Ellie all but preened as Finn walked toward them.

Finn had barely said a word to her as they'd dressed that morning. Not certain what to say or to reveal how tired she was after a nearly sleepless night, she hadn't spoken to him, either.

Pretending to be his wife, having to share his bed, was proving to be far more difficult than she'd imagined. She'd hardly slept a wink, all too aware of his powerful body so close to her scantily clad one, and even more aware of her own lustful desire, which must and would be subdued.

Wimarc frowned with concern as he drew near, drawing her attention away from Finn, and her memories of the previous night. "My lady, I thought you would be done that task by now, or I would have had Ellie save you the trouble."

"It's my fault," she replied, giving him a smile. "I am an indifferent seamstress."

"You seem well rested, at any rate," Wimarc remarked, "unlike your husband. I fear the walk around my castle has wearied him."

"He does look tired," she agreed. Had he had as sleepless a night as she?

"Perhaps while the servants prepare the hall and he rests above, you'd take a short turn about the lady's garden with me?"

Finn opened his mouth as if about to speak, but she rose and answered before he could. "I'd be delighted."

She put her hand on Wimarc's arm. "You have a nap, Gilbert, until the evening meal."

So saying, Lizette let Wimarc lead her from the hall. She didn't look back—or she would have seen Ellie talking to Finn, then gathering up her sewing and following him up the stairs.

LIZETTE SOON FOUND HERSELF in a very charming, if not large, garden. Since it was September, it wasn't at its blooming best, yet roses still decorated the walls and trellises, and other late-blooming flowers colored the beds that bordered a stone walk. A wooden bench was in the center, sheltered by another rose-covered trellis.

"This is lovely. Did your wife plan it?" Lizette asked, genuinely impressed even as she wondered if there was another exit to the garden, or a way to get out without being seen.

Perhaps they could scale the wall somehow and land…where? A quick glance confirmed that anybody climbing over the wall would be easily spotted by men on the wall walk, certainly during the day.

At night it might be possible. The trellises looked too fragile to act as ladders, but the bench, perhaps—

"No, my lady, I planned it," Wimarc replied. "Roslynn takes little interest in such things. Indeed, she takes little interest in wifely duties of any kind."

He spoke without any hint of displeasure or double meaning, yet Lizette couldn't help wondering why he would say such a thing to her, unless he meant to imply he was unhappily wed and thus gain her sympathy as a start to his seduction. "My husband might say the same of me. I find domestic duties tiresome."

That wasn't completely a lie. She did find domestic tasks extremely tiresome, unlike Gillian, who seemed to revel in them. She preferred to be alone, making up stories to pass the time—exciting tales of exotic places that always ended with Lizette triumphant, vanquishing her enemies, who would try to imprison her or do her harm.

Now she knew the fantasy was much more pleasant than the reality, which was much more dangerous, too.

"When one is a lily of the field, one shouldn't have to trouble herself with irksome tasks," Wimarc agreed, his voice a little lower and a little deeper.

He wasn't very close to her. He certainly wasn't touching her, but she felt a prickling sensation of discomfort down her back nonetheless. Yet she wasn't going to flee and waste this chance. "I'm surprised you aren't at court."

"I doubt I'd be welcome there."

"Oh, I'm sure a man like you would be very welcome—by the ladies, at least."

"It seems I'm not the only one capable of flattery," Wimarc wryly observed as he handed her down onto the bench.

It was only after she was seated and he'd joined her that she realized how well screened they were by the trellis.

"I prefer not to spend any time near our august sovereign," Wimarc admitted.

"That I can more readily understand."

"You don't like our king?"

"Does anyone, except those he so obviously and unfairly favors?"

Wimarc wagged a cautionary finger at her. "Have a care, my lady, to whom you say such things. They could be accounted treason."

She widened her eyes. "You won't tell anyone, will you? I…I haven't even said such things to my husband." She ran a hand over her brow. "I can't think what's come over me!"

Wimarc took hold of her hand and looked into her eyes. "Perhaps you fear he won't sympathize with your feelings?"

"Oh, it's not that! He hates…"

She fell silent, as if confused and upset as she pulled her hand from his. "That is, I don't think he would chastise me too harshly for criticizing the king." She gave Wimarc a beseeching look. "You just seem so much easier to confide in."

"Now I am truly flattered, my lady."

She relaxed a little more, or seemed to. "I think if I were to ask you questions, you'd answer. Gilbert treats me like a child and won't tell me very much at all about the king or the other courtiers. Why, just before we left to come here, a traveling merchant told me Lady Adelaide d'Averette was recently wed. I asked Gilbert about it, and he told me he had no interest in who married whom, or what she wore, or how she looked."

Wimarc chuckled softly and moved a little closer. "I can assuage your curiosity on that point. Lady Adelaide did indeed recently marry. Her husband is Lord Armand de Boisbaston, a man completely loyal to the king."

Lizette clasped her hands together and tried to remain calm. Adelaide was married. Really married. To a man loyal to the king. A man neither she nor Gillian had ever met—and after all Adelaide's talk of honor and duty and keeping one's word! Adelaide had always acted as if she were certain Lizette would break their promise, but in spite of all her admonitions, it had been Adelaide who broke their vow.

"Perhaps your husband didn't care to speak of Lady Adelaide because he wanted to marry her himself," Wimarc suggested, leaning closer still. "No doubt he no longer regrets the loss, although I fear Lord Gilbert doesn't truly appreciate the prize he has in you. Such a beautiful, desirable prize."

She rose abruptly, as if distressed. "Excuse me, my lord. I should see if Ellie's finished with that gown."

"Until later," Wimarc smoothly replied, rising and bowing as Lady Helewyse scurried away from him like a startled rabbit.

Give her a few more days, he thought with smug satisfaction, and she'd come running eagerly back. Right into his arms.

LIZETTE PLUNGED into the dimmer confines of the hall and crossed the rush-covered floor, ignoring the few men already awaiting the evening meal and their curious, lascivious eyes.

A few of Wimarc's hounds lumbered to their feet as she swept past; once she'd gone by, they returned to their places by the hearth. They were some of the biggest dogs she'd ever seen, and more than one sported a studded collar.

Gathering her skirt in her hands, panting slightly because of the tight bodice of her gown, she hurried up the steps and reached the door of the bedchamber, then hesitated as she put her hand on the latch. Perhaps Finn was asleep.

It would be a relief if he were. She didn't want to have to talk to him. She wanted to be alone. To stop pretending, if only for a little while.

She eased open the door and saw that the bed was empty.

Perhaps he'd gone somewhere else, seeking to learn more about the castle, including ways to escape it, she thought as she opened the door wider and stepped into the chamber.

No, he was there by the window.

Kissing Ellie. Kissing her passionately, the maidservant pressed full against his powerful body.

As he had kissed *her* in the courtyard.

Rage and hurt boiled through Lizette. What a stupid, lustful fool she'd been! What a selfish knave he was!

She stormed toward them and yanked Ellie away. "Get out!" she shouted at the stunned maidservant. "Get out *now!*"

"My dear," Finn began, spreading his hands in a placating gesture, a look of baffled innocence on his face.

"You get out, too! You cheating, adulterous cur! You rutting dog!"

Only Finn's eyes moved as he watched her warily, as if she might explode or fly right out the window, while Ellie fled the room.

God help her, she must look—and sound—like a jealous fishwife. But she wasn't jealous. She couldn't be. Not of a thief and a maidservant.

She shouldn't be. After all, he wasn't her husband. If he wanted to kiss another woman, if he didn't care about her as much as she thought, if he'd kissed her in the courtyard and here in this chamber only to maintain the ruse, that was as it should be.

Embarrassed and ashamed of her outburst, she looked away from Finn. Her gaze fell on the tapestry and it galled her to think that someone might be spying on them now, too.

Suddenly she saw an opportunity to end that, as well as explain her rage that would spare her pride.

With a growl like a lioness, she strode toward the wall, grabbed hold of the tapestry, ripped it from the wall and threw it at Finn. Dust flew from it as it hit his broad chest. Bundling it in his arms, Finn sneezed, then glanced at the hole in the masonry exposed by her action.

"What are you looking at?" she demanded.

He appeared confounded as he answered. "Nothing."

"You're right, it's nothing. Only some missing mortar. But you'll stare at it rather than me because you're too ashamed to look your wife in the eye—as you ought to be! I'll *make* you look at me!"

She grabbed a cloth from the washstand and shoved

it in the hole, blocking it. But she wasn't finished. She marched to the door and flung it open, to see the hem of Ellie's skirt as she disappeared down the steps. So, she *had* been listening.

Although the young woman was gone, Lizette slammed the door. Then she turned to face Finn, her hands on her hips, triumph on her face as if she'd been playacting all along. "*Now* we are alone."

CHAPTER TWELVE

FINN CHUCKLED and tossed the tapestry onto the chair. "Very nice, my lady."

"I thought so," Lizette replied, forcing herself to sound far calmer than she was, lest he realize how upset she'd been by the sight of that kiss.

She sat at the dressing table and started to unpin her hair. There was no mirror—Wimarc's wife would have taken such an expensive possession with her—but she wanted to have an excuse not to be facing him as they talked. "I assume you hope to seduce Ellie so that she'll help us escape? Will your new paramour be coming with us, then?"

He crossed his arms and leaned against the bedpost. "I'm just doing what you're doing with Wimarc. If it's all right for you to use your feminine wiles to get information from him, why can't I kiss a maidservant if I think she'll tell me things?"

She pictured him kissing Ellie again. "No doubt she will, with a great deal of flattery, I'm sure."

Finn came to stand beside the table, his jaw tight with tension. "Do you enjoy flirting with Wimarc?"

"That's a necessity."

"I considered it a *necessity* when I kissed Ellie, too, although I didn't particularly enjoy it. It's quite obvious Ellie wants something of me, my lady—money, or some other sort of gift, perhaps. There was more commerce than passion in her kiss."

She would not be pleased. She would not.

Her hands trembled as she put down the comb and she clasped them in her lap. "If you want to be with her, be with her. I don't care—as long as it doesn't interfere with our plans."

"Do you think I'd risk my brother's life just to get under a maidservant's skirts?" he demanded incredulously.

"I don't know *what* you're capable of!" she returned, immediately ashamed of her accusation, but too proud to take it back. "And I don't care with whom you make love unless it complicates our plans."

"I shall bear that in mind should I ever decide I require your permission," he sarcastically replied. "It so happens I learned many valuable things today. Ellie told me there are over two hundred mercenaries in this castle. That Wimarc pays well, with food and wine as well as coin. And women, too, I suspect, for Ellie seemed quite confident that I'd be delighted by her attention even though I'm married. More importantly, Ryder is alive."

She was so relieved to hear that, she forgot her anger and dismay and turned on the stool to smile at him. "Oh, I'm glad!"

Finn's stern expression softened a little. "I'd be happier if there was more than one way into that dungeon," he grimly replied before he threw himself into one of the chairs and ran his hand through his hair. "God, it's an awful place! Like hell itself. And to think of Ryder alone and starving there…"

She rose and went toward him, wanting to console him, to touch his shoulder or caress his cheek to show him he wasn't alone in his concern, but she didn't dare after what she'd just said to him and with the bed so close, and her heart racing and her skin flushing with warmth, the memories of Finn atop her coming fast and unbidden and tempting.

He raised his eyes and thankfully she saw no anger there, but only curiosity. "Did you learn anything of use from Wimarc during your tête-à-tête in the garden?"

"He confirmed that Adelaide really is married to Lord Armand de Boisbaston. It's also clear Wimarc believes Armand is completely loyal to John. Your suspicion as to his motive for wanting to abduct me may have been correct."

Finn's right brow rose slightly and a little smile played about his fine lips. "What's this? My lady was mistaken? The lowly outlaw may have known something of import after all?"

Of course she'd made mistakes; she wasn't perfect—and she'd had enough people tell her so all her life that she didn't need one more.

She went back to the dressing table, sat on the stool and picked up the comb again. He rose and drew near, yet she continued to comb her hair with brisk, hard strokes, hating her natural curls, wishing her hair was straight like Gillian's. That she was calm and cool like Adelaide. That she was home.

"What else did you learn, my lady?"

"Only that there is no way to get out of the garden except through the hall, so it will be of no use to us. Even if we could climb the wall, we would be seen by the sentries."

"Of which there are many," he added, his voice lower.

She tried to ignore him, and the heat threading through her body, the desire rising, the need building.

He took the comb from her hand. "Let me, before you break it," he said, running the comb through her hair before she could protest. "I know your sister's marriage disturbs you, but I can tell you that she could do a lot worse than Armand de Boisbaston. The worst thing I can say about him is that he's loyal to a fault and takes his honor too seriously."

She should make him stop. She should take the comb from him, or stand up, or do something other than sit here with her eyes closed, lulled and comforted by the sensation of the comb running through her hair. Adelaide used to comb her hair when she was little and tell her everything would be all right.

"Not all noblemen are chivalrous, despite the oaths they swear. He is—and better yet, he loves your sister as few men love their wives, or their mistresses, either, for that matter."

She didn't want to hear Finn speak of love, or marriage, or mistresses.

"Have you ever been in love, Lizette?"

He called her Lizette. In that marvelous, deep, lyrical voice of his.

She put her hand over his. "That's enough," she

whispered, hoping he would put down the comb and move away.

He didn't. He let his hand rest where it was, lightly on her head, warm and strong and vital beneath her palm. "I didn't mean to upset you, my lady. Sometimes I speak without thinking."

Sometimes, so did she. But she must think now— especially now. Intending to tell him to stop, she took a deep breath—and realized she'd torn the side seam of her dress from armpit to waist.

"I've ruined it!" she cried as she rose to examine the tear. It wasn't hers, and she'd ruined it.

"Thank God for that," he said, putting the comb back on the table. "Wear that again, and Wimarc might go blind staring at your breasts. So might half his men."

"If I thought the sight of my breasts could do that, I'd go naked," she muttered, her attention more on her dress than Finn at the moment.

"Would you really?" he asked, his voice low and husky.

Seductive. Capturing her full attention, although she continued to finger the tear as if wondering how to mend it. Her whole body seemed to flush with passionate anticipation. "Of course I'm not serious."

"Good." He spoke lightly, but there was a tone in his voice that betrayed him. He really meant that and when he laughed, it sounded false and hollow. "Otherwise I'm liable to go all over angry and draw my blade to punish them for staring, and then where will we be?"

"You'll simply have to control yourself," she said, her voice a whisper.

"Maybe I can't," he replied, his eyes seeming to ask

a host of questions. She wanted to answer each one with a yes as he put his hands on her shoulders. "I think if you were to be honest with me, my lady, you'd admit you enjoy my kisses."

She didn't—couldn't—resist as he pulled her into his embrace. Closing her eyes, she yielded, relaxing against him, giving herself up to the desire he inspired.

"I think if you were truly honest," he whispered, "you'd even admit you want me in your bed."

He had gone too far and awakened her to a new danger—her own weakness. It was one thing to want him, to ponder taking the risk of being his lover, but now, when the opportunity presented itself, when the fantasy could become reality, she knew it must not be. There could not be—must not be—such intimacy between them. If she were to give in to her desire and get with child, she would be risking scandal and shame not just for herself, but Adelaide and Gillian, too, and that she could not do. Not even to be with him.

She must ensure that she could not be tempted. She must make certain that he never kissed her again, unless it was part of the ruse. So she shook off his grasp and regarded him with an air of cool disdain. "You're good-looking in a common sort of way, I suppose, and well-spoken for a peasant. But I could never *really* want a man like you."

Finn stared at her with disbelief, and she watched as disbelief became scorn and anger. With every beat of her heart, she felt worse and hated herself more for what she'd said, whether it was necessary or not.

And then he turned on his heel and marched from the room.

FINN SLAMMED THE DOOR behind him and stomped down the stairs. Damn the woman—and damn all the nobility, with their pride and arrogance, using peasants for their own gain, treating them like dung beneath their heels. And lying—oh, yes, lying worse than the most dishonest thief in England, because, say what she would, Lizette had responded to his kisses with more than playacting. She'd been as aroused as he.

He should welcome a rebellion against the king. Let the nobles kill each other…except that if it came to war, it wouldn't be the nobles who suffered most. It would always be the peasants and the foot soldiers who bled, suffered, starved and died, while the nobles would merely be captured and released upon payment of a ransom.

Unfortunately, he needed Lady Elizabeth of Averette until he could free his brother and get out of this place. But Jaysus, he'd never touch her again, ruse or no!

And by God, she'd better find another gown to wear—something with a collar that went up to her chin. He could hardly think with her in that red-and-gold dress, and after last night, he found it even more difficult when he remembered the sensation of her body beneath his. He'd hardly slept at all last night, fearful that he'd inadvertently touch her and be unable to resist the urge to kiss her.

God help him, he'd never wanted a woman so much in all his life, and having her pretending to be his wife, sharing his bed, being so intimate yet not, was proving to be far more difficult than being Lord Gilbert of Fairbourne. Or at least it had been.

It would be a hell of a lot easier now.

He marched into the hall. Wimarc was there, sitting on the dais by the table set for the evening meal.

Finn's jaw clenched as he slowed his steps and considered what part he should act—the enraged husband? Easy enough to do. He *was* enraged.

The scolded henpecked spouse?

Not so easy. He'd never bow down before an arrogant baggage like Lady Elizabeth d'Averette, who thought herself so much better than he and likely any other woman in the kingdom, too.

The errant husband who takes pride in his adultery, at least with other men of equal rank and status? Better.

Better yet, he would be the husband who's angry because he'd been caught in near adultery, but really proud of his near seduction of a servant. It was a common conceit among noblemen that they were irresistible.

"You look upset, my lord," Wimarc ventured as Finn came to stand near him beside the hearth where a fire burned to ward off the chill of the autumn evening.

"I'm sure you can guess why," Finn answered as he leaned one arm against the mantel and traced the edge of a flagstone with his foot. "My wife's shouts were surely heard out in the yard. And I regret to tell you, my lord, she tore the tapestry right off the wall of the chamber."

"God's blood, a fiery temper indeed!" Wimarc replied. He waved his hand dismissively. "No matter about the tapestry. It can easily be repaired and replaced."

"Along with some of the mortar. It's fallen out between a few of the stones."

Without a hint of dismay, Wimarc inclined his head

and then sighed. "Women are so easily upset. They should understand that men have their appetites, and a little dalliance with a maidservant is meaningless."

"Yes, they should. You'd think I'd despoiled our marriage bed on our wedding night. It was just a kiss."

"And Ellie is easily persuaded to a kiss, and often more," Wimarc said with a wink. "My nights here would be very lonely without her."

Finn regarded his host warily. "I hope I haven't offended *you*, my lord. I didn't realize you might—"

"I'm more than willing to share," Wimarc said. "Ellie's merely a servant, after all—albeit a very skilled one. However, if I could offer a piece of advice from one married man to another, it's best to take your sport where your wife is not likely to discover you."

"Yet I note Ellie is here."

Wimarc laughed in that odd, noiseless way he had. "She is only an *occasional* comfort when my wife is not in residence. I have other women elsewhere when Roslynn is at home."

"You're a wise man, my lord," Finn replied, apparently impressed. "Would I had been so." He sighed heavily. "I fear my bed is going to be cold as ice for several days."

It would have been better if it had been cold as ice last night. Then he might not have given in to the urge to take Lizette in his arms today, although he would then still be ignorant of her true and arrogant nature.

"It need not be. Apologize, tell her you were wrong, give her a trinket, and her heart will soon soften toward you."

"Apologize? To my wife?"

Wimarc's eyes gleamed with sly purpose. "What harm to act the penitent if it gets you back between her legs?"

So saying, he took off a small silver band from the fourth finger of his right hand. "Give this to her to soothe her ruffled feathers."

"That's most generous of you, my lord," Finn said, tucking it into his belt. "I'll repay you."

Smiling, Wimarc shook his head. "No need for money to change hands between friends. It is my gift."

Likely not without some hidden cost, Finn thought, or so Wimarc probably planned. "Again, I thank you. I've heard you're generous to your friends."

"Indeed I am," Wimarc genially agreed. "Tomorrow should be a fine day, and my huntsman tells me he's found a boar's wallow. A huge beast, apparently. I was thinking we should have a hunt. Would you care to join me chasing down the creature?"

"I think not, my lord," Finn replied. "I believe I might better spend my day here with my wife."

Making certain she didn't do anything unexpected, or cause anyone to doubt who they were.

And he should be seeking more information about the fortress, and ways to get out of it without being seen.

Moreover, he was no great hunter, never having been properly taught, as most noblemen were in childhood. His inexperience might raise suspicions.

"Ask her to join us," Wimarc proposed. He glanced at the stairs. "Here she comes now."

Finn turned to look at Lizette. Mercifully she wore

a new gown, the one she had been altering, of doe-brown with green trim and a touch of scarlet about the neck and cuffs lined with a deeper green. She had her own leather girdle about her hips, which seemed to emphasize the unconscious sensuality of her walk.

Despite what she'd said to him and the way she'd made him feel, in spite of his own resolve never to touch her again, there was no denying that she was the most desirable woman he'd ever met.

Unfortunately, her appeal wasn't merely physical; she might have been easier to ignore if it was. He wanted to know her spirited mind, how she could be both bold and shy, determined and timid—for timid she'd certainly been when they were in that bed.

He told himself the strain of pretending to be her husband, of knowing Ryder was so close and yet still suffering, being in this terrible place with this band of ruffians and their smooth-talking, lascivious master, must be confusing his wits.

Wimarc leaned a little closer and whispered. "I shall be your ambassador tonight. Let me soothe her ire a little, then you give her the ring when you are alone. I'm sure that will put her in a forgiving and generous mood."

"A most excellent suggestion," Finn replied, although in his heart, he squirmed with discomfort. Regardless of their plan, he didn't want Wimarc anywhere near Lizette.

So he was not pleased as he watched Wimarc approach her, all charm and condescension.

"Good evening, my lady," he said. "You look like the very goddess of the season, giving us mere mortals a taste of your beauty before the harsh winter comes."

"Thank you, my lord," she said, darting a pert glance at Finn.

She could look at him all she liked—he was never going to forget what she'd said to him. Nor did he move as the two of them came to the dais.

"Lord Wimarc plans to hunt a boar tomorrow," he said when they reached him. "He's asked us to join him."

"More graciously than that, I'm sure," Lizette replied with a hint of displeasure before she gave Wimarc a sad smile. "Unfortunately, my lord, I do not enjoy the sight of blood."

"Then we shall not go," Wimarc gallantly replied.

"Oh, no," Lizette cried, her pretty eyes widening with distress. "I don't want to keep you from your sport." Her gaze went to Finn. "I think the fresh air and the company of such a fine gentleman would do my husband good."

"Then it's settled," Wimarc said quickly, clearly trying to prevent another public quarrel. "We men shall hunt, although I don't like leaving you with no one to entertain you, my lady."

"Unlike *some* people, I can amuse myself," she returned, giving Finn a look that, if it had been fire, would have burned him to a crisp.

"You shall have the finest cut from the boar," Wimarc promised. "Now, shall we dine? Regrettably, I cannot promise anything so fine as boar tonight, but I hope you'll find the fare to your liking."

"I'm sure I will," Lizette assured him, letting Wimarc lead her to her chair.

And ignoring Finn completely.

PAYING NO ATTENTION to the look of enraged scorn on Lord Gilbert's face, Garreth finished patting down the nobleman, seeking any hidden weapons. Beside him, Keldra blushed as red as a cardinal's robes while she did the same to Lady Helewyse, who stood as erect as a statue, a look of outraged pride on her pretty face. Both nobles were in their briefest garments—the lady in her shift, her arms wrapped about herself, the lord in his breeches—and both were barefoot and shivering despite the glowing coals in the stone circle in the middle of the hut.

"I'm sorry, my lady," Keldra murmured. "Garreth says we have to make sure that you haven't made a weapon out of a stick or bit of wood."

"Then you intend to perform this indignity every day of our captivity?" Lord Gilbert demanded.

"Aye, my lord, I do," Garreth replied with absolutely no contrition. "I've seen what some men can do with a sharpened stick, and I won't take no chances."

"You might at least allow my wife some privacy."

Garreth grinned as he finished. "She ain't got nothing I ain't seen before, my lord."

Keldra's blush deepened as she went to the door and waited for him to join her.

"If you want to live, you should let us go," the nobleman declared.

"Can't do that, my lord. Not while Finn's life depends on it."

"*Your* life will be forfeit if you don't, because I assure you, you're going to be found and—"

"Aye, hung for a thief. I know," Garreth replied. "I've

had that fate awaiting me all my life, so you might as well save your breath."

He waited for Keldra to exit while, with a sob, Lady Helewyse threw herself into her husband's arms.

"You don't have to be so rude," Keldra charged after Garreth had replaced the heavy stick against the door, and they were back by the fire. Dark clouds were forming in the sky and threatened rain, but they were nothing compared to the storm brewing in her eyes. "Why can't I search the lady alone?"

Garreth kicked at a bit of wood sticking out of the fire, shoving it back into the flames. "Because it's too risky."

"You could take Lord Gilbert outside. Tie him up first, of course, so he can't escape, and then I could search Lady Helewyse without you watching—unless you enjoy that?"

Garreth's scowl deepened as he glared at Keldra, his hands balling at his sides. "It's necessary. They're probably planning an escape right now—that's what I'd be doing if I was them."

"Well, you're not—and you obviously don't understand a gentle lady. Poor Lady Helewyse—"

"Has had servants to tend her all her life. I'm sure I'm not the first person to see her in her undergarments."

"You could be the first man not her husband!" Keldra retorted. "What's wrong with my way? Or is it just that it's *my* way? Or do you fear Lord Gilbert will escape from you?"

Garreth crossed his arms and leaned his weight on one leg, the way Finn often did. "All right, we'll do it your way."

"Good."

Obviously pleased, Keldra bent down to stir the rabbit stew in the pot. Garreth flopped down on a nearby log, frowning as he picked up a stick and made designs in the dirt.

Keldra's stirring slowed, then stopped, and she glanced at him. "Do you think they're all right?"

She didn't have to say to whom she was referring.

"Of course," Garreth muttered, his eyes on his drawing as if he was considering its artistic merit. "Finn can do anything he puts his mind to."

"Which is why he's just a thief?"

Garreth leapt to his feet. "He's the *best* thief!"

Keldra pursed her lips and kept stirring.

"All right, Lady Lacking, tomorrow I'll go to the village and see if I can hear anything about visitors to Castle de Werre, if that'll make you happy."

Keldra straightened, but there was no gratitude in her expression. "You should. We have to find out if the plan's failed."

"I'm sure it hasn't."

"I hope you're right," she said with more hope than anger as she went back to stirring the stew.

He watched her another moment, trying not to notice how gracefully she moved, or think about her shining green eyes.

He certainly wasn't about to tell her that he'd already considered going to the town because, despite his faith in Finn, he was worried, too.

CHAPTER THIRTEEN

LORD WIMARC might not have had boar on his table that night, but he had a host of other excellent food: venison, mutton, carp, eels in batter, salmon from Scotland, a pottage of leeks and dumplings, a fine pudding and baked fruit.

If Lizette hadn't been so upset, she would have eaten until she felt ready to burst, for never at Averette or anywhere else had she enjoyed such food, and such variety. Yet she was upset—by the part she was playing even though it was of her own volition, and especially by the knowledge that her words had so obviously hurt and offended Finn.

It didn't help that as the evening meal proceeded and Wimarc did his best to charm her, Finn sat silently beside her, eating and drinking and rarely speaking.

What else could she expect after what she'd said to him?

She'd said those horrible words to make him keep a necessary distance, to prevent her desire for him from growing any deeper until she forgot who and what they were, and gave herself up to the passionate longings he inspired.

Despite her very real dismay, she took some small comfort from the fact that Ellie came nowhere near the dais.

As the servants cleared away the last of the meal, Wimarc clapped his hands and a pair of jugglers entered the hall from the kitchen corridor. The men were tall and dark skinned, 'Gyptians most likely—itinerant vagabonds who traveled with their kin from place to place telling fortunes, playing music, dancing and otherwise entertaining whoever would pay them.

"I thought we could all use some amusement this evening," their host explained.

"A welcome distraction," Lizette agreed.

After bowing to Lord Wimarc, the men began to perform, tossing round wooden sticks back and forth in a flurry of motion too hard to follow with the naked eye.

Lizette clapped, and the folk in the hall cheered and stamped their feet with approval, then let out a roar when the jugglers changed from sticks to knives. Lizette, however, held her breath, afraid one of the knives would go astray.

"No need to be afraid, Helewyse," Finn said with a patronizing air. "I'm sure they know what they're doing. Men like that learn the art in the cradle."

"Your husband is quite right," Wimarc agreed, giving her another smile. "I've had these men here before, and they're very good. Just wait until they bring out the axes."

Axes?

"If you'll both excuse me, I shall return in a little while," Finn said. "That wine has run right through me."

It was not the first time Finn had left the hall that

evening and as before, Lizette's gaze instinctively
sought out Ellie, who was seated on the lap of a huge
fellow with close-cropped hair who was missing his
right ear. She shouldn't be so relieved that Ellie was still
there while Finn was not, but she was nonetheless. She
had been the other time, as well.

"Have no fear, my lady," Wimarc quietly assured her.
"I've forbidden Ellie to go anywhere near your husband
on pain of branding."

Lizette wasn't pleased to hear that. Seeing Ellie with
Finn had upset her, but the girl didn't deserve such a
harsh punishment.

"I thought her pain should equal any distress she
might have caused you today."

"Couldn't you just send her away until we go home?"

Wimarc regarded her as if she were a child who
didn't understand the rules of a game. "Surely if she
keeps her distance from your husband, my men need not
lose their toy."

No doubt that's all women were to him, whether high-
born or low—toys for his amusement, to be discarded
when he tired of them. In that, he wouldn't be different
from most men. To them, women were playthings, or
chattel, or potential mothers of heirs. Amusements or
tools or trade goods, one almost interchangeable with
another.

Many of Adelaide's unsuccessful suitors had been
such men, easily changing their target from Adelaide to
her sisters when their wooing proved unsuccessful. Fortunately, their father had been adamant that his eldest
daughter marry first and well to establish a precedent.

She'd had no qualms at all about teasing those suitors and pretending to be flattered by their attentions, or too stupid to guess their real intentions.

"Very well, my lord," she replied at last. "This is your household, after all, not mine."

"Now I've upset you," Wimarc replied with every appearance of genuine dismay. "If you'd truly prefer I send the girl away, my lady, I will."

Lizette was very tempted to tell him to do just that, except that Finn was right; Ellie might be able to help them, or provide some necessary information.

So she gave Wimarc a wistful smile and shook her head. "No, that won't be necessary. I'm sorry I made such a fuss. I know men have their needs, and noblemen are no different, but I didn't expect to find…to see…"

She put her napkin to her eye as if brushing away a tear. "We are but newly wedded, and I thought Gilbert would be content with me for at least a little while before…before…"

Wimarc put his hand on her knee. "If it's any comfort, my lady, I begin to think your husband a great fool, to have such a jewel and try instead for the lump of coal."

His hand slid up her thigh a little, and her blush and anxiety weren't entirely feigned as she shifted. "My lord, please! Just because my husband is willing to break our marriage vows—!"

"I meant no harm, my lady," Wimarc quickly asserted as he removed his hand. "I forgot myself. But to see you so distressed, and for such a cause…"

"No axes yet?"

They both started and looked up at Finn as he resumed his seat. Lizette had no reason to feel guilty, no real need to blush, but she did anyway. Wimarc, however, remained as cool as always.

"No, no axes yet," he replied. "You there, Jacapo!" he called to one of the entertainers.

Both jugglers caught their knives and looked at him expectantly.

"Show our guests how you toss the axes."

Wimarc rose and pulled Finn to his feet as the jugglers went to a large wooden box by the corridor. "You should see this demonstration up close, my lord."

While the mercenaries nearby pushed their benches farther back and talked excitedly among themselves, Wimarc led Finn to the center of the hall. The others clearly knew what to expect, and Lizette could tell that bets were being made.

The juggler called Jacapo pulled out two large axes whose heads gleamed in the torchlight—big, sharp axes that could probably cut a man's head in two.

Fear rushed through Lizette and she half rose in her seat. "My lord!"

"Have no fear, my lady," Wimarc said. "Jacapo and his brother are very good. No harm will come to your husband." He addressed Finn. "Stand in the center, my lord. Trust me, they won't miss."

"I sincerely hope not," Finn said as he nevertheless did as directed.

"Keep your arms at your sides," Jacapo instructed while his brother brought out two more large axes and Wimarc returned to the dais. "Stand still and don't move."

"My lord!" Lizette protested again, suddenly worried

this might be some scheme of Wimarc's to hurt or even kill Finn. That Wimarc had somehow guessed they were deceiving him and had decided to end the ruse in a cruel and bloody way. "Please, don't!"

Finn crossed his arms and raised his brows. "What, all concerned, my lady? After the way you spoke to me this afternoon, I should think you would be pleased if one of these axes should go astray and make you a widow."

Ruse or not, there was no need for him to do anything so foolhardy—and was he forgetting his brother and her family? If anything happened to him… "No, my lord, I would not."

"Then come and give me a kiss for good luck."

Truly worried that Finn hadn't considered that this might be some evil scheme of Wimarc's, she rose at once and hurried to him. Throwing herself into his arms, she looked up into his dark eyes and whispered, "Be careful! This might be meant to hurt you!"

And then she kissed him. Passionately. Fervently. Possessively. As if they were not in Lord Wimarc's hall, but their own bedchamber. As if they were not pretending to be husband and wife, but were. To let him know she regretted what she'd said and the hurt that she had caused him, because she was terrified he was about to be killed before her very eyes.

When she drew back, Finn was breathing hard and his confused eyes searched her face. "God save me, woman," he murmured. "What are you doing?"

"Wishing you luck, and I sincerely hope not saying goodbye!" was all she trusted herself to say before she went back to the dais.

Only when she took her seat again did she realize Wimarc was watching her closely. "I see kissing brings a sparkle to your eyes," he said quietly. "Would that I could do so."

Lacing her fingers in her lap, she didn't reply as Jacapo lifted his arm and threw his ax.

Right at Finn's head.

Lizette didn't even have time to scream before the ax narrowly missed him. Then another went past his side before she could draw breath.

Beside her, Wimarc chuckled, the sound low and mocking. "You see, my lady? There was no need to panic."

"Do you find my fear *amusing*, my lord?"

"I merely meant to reassure you that this is but a game."

"It's not one *I'm* enjoying," she retorted as the axes continued to fly past Finn, who stood as still as a statue.

Only when she saw the slightly irate expression on Wimarc's face did she recall the role she was supposed to be playing. She immediately turned away and sniffled, as if she was trying not to cry while keeping her attention on Finn.

Faster went the weapons, and faster still. The men in the hall grew more excited, and Lizette's heart pounded loud in her ears. How much swifter could Jacapo and his brother throw their axes? How much closer to Finn could they get before they hurt him?

At last, finally, and to the cheers of the spectators, they stopped. She drew in a great breath of relief—and again felt Lord Wimarc's unwelcome and annoying hand upon her knee.

"I hope you're not angry with me, my lady?" he asked as if worried.

She turned to him and managed to put a contrite little smile on her face. The words nearly choked her, but if she had to appease him, she would. "Not at all, my lord. As you said, I was worried for nothing."

IAIN GROANED. It felt as if every bone in his body was broken, every muscle and sinew torn—but this was different from before. He was warm, and dry, and sleeping on something soft. And the air smelled of lavender. Or maybe it was the sheets.

There was another odor, too. Medicinal.

Maybe he was in a convent or hospice, and the good brothers were tending to him. He had somehow gotten on that horse and ridden far enough to find help.

Perhaps Lizette was here.

Energized by that hope, he opened his eyes, squinting at the light from a candle spluttering near his bed. He tried to sit up despite the pain.

A pair of hands pressed on his shoulders and gently forced him down again. "You mustn't, sir!" a woman softly ordered. "Please, you're very hurt and need to rest."

Then a face loomed above him—a woman's face, plain and full of concern, her soft blue eyes gentle and sympathetic. "You must lie still and rest," she said, her voice gentle and soothing and sweet, like music.

He had to tell her who he was, and have a message sent to Averette about Lady Elizabeth and the attack on their cortege.

"Don't try to talk," the woman cautioned as she

reached out for something. "Your throat is still a little swollen. I think you must have taken a blow there. Fortunately, your ventail saved your life.

"I'm Lady Jane de Sheddlesby," the woman continued, "and you're in my manor, where you will be safe regardless of who attacked you. Now, I've got something for you to drink. It doesn't taste very good, but Brother Wilbur is quite sure it will help you."

She gave him a warm, encouraging smile of a sort he hadn't seen since… Of a sort he'd *never* seen directed at him, not even when he was a child.

But she didn't understand. She didn't know why he had to get up, what he had to do, what his duty demanded. He must find Lizette, or learn what had befallen her. Then he'd go back to Averette, either with Lizette, or to tell her poor sisters of the attack and fetch help with the search. "Please, my lady—"

"If you must speak, and I can tell by the look in your eye that you will whatever I say, wait until you've had Brother Wilbur's medicine."

She didn't give him a chance to argue. She cradled his head against her breasts and practically forced him to drink the foul-tasting brew. He would have gagged and spit it up, except that her grip was surprisingly strong.

She helped him lie back down and set the plain copper cup somewhere beside the bed. Folding her hands in her lap, she regarded him with a smile as well as curiosity. "There. Now you may tell me what is so important that it cannot wait."

She wasn't pretty, or at least most men would say so. But he'd seen beauty enough in his day and knew it was fleeting. There was strength in Lady Jane's face. Aye, and patience. She'd known suffering, like him. She'd learned how to live with it, deal with it and overcome it. Like him.

Yet his duty, first and foremost, was to the ladies of Averette. "I'm Iain Mac Kendren, the garrison commander of Averette."

"Averette!" Jane eagerly exclaimed, leaning forward. "Lady Adelaide's estate? I know her from the king's court." Her cheeks bloomed with a blush. "She's a good friend."

Iain was glad to hear it, although it increased his guilt over failing to protect his charge. Now Lady Jane would know of that failure, too. But it never entered his honorable head to tell her anything except the truth. "I was escorting her younger sister back to Averette when we were attacked."

Lady Jane's eyes grew as round as a full moon and she put her hand to her breast. "Elizabeth?"

"Aye. She's been abducted. I must get word to Averette, and Lady Adelaide."

Jane jumped to her feet. "Of course! I'll send a message there at once. And the court, too, in case Adelaide is there. Gillian will be at Averette for certain, though. Adelaide says she never leaves it. I'll write them both and—"

"My lady!"

She was halfway to the door when she halted and turned back. "Yes?"

"I would start a search for her from here."

She ran back to the bed and knelt beside it so that she was eye to eye with him. She took his hand and concern was etched upon every feature. "Of course!" She got a resolute look in her eyes that reminded him of the ladies of Averette. "Not today. You're still too weak. I'll speak to Brother Wilbur and ask him when you can ride again."

Her stern expression gave way to a hopeful, sympathetic smile. "Perhaps Lady Elizabeth escaped and is safe elsewhere. Maybe she's even at Averette and worried about *you*. I shall send a message right away. You'll have anything else required to find her if she is truly lost."

She blushed and lowered her eyes, so that her dark lashes fanned upon her cheeks. "You must take care, Iain Mac Kendren. I wouldn't want you to fall ill again."

Overwhelmed with gratitude, he brought her hand to his lips and pressed a kiss upon it. "Thank you, my lady. For everything."

"OOOOH, I KISSED HER THERE and there and then, I kissed her all over again. And again. Oh, I kissed her all over, all over again!"

Lizette sat bolt upright in the bed. That was Finn, singing loudly, like the most drunken buffoon in England, and unless she was much mistaken, that uneven gait staggering and stumbling up the stairs and along the corridor was his, as well.

"Oh, kiss me again and again, she cried. Oh, what can I say? I tried!"

The door flew open as if from a stiff breeze and Finn stumbled into the room, a wine goblet still in his hands and a sodden grin on his moonlit face.

He wasn't alone. Ellie did her best to support him and stop him from hitting the wall. She nearly succeeded.

To think she'd been lying here for so long since leaving him in the hall with Wimarc, all the while wondering and worrying about what was transpiring below! She'd even begun to fear their ruse had been discovered and Finn had been dragged to the dungeon. More than once she'd gotten up and examined the hole in the wall to ensure that it was still filled with fresh mortar. Instead, he'd been drinking and…and who could say what else he'd been doing?

"My wife, I am come!" he shouted as if announcing the king was in her presence.

"So I see," she said as she got out of bed. The stone floor was cold on her bare feet, and her thin shift didn't offer much warmth, either.

But she felt no chill. Her anger warmed her too well.

An anger that she took no pains to hide, and that made Ellie suddenly wary, and seemingly humble as she slipped out from under Finn's arm.

He gave her a loose-limbed imitation of a bow. "Thank you, sweet maid, for your kind assistance!"

"Yes, thank you," Lizette said through clenched teeth, glaring at the young woman who made her way swiftly to the door and shut it behind her with a bang.

"Are you mad?" Lizette demanded as she faced Finn. He was leaning against the bedpost, his arms crossed and apparently as sober now as he'd appeared drunk before. "You're not drunk!"

"No, although not for lack of Wimarc's trying."

She didn't know whether to be angry or relieved, and so was peevish instead. "I hope you kept your wits about you."

"Always, or I'd be dead in a gutter by now for sure."

As he looked at her, she suddenly became aware of the cold and what little she wore and hurried back to the bed. She bundled up the coverlet and shoved it onto the floor, then added a pillow to the pile. "At least the servants won't wonder if one of them comes in and finds you sleeping on the floor."

"I'd say everyone here is convinced by now that our marriage is a troubled one."

His tone was calm, unreadable. If he was still angry, he gave no sign in his voice, or the set of his shoulders as he strolled to the window.

"Good," she replied.

He turned and regarded her steadily, his face shadowed. "Although the way you kissed me before Jacapo threw his ax might have made them think otherwise."

She could hear slight accusation in his deep voice. "I want to keep Wimarc guessing," she lied, hugging her knees. "I don't want him to think I'll be easy to seduce. What were *you* thinking, agreeing to take part in that entertainment? Wimarc might have paid those men to hurt you. What if you had been killed? What would happen then, to me and to your brother?"

"I was in no danger of being hurt. Jacapo and I are old friends. I asked him if there was anything like that afoot when I first left the table before they began and he told me Wimarc had made no such suggestion."

"Jacapo knows who you really are?" she gasped, appalled.

"Aye," Finn replied evenly. "He assumed I'm here to rob the man. He warned me not to try it, good fellow that he is, and I said I'd heed his advice and leave soon. He also complimented me on my beautiful lover, for which I thanked him. I told him you were a courtesan from London hired to make my impersonation more believable."

A courtesan? She threw back the covers and got out of bed. "Could you not have come up with a less humiliating story?"

Finn shrugged with aggravating calm. "It was an explanation I thought he'd believe."

"But…a courtesan! That's so shame—"

She suddenly remembered his mother, and fell silent.

The corners of Finn's mouth tightened and his brows lowered. "Next time," he said through clenched teeth, "should there *be* a next time, I'll say you're a court clerk's daughter."

He reached into his belt. "Here. A gift of apology for kissing Ellie."

She caught the small thing he threw at her—a ring. "Where did you get this?"

"I didn't steal it, if that's what you're thinking," he said as he unbuckled his sword belt. "Wimarc gave it to me for you, so that you'd welcome me back in our bed."

She put it on her right hand. "Tell him I was suitably grateful."

"Then why would I be sleeping on the floor?"

He was right, and although no servant had come barging in unannounced yet, she wouldn't put it past the bold, inquisitive Ellie to do so.

She picked up the pillow and tossed it back on the bed. Then she gathered up the coverlet. "You wouldn't be. So come to bed, my lord, and we shall sleep together as we did last night."

When she got no rest at all.

CHAPTER FOURTEEN

TRYING NOT TO LOOK at Lizette as she spread the coverlet back on the bed, her thin, almost-transparent shift straining against her buttocks, Finn removed his sword and belt. When Lizette got into bed and mercifully pulled the covers up to her chin before turning onto her side away from him, he placed them on the chest before removing the woolen tunic Wimarc had lent him. Scowling, he pulled off his boots, leaving on his breeches as he got in beside her.

For a long time, unable to sleep any better this night than he had the last, all too aware of Lizette's shapely body so close by, he lay staring at the bed curtains. The only sounds that broke the silence were those of the watch exchanging muffled passwords, and Lizette's breathing.

She was slumbering like an infant. God, she was a cool one—except that she'd seemed genuinely upset at his possible demise in the hall this evening. Maybe she did like him and not just because he could be useful to her.

What if she did care about him? It was likely only the way some ladies cared for their dogs or horses or caged birds.

It was no good. Sleep would not come, despite his

exhaustion. Perhaps he should sleep on the floor after all. If a servant did intrude, they could always say they'd quarreled again over the accommodating Ellie.

He rose from the bed gingerly and gently tugged the coverlet from the bed. He took his pillow and made himself another bed—still finer than many he'd known—and was about to lie down when he decided to look outside. The moon was full and bright, not good for escaping, but excellent for seeing how many soldiers were on watch at this hour of the night.

At the window he leaned against the sill and surveyed first the wall walk, then the gate, then the courtyard. As before, there were a lot of guards.

He was about to draw his head inside when a furtive motion caught the corner of his eye. He searched the area near the stables—and saw a brief movement.

It was a woman, too plump to be Ellie, surreptitiously making her way to the side of the stable. He watched with growing excitement as she opened a narrow door and slipped inside.

If they were to create a diversion, there was nothing so good as a fire and frightened horses.

Was that door always unlocked at night? Did it even have a lock?

THE NEXT DAY, tired but not so much as yesterday, Finn rode beside his host. After seeing the women sneak into the stable, he'd felt a surge of excitement that had kept him awake a little longer, but when he'd finally gone to his makeshift bed, he'd slept like the dead.

For the first time since Ryder had been taken, he had

a real hope of rescuing his brother and getting successfully out of Castle de Werre.

He would have told Lizette, but she was still abed when he'd risen, dressed and gone down to join the others going on the hunt.

Ahead of them trotted the huntsman, who Wimarc claimed could smell a boar a mile away. Behind them came a portion of Wimarc's men, clearly looking forward to the hunt, or at least killing something, as well as the dog boy. He held the leashes of several large hounds that sniffed and lunged, as eager as the men to find a quarry on this fine day that seemed to belong more to summer than September. Wimarc rode a fine black gelding, and his short cloak was one of the finest Finn had ever seen, of soft gray wool lined with fox fur.

Likewise mounted on an excellent horse, Finn wore a short, dark green tunic that belonged to Wimarc, as well as brown woolen breeches and his own leather boots. Wimarc had offered him others, but Finn had demurred, claiming they wouldn't fit.

"You're looking better rested this morning," Wimarc remarked. "I hope that's due to a delightful truce."

Finn smiled. "The gift of your ring was most appreciated."

"I'm always glad to be of service to my friends."

Finn caught an undertone in his host's voice and realized this was no insignificant statement. "I hope you'll always consider me a friend."

"I believe I shall." Wimarc slid him a companionable glance. "I understand the king is not one for boar hunting."

"I don't think he cares much for anything that requires effort, unless it's bedding his wife," Finn replied like one who trusts his confidant. "That's why his latest campaign in France failed. He was too busy amusing himself with Isabel."

"I hear she's quite a little beauty."

"Little, and lovely, and not likely to stand up to him, unlike his mother."

Wimarc parted his lips in that silent laugh. "Eleanor would have stood up to the devil himself, I think! Even in her old age, she was a formidable woman. It's a pity John isn't more like her. He's as changeable as a weathercock."

"Except when it comes to his lands in France," Finn replied. "He's quite determined to get them back."

"I fear he's more likely to lose England in the attempt. Will *you* go to France if he mounts another campaign?"

"I'd rather not risk my life on such a venture."

"His allies are richly rewarded."

"While they bask in his favor," Finn replied, "but as you say, the king is notoriously fickle, and dishonorable, too. Look what he did to Armand de Boisbaston—left him to rot in a French nobleman's dungeon."

"John's compensated de Boisbaston well for that discomfort since his return, with the hand and lands of Adelaide d'Averette," Wimarc said.

Finn sniffed with disdain. "He's welcome to her. I much prefer Helewyse, especially after last night," he added with a wink.

"No doubt John also hopes to seal Armand's loyalty with such a marriage," Wimarc observed. "And his brother's, too, now that he's let Bayard de Boisbaston marry Gillian d'Averette."

Finn nearly fell out of his saddle. Bayard de Boisbaston had married Gillian d'Averette? How was that possible? It wouldn't be legal, or so he'd heard while listening to such discussions among nobles. "They're brothers. The church would never allow a marriage between people related in that degree."

"It was allowed, my dear fellow, because Bayard is no true son of Lord Raymond de Boisbaston. The true son died at birth and another baby was put in its place."

Bayard de Boisbaston was not Raymond de Boisbaston's son?

"The man's confessed to the king," Wimarc continued. "He claims he knew nothing of the truth until recently. John believed him and gave him Gillian d'Averette."

Finn's mind seemed to be in both a fog and fever. Bayard was not a de Boisbaston and he was married to Lizette's other sister.

"It *is* shocking, isn't it?" Wimarc said with another glance at his companion. "I'm beginning to think John will take a bribe for anything. I wouldn't be at all surprised if he started knighting anybody willing to pay."

"He may, if he loses the loyalty of any more of the barons and men like Armand de Boisbaston and the Earl of Pembroke," Finn slowly replied. "Many believe he's killed his nephew, who had a better claim to the throne. And now he has his niece imprisoned. I suspect he'll never free her, lest she take a husband who could lay claim to the throne."

Wimarc regarded him with greater respect. "I wasn't aware you were so knowledgeable about the succession."

Wary he'd overstepped, Finn shrugged his broad shoulders. "There was much talk of John at my wedding."

That was a safe enough guess, he was sure. Any time nobles gathered there was sure to be talk of the king.

"Let us hope his reign will be short, then. Sickness, an injury…so much can fell even a young man."

"That's true," Finn agreed, "but with Arthur dead, there is no clear succession until John has a legitimate son. If anything happens to John, it could mean war between the barons."

"Yes, it could," Wimarc replied. "But sometimes during such times, a more worthy king emerges."

The huntsman held up his hand to halt them. "Here, my lord!" he called out. "The boar's wallow."

Finn and Wimarc dismounted and got their boar spears—sharp, short weapons with a crossbar located about a quarter of the length from its tip. The bar was to prevent the speared boar from getting too close to the hunter, for even a speared boar would keep charging as long as it was alive.

Meanwhile, the gray-haired huntsman knelt beside the muddy indentation and laid his hand on the ground. "Still warm."

Finn knew that meant the beast was close by and, as if they'd understood the huntsman, the hounds began to bay.

"Let them loose!" Wimarc called to their keeper. The thin young man whose face was filthy and covered with spots, yet who seemed competent enough, slipped off their leashes and let them go.

As they took off at the run, Finn noticed the marks

on a nearby tree where the boar had rubbed against it. Judging by the height, it was indeed a big one.

"The trees are too close together," Wimarc said to Finn and the rest of the men. "We'll have to follow afoot."

They did, and soon a yelp of pain told them the dogs had found their quarry. They quickly came upon the lifeless body of one of Wimarc's hounds, its belly torn open from neck to tail.

Wimarc barely glanced at the fallen animal. The other men paid it little heed, much as they would a peasant killed in battle, Finn thought, as he, too, passed the body.

He gripped his spear tighter, hoping he didn't make a mistake or do anything that would reveal that everything he knew about boar hunting he'd learned by watching other noblemen, feigning knowledge he didn't possess.

He'd spent most of his life pretending—pretending not to care when somebody berated and insulted him, or his mother, or his brother. Pretending not to notice when his mother passed out from drink, or that it hurt when she struck him in her rages. Pretending not to care about anything or anybody, because it was safer that way.

Until Ryder had found him and he'd met Lady Elizabeth of Averette—spirited, bold, stubborn Lizette, whose initial regard had warmed his heart and aroused his desire.

The noise of the dogs grew louder and more excited, tearing him from his troubled thoughts.

"They've got him cornered!" the huntsman called out ahead.

Finn was tempted to stay where he was, but how would that look to Wimarc and the others? And didn't he face dangers equal to an enraged boar all the time?

Perhaps not to quite the same degree, he thought when they came upon the creature cornered in a thick grove of trees, its humped back against the trunk of a fallen oak. The hounds faced it in a half circle, barking madly.

Its mouth flecked with foam, the beast's beady eyes flicked madly from side to side, the sound of its gnashing teeth sickening.

The huntsman was, wisely, behind a tree and the other men stayed back as Wimarc took a kneeling position in front of the boar, his spear tilted, its butt pressed against the ground.

The nobleman looked at Finn. "Whenever you're ready."

Thinking he would never really be ready to face a charging boar, Finn knelt beside the nobleman and braced himself and his spear. He silently prayed the boar would go for Wimarc, or else escape completely. He'd seen the damage a boar's tusks could do to human flesh.

"Now!" Wimarc shouted, and the dog boy let out a sharp whistle.

Still barking furiously, the dogs directly in front of the boar nonetheless moved aside, giving the boar an avenue of apparent escape. With a roll of its demon eyes, the great beast charged, heading straight for Finn as if it sensed his ignorance and inexperience, spittle flying from its open jaws, its tusks gleaming like knives.

With a shout, more terrified than he'd ever been in his life, Finn shoved his spear into the beast's chest.

Still it came on, charging forward, its jaws snapping, until—thank God!—it hit the crossbar.

Then Wimarc struck, ramming his spear into the

animal's side with such strength and force, he pushed Finn to the side.

One of the boar's tusks caught Finn's leg.

"Get it off me!" he yelled as it ripped into his shin.

UP IN AN OAK TREE a few yards away, Garreth sucked in his breath and leaned as far forward on the branch as he dared, trying to see through the crowd of men and dogs.

At least Finn wasn't dead—his curses and sharp exclamations as the huntsman bound his bleeding leg told him that. Thank God. When he'd seen that boar charge and watched as it struck Finn's spear and kept going, he'd feared the worst.

He'd only had a moment's respite before that other man stabbed the boar, shoving it over onto Finn. And then seeing tusks rip into Finn's leg—

Suddenly feeling sick, Garreth clutched the branch tighter.

"I can ride," he heard Finn say. "Give me room!"

The men moved back, and the other fellow who'd speared the boar helped a pale and panting Finn to where their horses must be. Two others carried the boar, a huge thing, suspended from a long, thick branch. Soon the clearing was empty.

Wondering whether he ought to tell Keldra what he'd seen, Garreth climbed down from the tree. If he did, he'd add to her fears—not that there was anything to really worry about. Finn was alive and likely to stay that way. It was only a gash, or so the man who had to be the huntsman had said. He'd know if a wound was serious or not.

It was also obvious Finn was passing for Lord Gilbert; he could tell Keldra that to ease her fretting.

He felt the sudden stinging slap of a low-slung branch and muttered a curse as he moved it out of the way. He ought to be paying more attention.

Maybe if he'd been paying more attention earlier on his way back from the village where he'd gone to see if there was news of Finn and the lady, he would have heard the dogs sooner and found someplace better to hide than up a tree.

But if he hadn't been up the tree, he might not have been able to see what had happened to Finn.

He didn't decide what to tell Keldra until he saw her running toward him, anxiety and hope in her bright eyes, as lithe and slender as the deer he'd startled that morning.

A feeling he'd never experienced before stole over him. He couldn't name it, but he knew he didn't want to be responsible for dashing her hopes. He couldn't tell her Finn was hurt.

"They're safe," he assured her as she came to a halt. "I told you they would be, didn't I?"

For an old woman, Greseld could move with surprising speed, and Lizette found herself panting slightly as she followed her from the kitchen, presided over by a sullen foreigner, back to the hall. She'd already seen the pantry, larder and buttery, and been suitably impressed by the variety of foodstuffs, wine and ale. Lord Wimarc clearly enjoyed fine meals and spared little expense to keep his soldiers well fed, too.

While the men were hunting, she was doing a little exploration of the castle on her own, even though she'd like nothing better than to go back to bed. She'd barely slept a wink, whether Finn was beside her, or after he'd taken off the coverlet and lay down on the floor. She didn't know why he'd done that, or why he'd stood so long at the window. Nor had she asked him that morning. She didn't say anything at all to him before he left to break the fast. She'd pretended to be asleep until he left the chamber; that seemed the easiest thing to do.

"May I see the keep?" she asked Greseld. "I adore ancient buildings—so fascinating, don't you think?"

Greseld shook her gray head, which trembled even when she was still. "There's nothing in there for you, my lady. Just the dungeon and his lordship's solar above. He don't let nobody in there and he keeps it locked, even when he's inside."

If the man were planning treason, surely that would likely be the place he'd keep any incriminating documents.

"Not even his steward?" she asked, realizing that she hadn't been introduced to such a person. He could be collecting tithes elsewhere, she supposed.

"He don't have one. Keeps all the accounts himself, he does, and collects the tithes and taxes personal. Always has since his father died and they found out the steward'd bled the estate dry." Greseld's steps slowed a little. "He almost got away, but his lordship tracked him down like a man possessed, and when he got him, he flayed the man alive."

Lizette shivered.

"His father was a weak man, my lady. Weak and

foolish, and his wife not much better. My lord, though, he's strong and powerful and he'll keep us all safe, he will."

"I'm sure." Unless he's rebelled against the king and his castle was besieged. She wondered what Greseld would think then, as she slowly starved to death like the prisoners in the dungeon.

Greseld slid her an unexpectedly shrewd glance from her pale gray eyes. "He's handsome, too, ain't he, my lady?"

"Yes. His wife's a lucky woman."

Greseld's only answer to that was a sniff. "A spoiled brat, that one."

Wanting to learn more about the dungeon and the keep, Lizette said, "Actually, I'd like to see the dungeon. Lord Gilbert was very impressed. I think he wants to enlarge ours, too."

Greseld stopped and frowned, making her face look even more unpleasant. "I don't think my lord would like it."

Lizette put on an imperious air. "Since I'm his guest, I'm sure he won't mind."

Leaving the gaping serving woman, she walked briskly toward the keep.

CHAPTER FIFTEEN

A SHORT TIME LATER, Lizette smiled despite the stench as she sat perched on a stool in the guardroom at the head of the steps leading down into the dark depths of Wimarc's dungeon. This was as far as she'd gotten into that horrible place, and it was already far enough.

No wonder Finn had had that haunted look in his eyes when he spoke of his visit here—but at least he had learned his brother was still alive.

"It must get very lonely on such duty," she said to the three gargoyle-ugly men in the small chamber.

"We find ways to amuse ourselves," the ugliest of them all, Uldun, answered, his voice as rough as a grindstone in need of grease.

"What sort of amusements?"

The three men exchanged glances, until Uldun shrugged his beefy and uneven shoulders. "This 'n' that."

No doubt she really didn't want to know. "Lord Wimarc must trust you a good deal to give you such a responsibility. And just the three of you!"

The short one, named Dolfe, said, "Oh, there's more than us three."

His one-eyed companion, Tark, nudged him hard.

"But we're in charge," Dolfe amended.

"Aye," Tark confirmed. "We're in charge."

"*I'm* in charge!" Uldun growled. He regarded the others as if daring them to contradict him. They didn't.

Satisfied, he smiled, exposing his rotting teeth. "We don't get many ladies visitin' here."

"I suppose most ladies don't appreciate the job you do," she said in her finest imitation of a simpering noblewoman. "They never think that if it weren't for men like you, there would be all sorts of robbers and outlaws preying upon them, instead of being locked up where they can't do any harm. And it's so much nicer to have them hidden away than hanging on gibbets along the road. As I said to my husband on our journey here, the sight of such corpses turns my stomach."

The three men stood a little taller.

She nodded at a bucket on the table, the remains of some sort of pottage stuck to the rim. "How often do you have to feed them?"

"Once a day, the first five days they're here," Uldun answered. "Then every two days, then every three a few times. Then they don't get no more."

Lizette wasn't ignorant of torture, but this slow starvation appalled her. "How do you know when they're dead?"

"We look in from time to time. You'd be amazed what some o' 'em will do to live a little longer," Uldun said, warming to his topic. "Eat their own—"

"I can imagine," Lizette interrupted. She didn't want to hear more.

"The weight of such responsibility must be very heavy," she said sympathetically. "I hope Lord Wimarc ensures that you have time away from here to refresh yourselves."

"Oh, we can take it," Uldun bragged.

"And Lord Wimarc only has one o' us on at night," Dolfe supplied. "Not that any o' them below know when it's night or day," he added with a snorting laugh, like a grunting pig.

She managed not to look disgusted. "And you're given wine to help pass the time, I see," she said, nodding at a large, nearly empty wineskin.

"Would you like some, my lady?" Tark offered, pulling out the stopper and wiping the rim of the opening with the bottom of his filthy jerkin.

"No, thank you," she said. She gestured at the shackles attached to the wall. "The prisoners are chained here sometimes?"

"The really bad ones," Uldun replied with a smirk.

She rose and approached the wall, trying to look fascinated, but in reality, nauseous. There was blood on that wall, and other things she didn't care to examine too closely.

She glanced at the guards over her shoulder. "My husband and I play a little game sometimes. With chains and shackles—not locked, of course. They provide a certain…excitement. Perhaps I'll come back with him later, if you'll let us have some time alone."

Uldun shook his large, shaggy head. "Couldn't allow that, my lady. Lord Wimarc'd skin us alive if we did."

Given what Greseld had told her, that was no exaggeration.

So she gave Uldun a seductive smile as she sauntered toward the door. "Then you'll have to stay…and watch."

Leaving them with that thought, she entered the yard

and drew in a deep breath of the blessedly fresh air with nearly as much relief as when Finn had saved her from Lindall and his men.

She must try to get evidence of Wimarc's treachery soon! They had to get out of this wretched place.

Finn must know how to open a lock. She and Finn could slip into the solar during the night and search for evidence of Wimarc's treason and treachery. Then they could get Ryder from his cell and escape…somehow.

A cry sounded from the gatehouse. She halted, wondering if the hunt had ended early as the thick gates swung open, and grooms and stable boys hurried from the stables.

Wimarc was first through the gates, his hair disheveled and his tunic muddy and blood-spattered. A woman who didn't know better might mistake him for a warrior, yet she was sure Wimarc would do everything in his power to avoid the field of combat, where he didn't have huntsmen and a bevy of mercenaries to protect him.

Finn rode in next. Unlike Wimarc, he was slumped in the saddle, his head bowed, his face pale—and his right leg was covered with blood.

"Finn!" she cried in dismay as she gathered up her skirts and rushed to him.

He lifted his head, his face racked with pain and a warning look in his eyes.

Sweet heaven, she'd called him by his name, and with Wimarc only a few feet away!

Despite her disastrous error, Finn smiled weakly. "It's not so bad, Buttercup. Just a flesh wound."

Buttercup? Of course. They could say they had pet names for each other. Hers would be Buttercup, and his could be Finn.

That error suddenly explainable, his smile reassuring her, her heart started to beat again. "Can you dismount unassisted?"

"I'd rather have help."

She went to stand beside him, until he gestured at one of the guards. "You there, lend me a hand. I'm too heavy for my wife."

She stood aside as one of the mercenaries came to offer his support. Leaning on the guard, Finn headed for the hall. She was about to follow when Wimarc laid a hand on her arm.

"I don't believe his wound's a serious one," he said. "It's a most magnificent boar, my lady. You can be proud of your husband for killing it."

"I will be, as long as you're right and he's not seriously injured," she replied, anxious to go after Finn.

Still Wimarc held on to her arm. "Yes, we wouldn't want his wound to worsen, lest he die and leave you a youthful widow. Of course, should that fate befall you, you can be sure of my protection."

Wimarc wasn't wishing a speedy recovery to her wounded husband; he was telling her what she could expect from him if her husband died, whether by accident or design.

"Even with your protection, the king or my family could order me to marry somebody else," she replied dubiously. "I couldn't go against the king."

"If John still rules," Wimarc said as he finally let go of her.

"Yes, if John still rules," she replied as she hurried away.

"Something's wrong," Gilbert whispered, his ear pressed to the hut's door.

"What do you mean?" Helewyse asked, huddled beside him.

"That thief—Garreth. He's worried. More anxious. I could see it in his face when he searched me."

Satisfied their jailers weren't nearby, Gilbert turned to Helewyse. Her hair was a tangled mess, her gown stained and muddy, her face pale, yet even that couldn't diminish her beauty. "What about the girl? Did she seem more afraid?"

Helewyse shook her head. "No. If anything, she was happier."

Gilbert frowned and moved to the far side of the hut. "Then he hasn't told her."

"Told her *what*?" Helewyse asked as she followed and helped him remove his tunic, so that he was half-naked.

"Whatever it is that's worrying him," Gilbert answered as he knelt down beside the wall and pulled out the wide, flat stick he used to dig from beneath their rustic bedding. "Maybe he was expecting Lizette and that Irishman to be back by now. Or maybe he heard something when he went off by himself, something that's frightened him, or at least made him uneasy."

Helewyse moved the straw away from the hole Gilbert had started and spread her veil beside him. They piled the dirt there, then scattered it over the floor so that their captors wouldn't realize what they were doing. "Maybe we should stop trying to escape and wait to be rescued," she proposed.

Gilbert shook his head as he began to dig, his muscles bunching. "And risk getting killed? I don't trust that Irishman—or Garreth, either. They might decide it's better to murder us than let us go."

Knowing he was right, Helewyse got another stick, and knelt beside him to help dig their way beneath the wall to freedom.

"YOU'RE NOT HURT, MY LORD?" Greseld asked worriedly as she entered Wimarc's bedchamber.

"Do I look like I am?" he retorted as he removed his hunting tunic and sweat-stained shirt.

She hobbled to his chest of clothes and took out a fresh shirt for him. "I always worry when you're hunting. Dangerous, it is. Men can so easily get killed and leave their wives a widow. Like Lord Gilbert almost did today."

"Gilbert got careless," Wimarc muttered as he sat on his chair and let her pull off his muddy boots. "I'm never careless."

"His wife's a strong woman," Greseld said as she set the boots aside for cleaning later. "She went to see your dungeon this morning. Said her husband's thinking of doing the same at his castle."

"He was impressed, as well he should be." That work had cost a small fortune.

Wimarc rose and took off his mud-and-grass-stained breeches, kicking them aside. Greseld let them lie and went to fetch him another pair. "Helewyse'd make a good wife—for the right man."

Wimarc paused as he tied the drawstring of his breeches. "You don't think Gilbert is the right man?"

Greseld shook her head. "No. He'd be fine for an alliance—the sort you could lead with your little finger, my lord—but Lady Helewyse's wasted on him. She's not weak and squeamish. She'll birth fine, strong sons, too, not like that barren bitch you married."

Needing money to finish his dungeon and fortifications, for weapons and gifts to create alliances, he'd been thinking only of her dowry when he'd married Roslynn. But it wasn't Greseld's place to criticize her betters. "It's only been a year. Who's to say Helewyse is any more fertile?"

Greseld sidled close to the man she loved more than her own life, who was more her son than anyone's. "If Lord Gilbert's wound were to fester and worsen, and Roslynn meet with an untimely accident…?"

"It would look bad if Gilbert died while my guest," he replied sharply.

Yet in his mind, Greseld's words took root. If Gilbert's comely wife became Gilbert's comely widow with all his money and lands, she would be worth wedding. As well as bedding.

FINN WINCED as Lizette removed his boot. Kneeling in front of him, she lifted his foot into her lap, then rolled down his hose, exposing the long gash.

Jaysus, he thought as he regarded the bloody wound and tried not to cringe as Lizette washed away the blood.

How was he to run or ride with such a wound? How could he rescue Ryder and hope to escape? "How bad is it?"

"It doesn't need to be stitched, thank God," she replied, reaching for more fresh linen to make a bandage, "although you shouldn't put your weight on it for a day or two lest it open and start bleeding again."

A day or two? "Damn that boar!"

"You're lucky it wasn't worse."

"Aye," he agreed, "but the longer we stay here, the riskier it is. Who knows how much longer Ryder will live? And then there's Garreth and Keldra. They'll be thinking something's gone wrong."

She sat back on her heels. "It *has*, but there's nothing we can do." Her scrutiny grew more intense. "What exactly happened, Finn? Was it really an accident? I can believe Wimarc tried to hurt you, if not kill you."

Finn thought of the boar's charge and how it had ended. "It's possible, but if he wants Gilbert's alliance, why would he try to kill him?"

"It would depend if he wants the man, or just his men and money," she replied as she removed his foot from her lap and gathered up the bloody linens she'd used to wash the wound. "If he has Gilbert's widow in his bed, he'd have the men and money and no need for Gilbert."

"He'd think that way," Finn agreed.

"After what Greseld told me today, I can believe that man is capable of anything," she said as she rose and picked up the basin full of soiled linen. "He flayed a man alive."

Finn winced. "What else did Greseld have to say?"

he asked, for he was sure Lizette wouldn't have let the conversation end there.

"She takes great pride in her master and clearly considers him a great lord," she replied as she put the basin on the washstand and brushed away a lock of hair with the back of her hand. "She also told me about his solar. It's in the keep, above the dungeon, and kept locked at all times. I'm sure that we'll find the proof we need of Wimarc's treason there."

Finn let out his breath in a whistle. "Aye, that sounds likely."

Somebody scratched at the door, like a large and tentative mouse.

"My lady?" Greseld croaked, "'tis time for the evening meal. Lord Wimarc bids me ask if you'll be joining him in the hall."

Lizette went to the door and opened it. "I'll be there shortly," she said to the servant. "My lord husband will sup in our chamber. Please have food brought to him here."

"Yes, my lady," the old woman humbly replied.

Jealousy bit him, but he fought to subdue it when she closed the door and faced him. "That's necessary, I suppose?"

"He must believe I'd rather be dining with him than tending to you. I also have to explain why I called you Finn, and how I earned the nickname Buttercup."

Of course. Just as he should tell her about her other sister's marriage. Eventually. Not now, not in haste. "Tell him the first time I saw you, you were wearing a yellow dress and sitting in the sunlight in a garden.

You looked so fair and fresh and sweet, I called you Buttercup."

"You ought to have been a troubador or minstrel with your knack for making things up," she said as she smoothed her gown over her slender frame, drawing his attention where he really didn't want it to go. "What about Finn?"

"Tell him it's like the part of a fish," he replied, remembering what she'd said when she'd asked about his name, "because I like to swim."

CHAPTER SIXTEEN

AFTER LIZETTE LEFT the bedchamber, Finn hobbled to the bed to lie down.

Maybe his wound wasn't so bad, he told himself. Perhaps a good night's rest would set it right, or at least enough to escape tomorrow night, now that he had a good idea where Wimarc kept his papers, and knew what cell held Ryder.

Another knock sounded on the door.

His meal, he thought as he eased himself down onto the bed and wondered if Ryder was getting anything to eat at all. "Enter."

The door opened to reveal not the ancient Greseld bearing a tray covered with a square of linen as he expected, but Ellie.

He wanted nothing more to do with the woman. She was trouble, and not just because kissing her had upset Lizette—who *had* been upset by that, no matter what she said. He was quite sure Ellie's presence here, especially after Lizette's tantrum, whether real or bogus, had a motive more than kisses and caresses or a few coins.

The question was, what was he prepared to do to

find just what those motives might be, and if they were hers alone?

"My lord?" Ellie inquired as she slipped inside and closed the door behind her.

"Here, on the bed."

"I've got beef stew and bread and mead—to start," she said, sidling closer and setting the tray down on the bedside table. As before, that calculating look came to her eyes even as she smiled.

He'd seen that greedy look before. Many women who sold their bodies were desperate, like his mother, and had no choice unless they wanted to starve. But there were others who saw prostitution as a way to live in comfort, and they could be as heartless as the men who used them. "Excellent. My wife tells me I need to keep up my strength."

"I think you're plenty strong enough already, my lord," Ellie purred as she removed the cover from the bowl of stew, the bronze goblet of mead and a plate of thick slices of bread.

As she spread the napkin across his lap, her motions a bold caress, he thought she'd likely had years to perfect her methods of seduction, although he doubted she was older than two and twenty.

Sitting beside him, she reached for the bowl and spoon, leaning forward to give him quite a view of her cleavage, which was no doubt her intention. "Here, my lord, let me help you."

She wasn't subtle, but some of the ladies at court who'd wanted the man they believed to be Sir Oliver de Leslille had been even more blatant and immodest.

"I was so upset when I heard you'd been hurt," Ellie said as she lifted the spoon to his lips.

It proved to be excellent stew, and he was very hungry.

"It's not a bad wound," he said lightly, reaching for the mead.

He took a sip and discovered it was the finest he'd ever tasted.

"If I was your wife, I'd be here with you, not in the hall flirting with Lord Wimarc," Ellie said with a toss of her nut-brown hair as she fed him more stew.

"My wife's flirting with Lord Wimarc?" he asked, taking another sip of mead, the sweet drink slipping down his throat.

Ellie nodded. "I don't mean to speak ill of your wife, but when I went by, she was laughing and smiling—and you here all by yourself and in pain, too!"

"I'm not all by myself now. You're here," he noted. "Pass me a piece of that bread, will you?"

Ellie readily did as he asked. "Anything for you, my lord."

He was quite sure she would do anything he asked, provided she thought she'd gain by it.

The bread was very good, too. He said so, then added, with a sly little smile, "Lord Wimarc only has the best, doesn't he?"

Ellie expertly feigned a blush. "Yes, he does."

"And he shares his good things with his friends?" he suggested, running his hand from her shoulder down her arm.

"Sometimes," she breathed, inching forward until her lips were very close to his.

"I thought maybe you'd been told to stay away from me after my wife's little fit of temper."

Ellie gave him a bold smile and an even bolder caress. "I was warned to keep clear of you and your wife."

"Yet here you are."

"Yet here I am," she seconded, leaning in to kiss him.

WHILE THE SERVANTS cleared away the remains of the meal, Lizette smiled at Lord Wimarc. Tonight, he was attired in a long tunic of fine scarlet brocade that seemed to accentuate his dark brows and hair and matched the ruby ring he always wore. His black leather belt was studded with bits of gold, and he had a wide gold chain around his neck.

"And that's why he calls me Buttercup," she concluded.

"How charming," Wimarc replied, refilling her goblet and not questioning the tale. "Did I hear you call him Finn?"

Relieved at her success thus far, she giggled like one of the giddier ladies who'd visited Averette. "He likes to swim, like a fish."

"Do you enjoy watching him swim?" Wimarc inquired, a little smile on his lips and overt curiosity in his eyes.

"Oh, yes," she sighed, looking down into the wine as it swirled about in her silver goblet.

It was easy to imagine Finn swimming naked in a moonlit pool. Indeed, she was reminded of the first time she'd met him, when he'd waded across that stream and emerged with his soaking clothes clinging to him. Then more visions came to mind, of Finn in a moonlit pool, naked, with her. Likewise naked.

"You seem amused, my lady."

"He likes to do other things in the water," she lied, leaving just what sort of things to Wimarc's imagination.

Obviously not content to simply imagine, Wimarc shifted closer and when he spoke, his eyes gleamed with interest and his voice was low. "What sort of things?"

She grabbed for her goblet as the servants came to take down the trestle table. "I think you can guess, my lord."

"Perhaps I can at that," Wimarc murmured as he offered her his arm to help her stand.

She stumbled a little as she rose.

"The floor must be uneven there," she said as he steadied her.

"Perhaps I should have warned you, my lady, that my wine is a little stronger than most."

She'd suspected getting her drunk had been his plan, and she would continue to let him think he'd succeeded. At least tonight she had on one of the altered gowns— this one of red, too—so she didn't feel nearly as exposed and vulnerable.

"It's all right, my lord. I'm sure I can trust *you* not to besmirch my honor," she said, giggling again as she poked his chest.

He was more muscular than she'd anticipated. Perhaps he practiced with sword and lance and mace more than she supposed.

"Of course. Will you sit here by the hearth?"

"De-lighted!" she cried, falling heavily into the proffered chair. "I wish we could have wine like this, but Gilbert is so miserly! Why, do you know he won't let me have a penny of my dower money to spend? Not a penny!"

"Terrible," Wimarc agreed, sitting opposite her and twisting his ruby ring around his finger. "A woman as lovely as you deserves fine things."

"That's what I think, too! But no," she cried, gesturing wide with the goblet. "He says we must save our money to pay for soldiers! Why? say I. The country is at peace. What need for so many men?"

"Things change, my lady," Wimarc replied, the light from the hearth flickering across his sharp features. "I'm sure your husband only wants to ensure that you and your home are protected."

She sniffed as she set aside the goblet. "He doesn't care about me at all, except to give him sons," she pouted, "and indulge his lust."

She put her cuff to her eyes as if wiping away a tear. "He can be so mean to me!"

Wimarc's gaze darted to the soldiers nearby, who all obediently looked away and busied themselves with their own conversations. Then he pulled his chair closer and took her hand, caressing it with his long, cold fingers. "I'm very sorry, my dear, that you are so unhappy. Truly."

She pulled her hand away as if feeling guilty, and not simply disgusted by his touch. "Yes, well, he's not mean *all* the time. Sometimes he can be kind. And in bed, he—is there any more wine?"

A look of discontent flashed across Wimarc's face, but he dutifully called for a servant to bring more wine, and Greseld tottered as fast as she could onto the dais with a carafe.

Not Ellie, Lizette noticed.

Was she with Finn? Wimarc had said he'd ordered her to stay away from him, but she couldn't trust Wimarc, or Ellie, either. After all, Finn was a very attractive man.

And he'd said Ellie might provide information. Who could say what he might do for that information? He'd already kissed her....

Greseld set the wine beside her master, then tottered off again, leaving Wimarc to fill Lizette's goblet. As he did, he loomed over her, blocking the light from the hearth like a grim shadow.

A shiver ran down her spine and she wanted nothing more than to leap up and return to her bedchamber; nevertheless, she smiled instead. "You're so generous!"

"I can be more so," he quietly returned, his breath hot on her cheek.

She took refuge in another sip of wine while he mercifully returned to his seat. She felt as she had in her childhood when she'd avoided a blow from her father's fist.

"Tell me, how many men does your husband consider necessary to protect you?" Wimarc genially inquired.

She waved the goblet dismissively. "Oh, two hundred or so."

"And knights?"

Obviously they weren't the only ones seeking information in Castle de Werre. "Plenty of them, too," she replied. "I don't mind them so much. Some of them are quite well mannered and handsome."

She gave Wimarc a coy smile over the rim of her goblet. "You have lots of men, too."

"About two hundred," he replied with a smile, although she was quite sure there were more.

"And knights?"

"I have many allies—but none of them are handsome."

She wondered just how many he meant. "At least none as handsome as you," she said, then she swiftly lowered her eyes and bit her lip as if she was embarrassed by that comment.

His eyes gleaming, Wimarc leaned forward and laid a hand upon her thigh. "I'm delighted you think so, just as I believe you're one of the most beautiful women I've ever seen."

It was blatant flattery, and he must think her simple to believe it. Adelaide was a beauty; their poor mother had been a beauty; she was not.

However, since it was to their advantage to have him continue to think her stupid, she smiled and simpered like the most vacant-headed ninny at court while she lightly slapped his hand. "Oh, you can't mean that!"

His hand stayed right where it was. "I assure you, I do."

Once more she feigned a blush, lowering her eyes and looking away. "I hope my husband doesn't hear you say such things!"

"I would rather say them where there would be no danger of anybody overhearing us, or seeing us together," he said softly, moving his hand a little higher on her thigh.

She'd put out enough bait for one evening.

Putting her hand to her head, she rose unsteadily. "I should retire now, my lord. I—I'm feeling a little dizzy."

Lord Wimarc got to his feet and again offered her his arm. "It's been a fatiguing day," he agreed. "Please allow me to escort you to your chamber."

Seeing no way to refuse without undoing all that she'd done to tempt him, she nodded and let him lead her to the curved stairway that led to the bedchambers.

When they were out of sight of those in the hall, he paused and turned to her, his expression so fierce and unlike his usual genial demeanor, it was like looking at another man entirely.

And then he grabbed her shoulders and pushed her back against the curving wall. "Gilbert is a *fool*. If I had a jewel like you, I would do all in my power to keep you and make you happy. If you were my wife, I would treat you like a queen. By God, I wish you were! You stir my desire and my passion more than any woman I've ever met!"

Frightened by the sudden change in him, feeling the heat from his body and sensing his lust, she fought to remain in control. "But...but I'm already married!"

"What does that matter if you desire me as I want you? *Do* you want me?" he demanded, forcing her back against the wall, his face mere inches from hers.

"Yes," she whispered because she must, steeling herself for his unwanted kiss.

Before his lips took hers, she thought that she could endure his embrace if it helped their cause—but she couldn't. It was too terrible, like being kissed by a monster—hot and wet and punishing.

She put her hands on his chest and shoved him back. "My lord!"

"Isn't this what you want?" he challenged, his voice as sharp as the crack of a whip.

"Not here," she lied. "Someone might see us!"

She forced a regretful smile onto her face and even brought herself to stroke his chest. "I do want to be with you, my lord, but I would also keep my honorable name, so we must either be very careful, or I must continue to be miserable with my husband."

"We can meet in my solar," he offered, his voice low and rough. "No one else is allowed inside that chamber, and I always keep it locked, even when I'm alone. No one can interrupt us there."

She swallowed hard, but nodded as if eager. "When?"

"Tomorrow morning. Tell your husband he must rest his leg awhile longer."

She nodded, then regarded him warily. "The accident that injured his leg…it *was* an accident, was it not, my lord?"

His smile chilled her. "What does it matter how it came about, as long as it keeps your husband confined? Will you meet me after breaking the fast?"

To make Wimarc certain she wanted him, she threw herself into his arms. "Of course!" she whispered before she kissed him with feigned delight and tightly closed lips, hating every moment of this intimacy and loathing the very feel of his body against hers.

Then she broke away and ran up the stairs as fast as she could go.

While Wimarc slowly descended, running his fingers over his lips that tasted of wine, and his future bride.

OUTSIDE THEIR CHAMBER, Lizette furiously rubbed her cuff over her mouth, trying to wipe off the sordid taint of Wimarc's lips before she pushed open the door.

She more than half expected to find Ellie there, but she wasn't. Finn was alone, reclining on the bed with his head cushioned in his hands and a welcoming smile on his handsome face. A brazier full of glowing coals warmed the room and a thick beeswax candle on the table by the bed bathed him in a pool of golden light.

He looked like some mischievous sprite lying there.

"Here you are at last. Guess who brought me something to sate my appetite?" he asked with a roguish twinkle in his eyes, so different from the horrible, lustful gleam in Wimarc's.

"Not the ancient Greseld, I take it," she replied, quite certain it wasn't, or he wouldn't have that grin on his face.

"No," he genially agreed as he patted a spot beside him on the bed. "It was Ellie. And she wasn't just after feeding me stew and ale. I tell you, my lady, I would have feared for my virtue, if I had any."

Lizette regarded him quizzically as she walked toward the bed. "Are you drunk?"

"A little," he cheerfully admitted. "That's some mead Wimarc's got."

"His wine's excellent, too," she agreed, wondering just how drunk Finn was. "Wimarc told me Ellie had been ordered to stay away from you."

He reached up to pull her down beside him. "She told me she'd been warned to stay away from both of us. I was supposed to be impressed by the risk she was taking to be with me, you see, but a woman like that'd never go against the orders of a man like Wimarc, not for a bag o' gold, let alone a tumble with no promise o' reward.

No, for her to disobey him, she has to believe she won't be punished, or else there was no such order given.

"In fact, my lady," he said, caressing her hand in a way that set her heart racing. "I'd say it's more likely she'd been ordered to seduce me."

Lizette found it difficult to concentrate with him so close beside her, especially looking so roguish and pleased with himself and talking about seduction. "Why do you think he would want her to do that?"

"To drive a wedge between husband and wife, to encourage you to adultery, or me to join his cause. O' course I refused her advances, citing my terror of your temper."

He sighed while he continued to stroke her hand and regard her with shining eyes. "I hope you appreciate the sacrifice of my manly pride. Now Ellie thinks I'm completely under my wife's thumb."

"I do," she said, toying with the edge of the coverlet and not looking directly into his face. Although embarrassed by her curiosity, she had to ask. "Did you kiss her again?"

He laughed softly. "No. I told her my wife could come back to check on me at any moment, and if you found her here, you'd surely fly into a rage and I wouldn't be able to defend her, what with my wounded leg. That seemed to cool her ardor. What about Wimarc? Did he believe you about the nicknames?"

"Yes, although…" She hesitated, wondering if she should tell Finn what she'd added to the explanation. He probably wouldn't like that, either.

Finn's eyes narrowed. "Although what?"

Wimarc might comment about what she'd said on the

morrow, she realized, so she'd best confess. "I told him that I called you Finn because you liked to swim, but I also implied you liked to, um, do certain other things in the water."

"Certain other things?" Finn repeated, puzzled. "What *other* things?"

"Intimate things…with me."

Finn's eyes widened. "Jaysus! And you say I can make up lies!"

"I was trying to make him think I was adventurous. I also went to the dungeon and spoke to the guards there. I told them something that should not only avert any suspicion if we go there together, but should even make us quite welcome."

"What?" he asked warily.

She felt her cheeks warm with a blush, but gamely answered. After all, it *was* a good excuse to get into the guardroom. "I told them that we liked to play with shackles and chains."

"Jaysus!" he gasped, jerking upright, then wincing.

"Sit still or you're going to start bleeding again!" she commanded. She bit her lip with consternation. "I wish Gillian was here. She knows more about treating wounds than I do."

"Never mind about your sister for now. Where'd you learn about such sport?"

"I overheard two tavern wenches talking once. They were speaking of their customers, and one said that a no-bleman who frequented her bed liked to be bound when they made love. I thought such a tale would enable us to enter the guardroom without raising suspicion."

He shook his head with amazement. "God help me, my lady, your mind is a marvel. But I hope Wimarc doesn't hear about our little games, or he might ask to join and then where will we be?"

"We can say we prefer to sport in private." She might as well tell him all. "I also kissed Wimarc, just as you kissed Ellie to further our cause."

His eyes narrowed. "Wimarc settled for a kiss?"

"Not exactly. I promised to meet with him in his solar tomorrow. Alone."

CHAPTER SEVENTEEN

FINN CURSED, or at least she assumed that long, aggressively uttered string of words were curses.

"I'll be in his solar," she pointed out, determined to be dispassionate and make sure he understood the necessity of her decision. "It's not likely he keeps incriminating documents out in the open, even if the chamber's locked, and we'll have to be swift when we break in, especially since you're wounded. I can do a preliminary reconnoitre that will save us time later."

"I don't like the idea of you alone with him in a locked room," Finn grumbled.

"I have to meet him or risk making him suspicious."

Finn shifted his weight on the bed. "I suppose you can find out the size of the lock," he grudgingly conceded.

"Does the size of the lock make a difference?"

"It'll make it easier to know which tool to use."

"There are *tools*?"

"Aye. Picks, they're called." He nodded at his boots on the floor by the stool where she'd left them after tending to his wound. "Bring me my right boot."

When she did, he reached inside and produced a wide strip of leather that had been wrapped around the boot's shaft. It was folded and sewn into small pockets and from those pockets protruded long, slender pieces of metal of various sizes, with a variety of shapes at the end.

"Locks come in all sizes, and the obstructions within are made in a host of shapes," he explained as he took one of the metal tools out of its sleeve, "so I had a smith make me these."

"Do you ever regret stealing?" she asked, genuinely curious as she surveyed the various picks.

"Not when I steal from the rich. When I was a boy stealing from folk not much better off than me, it troubled me all the time."

"Even the rich may have things they treasure for more than their monetary value. Adelaide would be upset if somebody stole her crucifix not because it's worth much money, but because it's all she has that was my mother's."

Finn nodded, then a troubled expression came to his face. "Wimarc spoke of your other sister on the hunt. Gillian."

New dread knotted her stomach. "Have you news of her? Is she sick? She's not...*dead?*"

"No, no, she's well," he hastened to assure her. "However, apparently, my lady, she's recently married, too, to Bayard de Boisbaston, Armand de Boisbaston's brother—or rather, not his brother, but a changeling child of some kind, although that's news to me and the king and court, as well."

It took her a moment to comprehend his confused, and confusing, words, but when she did, what he'd said was even more unbelievable than the news of Adelaide's marriage. "That's impossible! Why, I'd sooner believe that the earth circles the sun than Gillian break a vow or marry anybody. She was even more against the idea of marriage than Adelaide."

"Who's married now," he reminded her.

"But Gillian *hates* men," Lizette declared, certain of that. "She always has. She wouldn't even speak to most of the knights who came to court Adelaide."

"You've never met Bayard de Boisbaston."

"Have you?" she countered.

"No," he admitted, "but I've heard of the man. The ladies at the court often talked about him. Handsome, charming, merry, they said. And the men liked him, too, which is stranger still.

"Not in that way," he said when he saw the change in her expression. "Never lost a joust, they said, although a more jovial opponent you'd never hope to meet. Sounds like a fine fellow to me."

Lizette began to pace like an anxious cat. "If you knew Gillian, you'd know that was the very last sort of man to appeal to her."

"Sometimes it's the person one least expects to find the most appealing who is," he noted.

She paused and looked at him curiously. "Why did Wimarc tell you about Gillian?"

"We were speaking of men loyal to the king, and the de Boisbastons are loyal to a fault. I think he was sounding me out, to know if I would be loyal to John, too—well, sounding Gilbert out."

"And you led him to believe you're not?"

"Aye, o' course."

Lizette rubbed her temples. "I wish I'd never heard of Wimarc, or the king, or this conspiracy. I wish there was no such thing as marriage. I wish Iain had left me at Lord Delapont's! I'm going to bed!"

With that, she grabbed the coverlet and pulled it off the bed. She raised an irate brow, obviously expecting him to vacate it, which he did. She tossed a pillow on top of the coverlet, hastily got out of her gown and onto the bed, closing the curtains with a few sharp tugs and shutting herself away.

As Finn made himself comfortable on the floor, he wondered if she regretted meeting him, too.

IAIN MAC KENDREN STOOD for a moment over Lindall's corpse. Then he spit in the dirt beside it and, head bowed, he walked back to the road where they'd been attacked. It had rained once in the interim, Jane had said, and most of the footprints had been lost in the mud.

When he came out of the wood, Lady Jane spurred her horse to meet him. She'd insisted on accompanying them in case he fell ill, and he'd brought her to this scene of bloody death and destruction, the men and the contents of Lizette's wagon strewn along the road. The bodies of the men of Averette had been stripped and left to rot, and so had those of the attackers his men had killed.

"Another body," he said grimly, "of the traitorous lout who led the attack."

"Then Lizette might still be alive!" Jane said fervently.

"Aye, maybe. We can hope." He had to hope.

"The messenger should have reached Averette by now."

"Aye." He mounted carefully, so he wouldn't hurt his shoulder more.

"I've sent for a wagon to bring the bodies of your men to the churchyard for burial. I'll send some servants to bury the ones who attacked you in the wood. They deserve no better."

"No, they don't," he agreed. "But tell your men not to bother with the one the farthest from the road. Leave him for the crows."

Lady Jane nodded. "I'm amazed you managed to make your way to the church, wounded as you were," she said after a long moment.

Iain didn't reply as he scanned the road and the trees lining the muddy verge, seeking some sign that somebody had gone this way. In his weakened, wounded state, he had gone the other way and taken a fork that had led, fortuitously, to Lady Jane instead of Castle de Werre. God had surely been guiding him that night, and keeping him alive, too.

Surely that same God was watching over Lizette and her maid, keeping them alive.

They rounded a bend and he spotted something lying on the road. To a man who'd never been in battle, it would look like a heap of clothes or a bundle that had fallen from a wagon.

Iain had been in many battles, and he knew what it was at once—another body, crumpled where it fell. He spotted another farther ahead on the side of the road as he spurred his horse to a trot.

There were three more, at uneven intervals along the road. And then nothing. No bodies, no sign of horses or

men. It was if these five men had simply fallen down…
except for the bloody wounds.

"What happened to them?" Jane wondered aloud.

"I'd say they were chasing somebody, somebody
who killed them one by one."

"Do you think they were chasing Lizette?"

"Maybe, but she couldn't have killed them. She's never
been taught to use a sword, and it would take a heavy one
to kill like this." Iain shook his head. "They were killed
by a strong man who knew was he was doing."

"Perhaps it was one of your men protecting Lizette
and Keldra," Jane proposed.

"As much as I'd like to think so, they were all there
on the road." Iain's brow suddenly rose with hope. "We
met an Irish nobleman some miles back by the river
when we watered our horses. He was with a hunting
party, he said. Maybe it was Sir Oliver de Leslille and
she's with—"

He fell silent when he saw how Jane's face had paled
and the look that came to her gentle eyes. "What's wrong?"

"Sir Oliver de Leslille's in Cornwall, recovering from
a fall. He's expected to be there for weeks yet."

"Maybe he got better. Physicians have been wrong
before."

"Iain, I hope and pray you're right, but there was a
man at court recently pretending to be Sir Oliver. He
fled before the truth became known."

"Oh, God," Iain whispered, aghast.

Jane's eyes filled with sympathy. "If it is the same
man, he didn't seem a cold-blooded savage. Perhaps
he's taken Lizette to Kent to ransom her."

"I hope so!" Iain fervently replied.

He couldn't bear to think of the alternatives, that she was alive and suffering, or lying dead where they would never find her body.

ALTHOUGH SHE WAS DETERMINED to get into Wimarc's solar, Lizette took as long as she dared to break the fast the next morning. She slowly spooned her brewis, broke her bread into tiny bits, toyed with the meats on the platter before her and took small sips of her ale.

Eventually, however, she and Wimarc were the last at table and the servants stood waiting to clear away the remains.

"Since you are finally finished, my lady," Wimarc said, betraying some impatience, "I'll take you to the solar so that you may write to your steward."

They hadn't agreed upon any such excuse, but clearly, she and Finn weren't the only ones capable of concocting a convenient story.

"Yes, I'd appreciate that," she replied, wiping her fingers one by one on her napkin before taking Wimarc's hand to rise.

She said nothing more as they crossed the hall to another set of steps that led, she discovered, to the upper floors of the old keep that joined to the hall. Wimarc's eyes seemed to burn into her back as she held her skirts, put her hand on the rail carved into the wall and made her progress upward.

It was like climbing a scaffold where the hangman waited, although she was seeking life for her sisters and Ryder, not death.

When she reached the upper level, she saw a bossed wooden door, and another door at the opposite end of the curved landing that must lead to another way outside. Two entrances, then, to this level—or two ways to escape, if need be?

Wimarc unlocked the door and gestured for her to enter. As she sidled past Wimarc, she studied both the large iron key in his hand and the lock itself. She was sure she'd seen a pick among Finn's tools that would fit it and whose head was of a similar shape.

Then she was inside Wimarc's inner sanctum, where they would be alone.

Unlike the rest of the rooms in this castle, the solar was Spartan in its furnishings. It was dark, too, the only light coming in through narrow loopholes. There was a large, plain table with writing implements and a small, square, unadorned wooden chest upon it, a single, equally plain chair behind it and an empty iron brazier.

She tried not to stare too obviously at the keyhole in the small chest as Wimarc closed the door, the sound like the shutting of the door of a tomb. And then he turned the key in the lock, imprisoning her with him.

Wrapping her arms around herself for both warmth and comfort, she didn't attempt to hide her nervousness as she faced him. "Perhaps I shouldn't stay. If my husband finds out I was alone with you—"

"All you need tell him is that you had to write a message to your steward at Fairbourne on some household matter," he said, strolling closer. "You *are* the chatelaine of his household, are you not?"

"Yes." She edged toward the table, closer to the chest and away from him. "What if he doesn't believe me?"

"Then he risks insulting me, and I'm sure he'll think twice about that—or he should."

The threat in Wimarc's voice added to her uneasiness and she shivered. "Yes, yes, I'm sure he won't want to offend you," she murmured, even as she realized Wimarc could trap her against the table. She sidled toward the window.

"Cold, my lady? Shall I warm you?"

"I'm only a little chilly," she replied, rubbing her arms. "I shall be fine soon."

"You aren't going to play the coy damsel now, are you?" Wimarc asked, his voice low and with an even greater hint of menace as he closed on her. "Not after that kiss."

She wished she hadn't done that. "I've never cuckolded my husband before," she said to excuse her apparent change of heart. "He has a terrible temper, my lord."

"Then we shall simply have to ensure that he doesn't find out," Wimarc said as he came closer still.

She tried to sidestep him. "He'll kill me if our adultery is discovered."

Before she could get past him, Wimarc grabbed her arm and pulled her close. "Do you think I'm some lovesick lad content to play flirtatious games, my lady?" he harshly demanded. "You knew what I expected when I invited you here and you agreed to come."

She tried to tug her arm free, but his grip was too tight. "My lord, please! You're hurting me! Surely a lady can change her mind."

"You made an offer, I accepted, and if you try to cheat me, my lady, you'll be sorry," he growled, his grasp tightening as she squirmed and struggled and fought to get free. "Renege now, and I'll destroy both you and your husband."

"But you need him and his men!"

He smiled, and a more evil smile she'd never seen or imagined. "There are other noblemen with as many men and arms as he. I can always find other allies, although they may not have such pretty wives."

His smile changed to a fierce scowl and his eyes glittered with lust. "I grow impatient, my lady, for what you've promised me."

Lizette forced herself to smile and relax in his arms. "I was beginning to fear you were not the man I hoped you were, my lord. I wondered what it might take to rouse the beast within."

Wimarc's eyes narrowed. "More games, my lady?"

"The kind I like."

His hold loosened, but he didn't let go, so she put her hands on his arms and drew him back with her until her hips were against the table.

How far was she willing to go to maintain this ruse?

As far as she must.

"You play dangerously," Wimarc noted, splaying his hands on the table, imprisoning her.

She tried to ignore the building panic and forced herself to stroke his shoulders and whisper, "I like dangerous men."

"I'm very dangerous," he assured her as he bent down to press his hot, moist lips against hers.

She submitted, telling herself she had to do this. Had to stay. Had to protect her family, Finn and Ryder, too.

Still kissing her, Wimarc lifted her so that she was sitting on the table. He would take her right here. Like a whore.

She was a whore, giving herself to him in exchange for information. But she had no choice. She had to—

A shout came from the battlements.

She started and pushed him back. "What's that?"

Wimarc cursed as he strode to the window and looked out into the courtyard. Scowling, he turned on his heel and snapped, "I have a visitor."

An unwelcome one, obviously, but she blessed the nameless guest, whoever he was.

Wimarc grabbed her arm and tugged her toward the door. "We'll finish this later."

Too pleased to be leaving, she didn't complain about his painful grip. "Who is it? Someone important, I trust."

"My wife."

CHAPTER EIGHTEEN

WIMARC'S WIFE was young and pretty. Seated on a fine mare, she had arrived with an escort of twenty men, as well as two baggage carts and five servants. Her gown, although plain as befit a dress worn while traveling, was of very fine burgundy wool, close-fitting until the skirt bloomed out in gored fullness. Slender vines embroidered in green decorated the bodice and cuffs. Her veil was of the thinnest silk and floated about her heart-shaped face like gossamer. It was held in place by a heavily embroidered cap, and her cloak was trimmed with fur.

Nevertheless, as Lizette walked toward her behind Wimarc, she pitied her, chained for life to such a vile man.

"Roslynn, what a delightful surprise!" Wimarc cried as he helped her dismount.

Given his annoyance when he looked out the solar window, Wimarc was as good an impostor as Finn, and as great a hypocrite as any man who had ever come courting Adelaide and sworn undying devotion while really coveting her dowry and inheritance.

Wimarc took his wife's hands and kissed her on both cheeks in greeting. "You should have sent word you were coming."

Lady Roslynn blushed and anxiously answered, "I hope you're not angry. I grew weary of Lord Bernard's hospitality and decided to come home."

She looked past her husband to Lizette. Her eyes narrowed with suspicion, and her expression darkened as she ran her gaze over Lizette's borrowed gown. "You have guests?"

Perhaps she was wrong to think this young woman meek and mild.

Wimarc turned, and it was clear he hadn't expected Lizette to follow him to the courtyard—and wasn't delighted she had. Nevertheless, he put on a smile. "Lady Helewyse, may I present my wife, Lady Roslynn.

"The cortege of Lady Helewyse and her husband, Lord Gilbert of Fairbourne, was attacked," he explained. "They were robbed, so naturally I offered her some of your gowns to wear."

The hostility fled from Roslynn's face as if it had never been there and she smiled, looking even younger and more lovely.

"Lord Gilbert of Fairbourne?" Roslynn repeated with happy enthusiasm. "Then you are nearly as fortunately wed as I! Lord Gilbert was quite the favorite at court— a most handsome, amiable fellow."

Lizette managed to maintain a calm demeanor, in no small part because Finn was lying injured in their chamber. If Roslynn knew the real Lord Gilbert, he'd have to stay there until they could leave.

"You look very familiar to me, my lady," Roslynn said. "Have we met before? In Kent, perhaps?"

Lizette's heart almost stopped beating as she remembered that Roslynn's brother had been one of Adelaide's many suitors. Roslynn had been in his party when he came to Averette.

"I don't believe so," Lizette lied, hoping that would content her. It had been a few years ago, after all, and they had both been younger.

"Perhaps I'm mistaken," Lady Roslynn agreed. "With such a husband as mine, one meets so many ladies. They swarm about Wimarc like bees to honey."

"Lady Roslynn, you look lovelier than ever!" Finn cried.

Lizette's stomach dropped. Turning, she watched as Finn limped toward them across the yard, a wide smile on his handsome face, as if he was truly happy to see Wimarc's wife. "What a delight to see you again, Lady Roslynn! Wimarc didn't tell us you would be joining us."

Why hadn't he stayed in their chamber? Or gone back into the hall when he saw a woman who'd been at court, and who must have met him there?

"I didn't know she would be," Wimarc coolly supplied. "My lovely wife took it upon herself to surprise me."

"How thrilled you must be she did!" Finn enthused.

Blushing so deeply she was nearly the same color as her gown, Roslynn looked as baffled as Lizette felt— as well she might, if she knew the real Lord Gilbert.

"Don't tell me you don't remember me?" Finn accused with a roguish grin. "I certainly remember you—but then, you were so much admired and sought after, I was forced to worship you from afar. I don't believe we ever exchanged so much as a single word at court."

"You were at court when I was there?"

Now it was Lizette's turn to be baffled, for Roslynn
had spoken as if she'd met him there.

"Not for long. I had to leave to go to my father-in-law's
estate for the wedding, but I saw you once or twice before I left and sighed to see such fresh, youthful beauty,
like a new blossom in a garden."

"I was told you were a good-looking, charming
man," Roslynn said, giving him a shy little smile. "I see
those reports were not wrong."

"If I'm charming, it's because you inspire me to be so."

Sweet heavens above! Finn *should* have been a
courtier. He was as smooth and flattering as any of
them, and at the moment, about as sincere.

A group of Wimarc's mercenaries rode through the
gate. One of them waved a hand at them, and Wimarc
nodded in acknowledgment. "A patrol has returned, so
if you'll excuse me, I should see if they have anything
to report," he said to them with an apologetic smile before he addressed his wife. "Do you not wish to get out
of those traveling clothes?"

He still smiled, although it wasn't really a question.

"Oh, yes," Roslynn said. "Excuse me, my lords, my
lady."

They nodded their adieus, and as Wimarc headed off
to talk to his man, Finn placed Lizette's arm upon his.
"I feel like taking a turn about the courtyard, my lady."

"What about your leg?" she inquired as she glided
along beside him.

"It's much better for moving about," he replied as he
led her toward the stable where grooms and stable boys
were taking charge of the lady's cortege and leading the

mercenaries' horses inside after they dismounted and, in a boisterous gaggle, sauntered toward the barracks.

More than one man eyed her speculatively, and her grip instinctively tightened on Finn's arm. "Must we go this way?"

"There's something I need to see," he replied as they continued toward the stable.

Seeing no servants or men nearby, Lizette leaned close to Finn. "Why didn't you stay in the bedchamber?" she whispered.

"I got bored."

She regarded him incredulously. "You risked our plan and our lives, and the lives of those we care about because you were *bored?* What if Roslynn had been at court? What if she'd met Gilbert there?"

"That would have been bad," he conceded as he halted in the shadow of a storeroom and leaned his weight on his uninjured leg. "However, I had not seen her there, and Gilbert had already left to go to Nottingham on the king's business by the time she arrived. You said she'd been raised on a remote estate prior to that, so I was fairly certain they'd likely never met. And since I shaved off my beard and kept my distance from most of the unmarried noblewomen when I was Sir Oliver, I didn't think she'd recognize me by that name, either.

"Otherwise, I would have hurried away as fast as this leg would take me the moment I set eyes upon her."

Lizette studied his face, trying to imagine him with a thick, dark beard. It would make him look older, surely, and perhaps draw even more attention to his dark, expressive eyes.

"Even so, you shouldn't have taken the chance. They could have met at another nobleman's castle, and you would have put us, and our plans, in jeopardy."

"No need to get so worked up about it," he returned, starting again to limp toward the stable. "By her own admission she hasn't met Gilbert before."

"Fortunately for us—but you should have stayed in our bedchamber!"

"And let Wimarc…?" She could see the effort it took for him to speak quietly. "All right. Tell me how wrong I was to be worried. That you don't need me to protect you. Rebuke me for my concern and remind me that you can take care of yourself. That you know what you're doing. You're not a child."

As they faced each other in their enemy's courtyard, she remembered how afraid she'd been in Wimarc's solar and how relieved she was by the interruption, and she couldn't condemn Finn for wanting to save her. "I'm not going to chastise you, or claim I don't need your protection," she conceded. "Wimarc's a cruel, dangerous man, and if Roslynn hadn't arrived, I would have been glad if you'd interrupted."

His shoulders relaxed. "Well. A miracle."

"What were you going to do to save me if Wimarc was attacking me?" she asked as Finn led her past the wide door to the side of the stable. He glanced up at the high wall around them, then, holding her hand, drew her into the narrow alley between the stable and the half-timber storehouse beside it.

"I was going to go to the solar claiming to have a question for Wimarc," he replied. "Finding you together,

I wasn't going to fly into a rage. I was going to pretend to believe whatever explanation you or Wimarc gave for your little tête-à-tête. Fortunately, Roslynn arrived instead."

"Very fortunately. It was terrible."

He turned to look at her, a smile on his lips—that suddenly died. "Kiss me!"

Before she could answer, he pushed her against the wall and covered her mouth with his. As she did, she heard the sound of deep, rough male voices. Some of Wimarc's men were nearby, perhaps at the entrance to the alley.

Understanding, she threw her arms around Finn and returned his kiss. Whatever the reason for their embrace, it felt so good to be in his arms, so right, that there was no need to feign passion.

The voices drifted away as the men moved on, but she didn't break the kiss. Neither did Finn as she relaxed against his powerful body. Pressing her back against the wooden wall, his tongue parted her lips and slid inside her warm and willing mouth. All thought of any other purpose was momentarily forgotten in the delight of being in his arms and feeling his desire building. Like her own.

His hand slid down her arm and glided across her ribs, rising to cup her breast as she arched her back, her own hands moving down his muscular back.

One of the guards on the wall called out for a cup of water. Startled, she broke the kiss and found herself staring up into Finn's intense dark eyes.

"There's a side door here," he said, "and I needed to see if that door has a lock. It doesn't and it's not visible from the wall walk."

"Good?" she murmured, her mind still dazed by the sensation of his lips and his hands upon her yearning body.

"Very good. Nothing like a fire and stampeding horses to distract the guards."

Fully attentive now, she raised her brows. "Tonight?"

"Tonight," he agreed.

So his kiss had only been another necessity.

"WHAT, THEY WERE ALL DEAD?" Wimarc demanded of the leader of his mercenaries as he faced him in the barracks.

"All," Draco confirmed. "Dragged into the woods and buried."

"Yet the wagon was still there?"

Draco reached into his leather tunic and pulled out some parchment. "And this."

Wimarc snatched it from his hand. "I suppose you and the rest of your party pilfered the rest of the baggage?"

Draco didn't reply.

Wimarc said no more, for Draco and his fellows were too skilled at their trade to anger.

"That was her cortege," he muttered after reading the mud-stained letter. He ground his fist, still clenching the parchment, into his palm. "I didn't think her men were so well trained. You found not a single one of their bodies?"

"No, my lord. Just your men." Draco regarded his overlord with blatant curiosity. "She was valuable to you, this woman?"

"To me and to others," he replied. Now he had nothing with which to neutralize the de Boisbastons.

Unfortunately, that also meant he needed Gilbert's alliance more than ever…or at least his men and wealth.

IN THE CHAMBER where Lizette and Finn prepared for the rescue and escape, a thick candle burned on the bedside table. The linen shutter was closed, keeping out the chill night air and light of the nearly full moon. It would be better if there were no moon at all, but that could not be helped.

Lizette had put on the gown she'd arrived in, now washed and mended. Because it was brown, it would make her harder to see, Finn said. He'd taken four picks from his leather strap and tucked them into his belt.

"Easier than taking off my boot," he explained. "Thank God Roslynn came, or Wimarc might be expecting you in his bedchamber tonight."

Lizette nodded as she tied back her hair with a simple leather thong. "Although I want to find evidence against Wimarc, I'm sorry for her. A traitor's lands and goods are forfeit to the crown. She could be left with nothing."

"She has a family to take her back, unless she's involved in the conspiracy, as well."

"I don't believe she is. Do you?"

Finn shook his head. "No, I don't. I don't think Wimarc would trust her enough to involve her in his plots."

She silently nodded her agreement, admiring his ease. Given what they were about to attempt, he was remarkably calm.

But then, he was used to such activity, and she was not. And when this was over, once they were safely away from here, she would go back to Averette and likely never see him again. She would probably never know what became of him. If he was alive, or dead. Well, or ill. "Finn, when this is over, what will you do?"

He shrugged and looked down at the stone floor at his feet. "The same as before."

Then he would probably die an early death. There were very few old thieves; the gibbets claimed most when they were even younger than Finn.

"You're so clever, surely you don't need to be a thief," she said, walking toward him, wanting to be nearer to him. "You'd be an excellent merchant, whatever you choose to sell. Women especially would be eager to buy from you, and Garreth could be your helper."

Finn shook his head. "He'd get bored in half a day and probably steal from the next stall."

"Not if you ordered him not to. I think he'll do anything for you, even to being honest. Won't you at least consider it? I...I don't want to be riding along a road someday and see your body hanging from a gibbet."

His gaze held hers, steady and intense. "Just as I don't want to hear someday that you're married."

"I'm never going to marry."

Not if I can't marry you.

The words burst into her mind and heart, and she felt the truth of them. For Finn, she would break her word, as her sisters had. She would give anything and everything to be his wife. To live with him for the rest of her life. To bear his children. But that could never be.

"I've taken a vow," she explained. "Adelaide and Gillian and I all swore a solemn oath after our father

died that we would never wed. That's why I was so upset when you told me they were married."

His brow furrowed. "I thought every woman wanted
to marry. My poor mother would have given her arm to
marry, even Judas if he'd appeared in a cloud and asked
her."

"Perhaps not if the groom was a brute like my father,"
Lizette replied. "We didn't want a life like my mother
endured—beaten and berated because she didn't bear
sons, despite the many times she tried. Between the strain
of pregnancy and childbirth, she became little more than
an empty husk and had nothing left to give her daughters."

"Save an aversion to marriage."

"Yes, save that—and in me, a desire for freedom. To
be at liberty to travel and move about, never tied to one
place."

"And if Adelaide cannot prevent your betrothal?"

"If John compels it by threatening my family, I'll
agree." She looked away, out the window to the sky and
stars beyond. "For too long I've been selfish and ungrateful despite all Adelaide and Gillian have done for
me. So if it's necessary for their safety that I obey the
king and marry, I will." Her voice fell and her heart beat
as rapidly as a galloping horse's hooves, but she would
tell him everything. Tonight, their last night, she would
tell him how she truly felt. "But I will not be happy."

He limped past her to lean against the bedpost.
"Don't say such things. And when this is over and we've
gone our separate ways, never think of me again. I'm
nothing but a thieving, bastard son of a whore, and
you're a noble lady."

She went to him, her gaze on his distraught face. "You're the finest, bravest, most clever man I've ever met. I'm proud to know you, Fingal. I'll always be proud to have known you. And if you were really Sir Oliver de Leslille, I would do everything I could to win your heart."

His chest rose and fell with his rapid breathing as he stared at her. And then he gathered her in his arms and held her close. "My lady, my lady, I wish I was! Oh, how I wish I was!"

Her heart full of sorrow and yet light to know how he cared for her, she clung to him, holding him tight for what could be the last time.

The last embrace. The last night. She raised her head and pressed her lips to his.

The last kiss.

With fervent urgency he returned her kiss. With anxious fingers he caressed her cheeks as she splayed her hands against his powerful back, feeling the coiled strength in his body.

Just because we won't marry doesn't mean we have to be celibate.

She herself had said those words when she'd made her promise with her sisters. She'd spoken half in jest, to break the tense mood in their father's solar, but now... now, here, with this man holding him in her arms, feeling the need and yearning and love coursing through her— "Take me, Finn," she whispered, pleading. "Please, make love with me."

He drew back, uncertain, but with the flush of longing in his face, his eyes dark with passionate need.

All that mattered, all that ruled her now, was her love and desire for this incredible man. To be with him as intimately as a woman could be. To show him how much he meant to her, so much that she would overlook the rules and restrictions of custom and honor to share his bed. Risk childbirth and scandal and shame. "Finn, make love with me! Now, tonight, before we part."

Although his body told her he was aroused and just as tense as she, he shook his head. "No, my lady. As much as I would like that, we have not the time."

Holding tight to her hands, he looked at her with a disappointment that equalled her own. "But oh, my sweet Lizette, if we had the time, and you looked at me like that and said those words, I would love you so long and so well, you could never doubt how much you mean to me."

He cared for her, he wanted her, and yet he was right. They had not the time. Not for love. Not now, not here.

And so never.

Full of regret and sorrow, but determination, too, she pulled away and, wiping the tears that would fall, led him to the door.

Even if she couldn't love Finn as fully as she wished, she could still help him save his brother and escape from this wretched place.

CHAPTER NINETEEN

HOLDING HANDS, Lizette and Finn crept out of their chamber. They moved quickly down the stairs and through the hall, where dogs and soldiers and male servants slumbered on straw pallets. The dogs rose and sniffed, but seeing them as no apparent threat, they went back to sleep. The men slept undisturbed, with only the occasional snort and snore to break the silence.

Purposeful and determined, Finn kept moving toward the stairs leading to the solar as if nothing or no one could stop him. Lizette followed, just as resolved to break into Wimarc's solar, find evidence of the conspiracy, rescue Ryder and depart. And if there was no evidence, they would still free Ryder and flee. Finn was right. It was too dangerous to stay any longer.

Hiding in the shadows, they were able to sneak inside the keep by the second entrance away from the guardroom.

When they reached the landing outside the solar, Finn took out the largest of the picks in his belt and worked it in and around until the lock opened. They entered the dark chamber and cautiously made their way toward the table, the only light coming from the moon through the loopholes. Using the smaller of the picks and a few deft motions, Finn soon had the chest open, revealing several rolled parchments inside.

"I'll have to see what they are," she whispered. "We can't take them all."

"I'll guard the door," Finn said with a nod. "Sit on the floor and light the candle. The table should block the light from the guards on the wall walk."

Lizette did as he suggested, and lit the candle using the flint she'd taken from the kitchen when she'd gone there to ask for more warm water before she changed for the evening meal. She pulled off the riband holding each scroll and quickly perused the contents, glad her father had decreed his daughters should learn to read to increase their value as brides.

Most were letters that seemed innocent enough; nevertheless, she took note of who had sent them. Some were from noblemen known to be opposed to the king, yet even those weren't very incriminating. They would surely not be enough to convict Wimarc or these other rich and powerful nobles of treason.

"There's nothing here that seems to prove a conspiracy against the king," she said, her voice heavy with disappointment.

"Feel around the side of the chest. Press in any indentations or anything unusual. There may be a secret compartment."

There was a small indentation near the back of the left side. She pressed it and the panel came down, like a little drawbridge, revealing a narrow opening—and more parchments.

Hope soared as she examined them. These letters

pledged support for Wimarc and his plans to overthrow
the king. The anger and hate for the monarch was almost
palpable, and she was amazed at the number of men
willing to rebel. A few suggested Wimarc take the
throne for himself, others that it should be a person who
had a just claim to the throne: the granddaughter of
Henry II and the murdered Arthur's sister, Lady Eleanor.
It was also clear a few of the conspirators hoped to take
their place at the young woman's side as her husband,
with Wimarc's help.

It was obvious Wimarc had promised more than one
ambitious nobleman that chance, as long as he supported Wimarc and his schemes. "These are exactly
what we need!"

"We can't take them all," Finn said grimly, "or he'll
know somebody's on to him and flee before he can be
arrested. Take two or three of the most incriminating and
leave the rest."

Nodding, she took the bottom three parchments,
rolled them up and slipped them into her bodice, then
retrieved three others from the bottom of the main part
of the chest, so that the hidden chamber would look as
full as before. She closed the secret panel and the lid of
the chest, then locked it before blowing out the candle
and putting both items back on the table.

When she was ready to leave, Finn opened the door
and ensured all was still and quiet beyond. He reached
for Lizette's hand and she grasped his, warm and strong,
ready to go on to the next part of their plan.

A woman's scream shattered the silence, coming from
the bedchambers as if someone was being murdered.

FINN FROZE. He'd heard screams like that once before. They haunted his dreams and sometimes his days, along with the memory of his mother's beaten, broken body.

He'd hidden that day. He'd let that brute kill her.

Never again. Never again would he stand by, helpless and afraid, while a woman was being hurt.

Despite that urge, he hesitated, torn between his wish to help, fear for his brother, and his need to get Lizette away from here. If he went to this unknown woman's aid now, he might not be able to free Ryder tonight. They would have to stay. And their theft of the papers might be discovered, their ruse revealed. Then Ryder would have no hope, and Lizette would be in Wimarc's power.

Another scream rent the air, and his decision was made. He couldn't abandon that woman to her fate. He couldn't leave another woman to die at a man's hands.

"Go to our chamber until I return," he ordered Lizette as he drew his sword. "Our escape will have to wait."

"I'm coming with you."

"Lizette!"

"Go!" she urged, and he did as she commanded, running down the stairs as fast as his wounded leg would allow and rushing across the hall toward the stairs leading to the bedchambers. Soldiers and servants started awake, and the hounds began to bark.

Finn paid them no heed. He took the stairs to the upper level two at a time, his ears straining for the sounds of a woman pleading or sobbing or moaning.

He heard what he sought behind the first door and with

all the power of his rage, kicked open the door to see Wimarc, his fist raised, standing over his cowering wife.

It was only with the greatest effort and knowledge that other lives depended on him that Finn held his anger in check and didn't strike the man down at once. None of them would get out of Castle de Werre alive if he attacked Wimarc.

Lizette rushed past him and threw her arms around the distraught Roslynn. Glaring at Wimarc, who slowly lowered his arm, she helped his wife to her feet. "You brute!"

Despite his order, she had followed Finn here.

He should have expected it. If she wouldn't balk from coming here in disguise and putting herself in danger, she wouldn't hesitate to stop a man beating his wife.

But that didn't lessen the risk, or that their ruse must be maintained.

"Enough, Helewyse," he said as Wimarc resumed his smooth, sophisticated mask. "She's his wife. We have no right to meddle."

"Married or not, he has no right to kill her," Lizette retorted.

Finn replied with stern arrogance. "I say again, she is his wife—his property, his chattel, as you are mine."

He knew the moment Lizette remembered who and what she was supposed to be, and why. Nevertheless, she continued to be indignant.

"You men are all the same," she charged as she helped the crying Roslynn to the door that now hung by only one twisted leather hinge. "Brutes, the lot of you! But although we are only women, we aren't utterly helpless. There are ways to deal with such husbands—beginning with *this*. *You*, my lord Gilbert, may spend the rest of the night in the hall, for you will find no welcome in our bedchamber tonight."

She helped the sobbing Roslynn out the door and, with another fierce glance of undisguised scorn, slammed the door behind them.

"Damn women," Finn muttered as he sheathed his sword. He really wanted to curse Wimarc for beating his wife, for his treachery, for his lust, and for ruining their plans of escape.

"I beg your pardon for the interruption, my lord, and the damage to the door. I was afraid it was an assassin attacking you. If I'd known you were just disciplining your wife, I would have left you to it."

"Your own wife has as impertinent a tongue as Roslynn," Wimarc remarked as he walked to the table near the bed and poured some wine from a silver carafe into two goblets.

Finn surveyed Wimarc's bedchamber. It was one of the most luxurious he'd ever seen, equal to the king's, and John didn't spare any expense when it came to his own comfort.

Handing him one of the bejeweled goblets, Wimarc sat on a delicate ebony chair. "Assassins, eh?" he queried after gesturing for Finn to sit in another chair opposite him.

"Yes," Finn answered as Wimarc delicately sipped his wine. "John's the sort of underhanded fellow who'd do something like that."

"Indeed," Wimarc replied. "I thank you for your concern."

"We who think John's a stupid tyrant must help and protect one another, until there's a new and better king on the throne."

Wimarc raised a querying brow. "So you agree England needs a different king?"

"I do, and as soon as possible. I wasn't sure *you* did, but now I believe we are united in our desire for a better king."

"And better wives," Wimarc added with a sly smile.

"More obedient and quieter ones, at any rate," Finn agreed with a laugh.

"It's a pity John's got such obedient and loyal men around him," Wimarc noted. "Otherwise, his own greed and excesses would be more obvious, and more men would agree he must be overthrown."

"Pembroke and the de Boisbastons will never be disloyal."

Wimarc twisted his ruby ring around his finger and regarded his guest steadily, his eyes reminding Finn of a lizard's. "Then we shall simply have to be rid of them, or bring them to our cause, willingly or otherwise. The de Boisbastons care a great deal about their family. Holding one of them hostage will soon bring them to heel. I thought I was going to have such an opportunity soon. Unfortunately, Lady Elizabeth slipped through my fingers."

They'd guessed that was Wimarc's aim, but to hear it put so cold-bloodedly made him want to draw his sword and run the man through.

Now more than ever, he had to get Lizette safely out of here before Wimarc learned the truth, or discovered those letters had been taken. With Ryder, or—please God, he hoped it need not come to this!—without him.

SITTING ON THE EDGE of the bed, Roslynn sobbed softly as she leaned against Lizette. Lizette stroked her hair and offered words of comfort, although the parchments in her bodice dug into her skin and her heart ached to think they'd lost the chance to rescue Ryder and escape tonight.

Yet she didn't fault Finn for rushing to Roslynn's rescue. To do less would mean he wasn't the good man she believed him to be, and they might have been guilty of letting Roslynn die.

Her selfishness had caused enough death.

Somehow, surely, they could keep up the ruse for one more day and do as they planned, provided Wimarc didn't notice anything amiss with his papers or the solar. Nevertheless, the longer they stayed, the more dangerous it was for all of them and the more likely Ryder would be starved to death before they could free him.

"I'm so glad you're here," Roslynn said, hiccuping as she sniffled. "I think Wimarc would have killed me if you hadn't stopped him."

Lizette could well believe he might have. Marriage was supposed to protect a woman—but it didn't protect her from her own husband, as she'd witnessed for herself. Her father had berated and beaten her mother, cursing her for giving him daughters as if her poor mother hadn't spent hours on her knees praying for a boy, visited every physician who came within fifty miles, and every soothsayer and alchemist, too. As if she hadn't

lost her health and nearly her sanity bearing and miscar-
rying for her unloving, ungrateful husband.

"Is there somewhere you can go?" she asked Roslynn
softly. "Are there family or friends who could take you in?"

Roslynn nodded. "I could go back to Lord Bernard's.
He's an old friend of my father's. Wimarc wouldn't
dare insult or threaten *him*. I should have stayed there,
but I thought…hoped…"

Her words ended in a choked sob. Lizette held her
close, thinking of the many times Adelaide had cradled
her thus after their mother had died and before that, too,
when she'd been upset by some trouble, and their
mother too sick to comfort her.

Yet in return, she had treated every order, every suggestion of Adelaide's as if it was a personal affront.

What an ungrateful wretch she'd been!

Roslynn sniffled and straightened, brushing back her
damp, messy curls from her cheek. "I'm sorry that you
had to witness my humiliation, Helewyse, and I hope
your husband will forgive you."

Lizette rose to get a damp cloth. "I'm sure he will."

She returned to Roslynn and gave her the cloth to
wipe her tear-streaked face.

"He told me I was shaming him with my behavior
with your husband at dinner," Roslynn said. "That I
was acting like a whore—but I promise you, Helewyse,
I had no intention of…I didn't want to…. It's just that
Gilbert is so nice…."

She dissolved into tears again, and as before,
Lizette hugged her gently. "It's all right, Roslynn. I
understand. My husband is a very witty, charming

fellow. And as chatelaine, you *should* be attentive to your guests."

Her comforting words only made Roslynn cry harder. Feeling woefully inadequate, Lizette made soft, shushing sounds as if the young woman were an infant. If only Adelaide were here! She would know what to say. Or Gillian.

At last Roslynn quieted. Wiping her face with the back of her hand, she looked at Lizette with red-rimmed, remorseful eyes. "I thought I loved Wimarc. I know now that what I felt was only desire—because he was handsome and rich and spoke so eloquently."

She rose and went to the window, studying the moon above the battlements. "What a fool I was! To think that I begged my father to bring the marriage about."

She turned and leaned back against the stone wall. "I realized on our wedding night I'd been wrong to believe Wimarc really cared for me." Her eyes lowered and her voice dropped until it was almost inaudible. "He was so...rough."

"Perhaps if you write to your father once you're at Lord Bernard's and tell him what's happened, an annulment can be arranged, some reason found to negate the marriage," she suggested. "I've heard of such things."

Roslynn shook her head. "I can't expect any help from him. He was against the marriage from the start, but I refused to listen."

More tears slid down Roslynn's cheeks as Lizette considered how stubborn *she* had been when she'd wanted something.

"Maybe Wimarc will regret hitting me," Roslynn said, brightening a little.

Lizette doubted that very much. "I wouldn't expect that if I were you. However, you do have friends to help you, and perhaps your father will be more forgiving and sympathetic than you believe."

With another sigh, Roslynn reached out to grasp Lizette's hand. "Thank you, Helewyse. You're a good friend."

"I'm glad I was here to help you."

Lizette *was* glad she'd been there to help Roslynn. She also pitied her and feared there was worse to come for the young woman. Unfortunately, she didn't dare warn Roslynn of her husband's crime. Once she, Finn and Ryder were safely away from here, she would try to find a way to warn her.

But not until then.

IN THE EARLY-MORNING CHILL, Garreth stood with his hands on his hips and eyed the pot simmering on the open fire outside the small hut. "Isn't that done yet?"

"I can't serve a lord and lady raw rabbit," Keldra replied as she stirred the contents.

"It doesn't have to be perfect. Haven't you noticed we're not in a castle?"

"That doesn't mean I'm not going to do my best. *Some* people take pride in what they do."

"*Some* people have reason to be proud," Garreth peevishly replied. "Other people are only proud because of who they serve."

Keldra straightened, the ladle dripping in her hand.

"Why shouldn't I be proud to serve a lady?" she demanded, waving the ladle at him. "Better a lady than a thief!"

"If you say so—but I don't serve Finn. We're partners."

"Oh, yes, partners. That's why you follow him around like a dog and brag about him all the time."

"I don't!"

"You do! Every time you open your mouth, it's to tell me another marvelous thing he's done."

"I saved his life!"

Keldra returned to stirring the pot. "I'd wager he just lets you *think* so."

"He does not. He trusts me—that's why I'm guarding the prisoners."

"So am *I*. Now are you going to help me take this to Lord Gilbert and Lady Helewyse or are you going to brag about Finn some more?"

With a disgruntled scowl, Garreth got the wooden bowls. After Keldra had ladled the thick stew of rabbit, leeks and peas into them, he led the way to the hut while she followed with the bowls. He lifted the thick branch that barred the door and, drawing his sword, entered the hut ahead of her.

"They're gone!"

Dropping the bowls, Keldra rushed inside to find that the small building furnished with some of the things from the baggage cart, including straw and thick blankets, was empty.

Garreth crouched at the wall opposite. "They dug a hole right under the wall. Must have done it in the night."

"When *you* were supposed to be standing watch!"

Keldra cried. What was going to happen to her beloved Lady Elizabeth if she were caught in that evil man's castle pretending to be somebody else?

"It doesn't matter when," Garreth snapped, rushing past her. "We've got to stop them."

She followed him around the back of the hut to the place where Lord Gilbert and his wife had crawled out.

"At least they didn't take a horse," Garreth said grimly. He pointed at footprints in the dew-damp grass leading away from their encampment. "He's not very clever."

He went back to the lean-to and grabbed his bow and quiver of arrows. "Come on, they can't have gotten far on foot."

"They wouldn't have gotten away at all if you'd paid attention and not been so full of yourself."

Garreth didn't answer.

CHAPTER TWENTY

LIZETTE COULD FEEL Roslynn tremble as they made their way to the hall the next morning. Wimarc and Finn were already seated at the dais, breaking the fast as if they were the best of friends.

The soldiers and servants in the hall glanced uneasily at the ladies, then quickly went back to their food, pretending they had no interest in what had happened, or what was to come.

Only Ellie stared with blatant curiosity, and a smug little smile on her face. As for Finn, she could tell nothing from his expression, which seemed deliberately inscrutable. Wimarc tried to look as genial as usual, but there was a glint in his eyes that told her she was not forgiven, and neither was his wife.

Nor was she the only one to realize that, for Roslynn sucked in her breath and stiffened.

Lizette feared Roslynn was going to lose her nerve, or even apologize to her husband—but she didn't. She stood before the high table and threw her shoulders back before speaking, although her voice was a little tremulous. "I'm going to return to Lord Bernard's household, Wimarc. Don't try to stop me!"

Wimarc's gaze flicked to Lizette. No doubt he was wondering if she'd put his wife up to that.

"You may do whatever you like," Wimarc replied as if he didn't much care.

"And I will!" Roslynn cried before she whirled around, her brocade skirt flapping about her ankles. Her back straight as a pike, she marched from the hall, leaving Lizette behind.

Out of the corner of her eye, she caught Ellie's satisfied grin. She could have Wimarc, Lizette thought, although she didn't doubt Ellie would one day be glad to flee his arms, too.

Finn rose from his seat. "If you'll excuse me, my lord, I believe I should speak to my wife."

She remembered she was supposed to be angry with him, too, for his arrogance last night. "Can it not wait until after I've eaten?"

"No, it cannot," he curtly replied, coming around the table and grabbing her arm.

As he pulled her toward the stairs and their chamber, she snatched a small brown loaf, much to Ellie's tittering amusement—until Finn darted a glance at her. Then the maid stopped laughing.

When they reached the bedchamber and opened the door, Greseld was inside, making the bed.

"Out!" Finn ordered.

With a sniff, the old woman hurried to obey and he quickly closed the door behind her. Then he pulled Lizette into his arms. "God, it's a mess. I never should have let you come here."

"You didn't *let* me," she replied, for the moment all her

fears and dread melting away. "I came because I wanted to—and if I hadn't, I would have missed being with you."

He caressed her cheek with his callused hand. "When you say such things, I don't regret it, either."

"I didn't dare take the letters out of my bodice last night," she explained, stepping back and pulling them out, then tucking them in her sleeve. "I was afraid Roslynn might awaken if I removed them, and it would be difficult to explain why I was carrying such things in such a place."

"That must have been uncomfortable." He shook his head. "Poor woman."

She knew he wasn't referring to her.

"She made a terrible mistake," Lizette agreed.

"That man's a vile thing. Last night after you left us, he suggested we amuse ourselves with Ellie."

"What, both of you?"

"Aye. I said she might object, and he said, 'What of it?'" Finn's lip curled with scorn. "I don't think she'd be the first or even the fiftieth he's taken against her will, or forced to do whatever he wants. I told him I was in no mood to do anything other than drink. He went off to find Ellie."

"Let's hope these letters and his attempts to abduct me will destroy him."

"Aye, let's hope."

She leaned back against the table, her anxiety and fear returning. "Oh, Finn, we've *got* to get out of here soon!"

He sighed and ran his hand through his hair. "We'd be out of here now if I hadn't—"

She went to him and put her fingers against his

lips. "You did right to stop him. Wimarc might have killed her."

Finn's sorrowful gaze held hers. "I hid the night a man beat my mother to death. I got Ryder and kept my hand over his mouth while we huddled by the hearth, and watched the man hit her with a piece of firewood." His voice fell. "I never so much as made a sound to stop him."

She took his cold hands and held them in hers, lifting her eyes to his anguished face. "And if you *had* tried? Perhaps you'd be dead, too. And Ryder. You were protecting him, Finn. I think that's what your mother would have wanted."

He swallowed hard. "Dear God, I hope so."

She thought of something else. "Who paid for Ryder to be in the monastery? It was you, wasn't it? You robbed so that he wouldn't suffer as you did."

Finn pulled his hands free and shrugged his shoulders as if the answer was obvious. "He's my brother."

Was it any wonder she loved him?

And was it any wonder she felt like an ungrateful wretch for taking for granted all the care and concern Adelaide, Gillian and even Iain had shown her over the years?

He lifted her chin and frowned. "I didn't mean to upset you, Lizette. And there's one good thing for the delay. Since I apparently upheld Wimarc's right to beat his wife, he's decided I'm worthy of being included in his conspiracy against the king. We're fast friends now, him and me, and we were right. He wanted to abduct you to force your brothers-in-law to join his cause."

"*You* were right," she corrected.

"But we've still got to escape tonight. The longer we stay here, the more dangerous it is for you. If Wimarc ever discovers who you really are…"

"Let's pray he doesn't," she replied. "All will be well, Finn. It has to be."

Yet when this was over and she was safe at Averette again, she would never really be completely happy again.

Because Finn would not be there.

"My lord?" Ellie called from outside the chamber.

"What now?" Finn muttered before he bade her enter.

She came into the chamber carrying a bucket of steaming water and made a little bow.

"Lord Wimarc sent us," she said, obviously more than a little disgruntled as she moved aside to allow more servants behind her to enter the chamber. They carried a large wooden tub.

Lizette slid Finn a glance. "I do believe Lord Wimarc's giving me a little present," he murmured.

As the import of his words struck her, Lizette blushed furiously. This had to be because of that lie she'd told Wimarc about Finn's name!

More servants came into the room bearing hot water with which to fill the tub. Greseld came tottering in at the last, carrying a pile of linen that reached to her nose, so high that she could barely see where she was going.

"He said you might welcome a wash after your night in the hall," Ellie said to Finn.

"Thank you, I would," he gravely replied. "Please convey my thanks to his lordship. Tell him my wife thanks him, too."

Ellie sniffed and, before Greseld shooed her and the rest of the servants from the chamber, gave Lizette a look that would have smote her to the ground if it had been a weapon.

"Oh, dear, Ellie's angry at us," Finn observed as he let go of Lizette and strolled to the tub, studying it speculatively.

"I do believe she hates me," Lizette replied, her heart racing and lust-inspired visions rushing through her mind as she followed him and slowly ran her hand around the rim, her fingers lightly brushing the linens laid in and over the side to cushion it. "I suppose Wimarc intends this as a reward for your alliance."

"I suppose," Finn agreed, coming up behind her.

She didn't move. He stood close to her, but not touching, in a way that was as exciting as a caress.

"I'd hate to disappoint the man by not using it," he murmured.

She closed her eyes. "It might not be good for your leg."

"I was afraid you were going to say that," he said, his voice full of regret.

They couldn't try to free Ryder again until nightfall. They had time. Today, they had time.

"Finn," she said softly, turning to him. "Make love with me."

His dark eyes widened, and then, to her delight, he gave her a smile of such promise and temptation, her very heart sang with the joy of it.

Until he frowned and moved away as if he feared contagion.

"I mean it, Finn, just as I did before—nay, more!" she

said, approaching him as carefully as if he were a horse that might shy away. "I want to make love with you."

Still he didn't touch her, and now she saw real dismay in his face. "What if you get with child?" he whispered.

And then she understood.

"Whatever the future holds for us," she assured him, "if I were to be so blessed, I would love the babe and cherish it with all my heart. And my sisters would never cast us out. We would be safe and your child would have a home—a real home, Finn. Always."

He let out a ragged sigh, then he gave her the ghost of a rueful smile as he reached out to pull her into his arms. "I remember what I said last night. God forgive me, I want you, too."

He kissed her, and as he did, she recalled his words about loving her so that she would have no doubt that he cared for her.

Excited and happy, determined to forget what might await them later, she broke the kiss and, laughing, steered him toward the bed. They might only have this one time, this one chance, and she would make the most of it.

"What are you doing?" he asked as he sat on the end of the bed.

"There's more than one way to bathe."

"There is?"

"Well, more than one way to get started, anyway," she replied as she turned her back to him. "Untie my laces, please."

"I'm to be your maid?"

"I thought you'd enjoy untying my laces."

He didn't argue with that and did as she asked.

When he was finished, she turned around to face him before wiggling out of her gown.

"Salome's dance couldn't be more tempting than that little wiggle you're doing," he observed, reaching out for her. "Maybe I don't want to wait for a wash."

Clad in her shift, softly singing a love song, she danced away from him toward the tub. The chorus counseled, "Patience, my lord, be patient."

"I'm not a lord," he noted, getting to his feet.

"Sit down or I'll stop," she warned. "I mean it, Finn. We have to be careful of your leg."

Muttering something under his breath, he obeyed.

She sang more of the song, letting her love come through in the words, happy to have him hear her, for singing was the one true talent she possessed.

And then, to her delight, he joined in, his deep, rich bass combining with hers to end the song.

"I learned that at court," he said, half rising again. "But nobody there sings as well as you."

"I'm flattered," she said, genuinely pleased as she motioned for him to sit. "Stay where you are and rest your leg."

Then she slowly, seductively wiggled out of her shift until she was naked.

"I hope you appreciate my restraint, Lizette," he said, his voice low and husky.

"Oh, I do," she replied, stepping into the tub and warm water. "I hope you appreciate mine."

She reached for the lump of soap Greseld had left within reach and began to lather her shoulders and breasts.

Finn sucked in his breath. "By the saints, my lady, are you after torturing me?"

"I'm after getting clean," she primly replied. "If you care to watch, that's not my concern."

"Liar."

She slid him a coy glance. "You're right. We're a fine pair of liars."

Despite her command that he sit, he came to the tub and took the soap from her hand. "I think you need a little help."

She didn't protest when he began to wash her, running the soap—and his hand—over her back and shoulders, her neck and collar bone, and then, finally, her breasts. Yearning and need and excitement kindled and burned, hot and anxious and ready for more.

"I think I'm clean enough," she said, opening her eyes. "Go back to the bed, my lord, and take off your tunic."

"Gladly," he replied, his voice thick with desire, his eyes dark with passionate need.

She rose and wrapped a large square of linen around her warm, moist body. Stepping out of the tub, she went to where he waited. His tunic was now on the bed beside him and with eager hands, she took off his shirt.

Then, swaying her hips in a blatant attempt to arouse him even more, she went back for a wet cloth to wash his chest.

As she began, moving the cloth in slow, titillating circles across his skin, he took hold of the linen covering her and, with a swift tug, yanked it off.

She gasped with the sudden chill, but made no effort

to retrieve the linen, especially when he put his hands on her waist and drew her forward, bringing her breasts to his eager tongue and lips.

Any pretense of washing was forgotten as he pleasured her, and she wound her hands in his thick hair. Then she kissed him. With slow, deliberate seduction she moved her mouth over his, feeling the need growing within her, the warmth and tension increasing, knowing it was the same for him.

Still kissing him, her hands made swift work of the knot in the drawstring of his breeches. Once he was free, he pulled her onto his lap. His hand slid around her waist, then up to her breast while she slipped her arms around his neck.

She felt him hard beneath her, and knew he was just as anxious to make love. Feeling more bold and wanton and free than she ever had in her life, she pushed him backward and straddled his muscular hips.

His eyes sparkled with both desire and amusement. "I'll have to thank Wimarc."

"Later," she whispered as she captured his mouth with hers, kissing him deeply and brushing her palm over his nipples, feeling them tighten beneath her touch.

"I think you like having me at your mercy, my lady," he said as his lips grazed her skin.

"I do," she breathlessly agreed as she stroked him.

"God help me, you're a wanton wench."

"I can stop if you want," she teased, although she hoped he didn't.

"I don't want to."

"Are you sure this isn't hurting you?"

"Not my leg, if that's what you mean," he replied. "In another way, it's a torment."

"Is it?" she asked innocently, caressing him more quickly.

"You know it is, you wicked woman," he said before he drew her right nipple into his mouth and teased it with his tongue.

Gasping from the excitement and ever-increasing need, one hand clutching his shoulder, the other encircling him, she lowered herself, moaning with pleasure as he entered her.

"Oh, yes," he sighed as he held her to him. He groaned when she began to rock, then whispered encouragement and directions to bring them both to a state of bliss.

Faster she moved as she kissed and caressed him, while he used his hands, his lips, his tongue, to bring her to the brink of ecstasy. His very breathing told her how to arouse him more, and she delighted in the knowledge that she was able to give him such delight, equal to her own.

But this was no swift coupling, over in a few brief moments. She varied the pace, savoring the sensations of his body joined with hers—the moist warmth of their mouths, the sinuous intertwining of their tongues, her soft, firm breasts against his hard, muscular chest, their bodies intimately connected, each one seeking to bring the other to completion.

The tension between them finally reached its height and breaking point. He stiffened and groaned, his mouth against her flesh, while she held him as if she needed him more than food or air or fire.

Sated, she relaxed against him, her eyes half-closed, certain in her heart she had never been happier than when she was in this man's arms.

Neither one had noticed that the hole in the wall opposite the bed was no longer blocked.

"GILBERT, I CAN'T! I can't run anymore!" Helewyse panted as she struggled to keep up with her husband. She stumbled over her skirts despite his arm about her waist as they ran through the forest, bushes clawing at them and slick mud beneath their feet. "Leave me and go on! Save yourself!"

"I won't!"

She tripped over the root of an oak tree and would have fallen if he hadn't held her upright. "I'm so sorry," she sobbed. "You would be far away by now if not for me."

Gilbert saw the strain in her exhausted face and how pale she was. Helewyse was gently reared, and delicate. Who could say what harm this headlong dash over rough ground might do to her health?

He stopped, and she collapsed against him, gasping for air.

He took off the water skin he'd taken from the hut and pulled out the stopper. "Drink this."

She eagerly gulped the cold water.

"I fear I've finished it," she said, her voice small and worried as she gave it back to him.

"It's all right. We'll find a stream and fill it again."

She nodded, clinging to him as she regarded him with large eyes that were no longer so afraid, as she'd endured their captivity with more courage than he'd ever expected.

Some of the water had leaked from its container and dampened the bodice of her gown, drawing his gaze to her breasts.

He felt himself rousing, despite this being the worst time for such a reaction. Yet in all the time he'd been married to Helewyse, he had never found her more attractive or desirable.

He caressed her cheek, marveling that he'd never noticed how soft her skin was, or how finely shaped her lips. He'd been a blind fool, marrying her only for her dowry when she was worth so much more.

"Helewyse," he murmured, "when we are safe—"

"Don't move, my lord," an unfortunately familiar voice demanded breathlessly from nearby. "You've led us a merry chase, but you're caught now, so unless you want an arrow through your leg, you'll both come back with us."

Helewyse turned abruptly, facing the young man who stepped onto the path. She held out her arms to shield her husband, ready to risk her life for his. "I'll die before I let you hurt him!"

God's wounds, she meant it! He *had* been a fool to underestimate her so. And in that moment, as Helewyse offered to sacrifice herself for him, when he saw the truly noble courage and spirit of the woman he had married out of ambition and greed, Lord Gilbert of Fairbourne fell in love with his wife.

He immediately tried to move her out of the potential path of the youth's arrow, but she wouldn't budge.

"Helewyse, stand aside!" he commanded.

The anxious serving wench appeared on the path. "If you'll both come back with us without any trouble, my lord, nobody need get hurt. Please, just come back with us."

Flushing with frustration, Gilbert clenched his jaw. To think that he was in the power of these two...two... peasants!

"Let my husband go, and I will gladly come back with you," Helewyse offered.

He came around her, putting out his arm to prevent her from going with their youthful captors. "No, take me, and let my wife go."

The damnable youth scowled, and although the maid didn't look pleased, there was something akin to sympathy in her face as she regarded them. "You *both* must return with us," she said. "We can't risk either of you causing trouble for Finn and my lady.

"Truly, we mean you no harm. Finn and my lady just need to be you for a little while longer, so they can rescue Finn's half brother and try to find out why Lord Wimarc sent men to attack our cortege and take my lady to his castle."

Gilbert blinked as he took in what she said. "Wimarc tried to abduct Lizette?"

"Yes, and since she'd never even heard his name before, she wants to know why. The best way she could think of was to get inside his castle and find out for herself."

"God's blood," Gilbert breathed as he considered the danger of what Lizette was doing and what could befall her if she was caught. "That's mad."

"No," Keldra replied with a lift of her chin. "That's my lady."

"Why wasn't I told of this sooner?" Gilbert demanded.

Garreth frowned. "Because you didn't need to know."

"The hell I didn't. I'm no friend of Wimarc. The Earl of Pembroke believes he's planning a rebellion and sent me to find out what he's up to."

His wife stared at him, stunned. "You never said."

He turned to her with regret. "I didn't think you'd come with me, and I didn't know then how brave a woman you are."

She blushed, her eyes shining, as he turned back to the maidservant and the young outlaw. "I can help."

Garreth didn't lower his bow, but continued to regard him warily. "How?"

"Free us and give us a horse. I'll go to the king and the Earl of Pembroke and tell them that Wimarc's tried to abduct one of his wards. Between that and the suspicions the Earl of Pembroke already harbors, the king will surely send a force against Wimarc."

"What suspicions?" Garreth asked warily.

"The earl's certain that the men recently involved in a conspiracy to overthrow the king weren't the only ones in on the plot and probably weren't the architects of it. The earl's intercepted a few letters that point to Lord Wimarc as the instigator. I was to try to find out if that was so, and what other nobles might be involved while feigning interest in joining the rebellion."

"We can't let you go, not when my lady's still in his castle," Keldra protested. "Lord Wimarc might hear of it, and then he'll know my lady isn't your wife."

"Aye, and that Finn's not you," Garreth seconded.

"No one need know who we are until I get to court. That's going to take at least a day. Surely by then Lizette and your friend should be out of there. If not, I regret to say I think their ruse has already been discovered, and if so, it's even more important that the earl learn what's transpiring in Castle de Werre."

Keldra clasped her hands, her eyes full of fear as she looked at Garreth. "You don't think…they probably aren't already…?"

"Wimarc and the others hunting thought he was Lord Gilbert," Garreth said firmly. "He won't fail."

"I truly hope you're right," Gilbert said, "but if not, you *must* let us go and alert the earl. The attack on Lady Elizabeth is enough to arrest Wimarc."

"How do I know if I can trust you?" Garreth demanded.

"I give you my word as a knight of the realm."

"That's not much."

"Garreth!" Keldra cried, aghast and indignant. "That just shows how little you know about the real nobility! He won't betray us—will he, my lady?"

Helewyse held on to her husband's arm, and her expression and voice were confident when she answered. "No, he won't. We'll help Lady Elizabeth and her companion. I give you my word, too."

Garreth still didn't lower his bow. Instead, he gestured with his weapon for Gilbert and his wife to start back toward the hut. "I have to think about this some more," he said as he followed them.

Keldra caught up to him and made no secret of her disgust. "Now you're just being stubborn."

"I'm being careful—and I'm in charge, remember? Finn said so."

"In a battle, you're the general. This isn't a battle.

This is *strategy*. Lord Gilbert can help us, and you should let him."

"If you're so sure about that, you can go with them."

Keldra came to a dead halt and regarded him as if he'd just accused her of being in league with the devil. "Abandon my lady? I will not! If they get away tonight, she'll be expecting me to be awaiting her, and so I will be!"

"Now who's being stubborn?" Garreth muttered.

"You go with Gilbert then."

"I can't leave you in the woods alone. Finn would have my hide."

"Then we'll simply have to trust them and let them go," Keldra said, an irritating note of triumph in her voice.

"Who said I was letting them go?"

"Garreth! You must! The earl and the king have to know what's happening here in case…in case…" Her lower lip started to tremble and she swiped at her eyes.

"Oh, don't start crying again! I'll let them go," Garreth grudgingly conceded, for in spite of what he said, he was really worried that Finn and Lizette had already been caught. It would take the earl's army to save them, and Ryder, too.

Keldra threw her arms around him and kissed him on the cheek.

"Enough of that," he muttered, although he suddenly felt ten feet tall and capable of anything.

CHAPTER TWENTY-ONE

"STAY A LITTLE LONGER," Lizette murmured as she reached out to pull Finn back down onto the bed beside her.

He reluctantly shook his head as he drew on his discarded breeches, wincing as he pulled them over his bandaged leg.

Lizette sat up, holding the sheet against her lovely breasts. "Is it bleeding again?"

"No, it's just a little sore."

"Come back to bed and rest. There's plenty of time before the evening meal."

"As much as I'd like to, I think I should thank our host for his present and try to get another look in the dungeon. I'm not going to have a lot of time to get Ryder out."

And if he also wanted to see if his brother answered his call again, that he was still alive, he wouldn't say, lest he distress her and ruin the pleasant afterglow of their intimacy.

"Then I suppose I should go below, too."

He gave her a roguish grin before putting on his shirt. "I could say I wore you out. Or that you're with child."

She looked away at that.

"I'm sorry," he said, regretting his hasty words. "I hope you're not."

Wrapping the sheet around her, she got out of bed. "If I am, the only thing I'll regret is that you won't see our baby. Or will you come to Averette one day?"

Our baby. Their baby. A bastard like him.

But it would be different. Having met Adelaide, he could be sure she would never abandon her sister, as his own mother had been cast from her home, and as Lizette had said, a child of theirs would always have a home.

Gathering Lizette in his arms, he held her close. "I'll come if I can. But if I don't, if something prevents me, I will always remember you. Of all the days of my life, these with you have been by far the best—even when we quarreled."

She held him tight, and her voice was a whisper of warm breath on his jaw. "And if someday you hear the king has made me marry, know that on my wedding night and every night thereafter, it won't be my husband's face I see when he takes me. It won't be his body I caress. It will be yours. Always, forever, yours."

They kissed again tenderly, as if they were newlyweds with all their lives before them.

Until he drew back. If he stayed here any longer, he was going to beg her to come with him.

But they would be poor, and she would no longer have the rights and privileges of her birth and rank. It was pure selfishness to even think of suggesting she leave her home for an uncertain future with him.

"Let me go, Lizette," he said, laughing softly to mask his pain. "Or I may never leave this chamber."

She did, albeit reluctantly. "As you wish."

How sad she sounded, how forlorn—as upset and woeful as he felt.

There could be no help for it. No other way. Because she was Lady Elizabeth of Averette, and despite what he'd told Adelaide and Armand at court, he was only Fingal, outside the law and bastard son of a whore whose father had been a merchant's son of no greater accomplishment than to get a gullible girl with child.

"I SUPPOSE IT'S ALL RIGHT," Dolfe said, his thick brow furrowed as he regarded Lord Gilbert in the guardroom of the dungeon. "Don't see why not. Just take a torch and mind the steps."

Finn nodded his thanks and grabbed a torch from the sconce at the top of the slick stairs. Keeping one hand on the damp wall, holding the spluttering torch aloft, he descended into the cool, clammy depths.

The priests described hell as fire and brimstone, the sulfurous air full of the screams of the damned. As Finn reached the lower level, he thought they were wrong. Hell was cold and damp and silence.

"Ryder!" he called as loudly as he dared outside Ryder's cells. "Ryder, it's me, Gally!"

He couldn't hear anything except the spluttering flame of his torch.

He got down on his hands and knees and slid open the narrow opening in the bottom of the door through which food was delivered, when there was any. He peered inside, but the only light came from his torch, and he didn't dare bring it lower lest it go out. "Ryder, are you there?"

Was he dead? Oh, sweet Jesus, was he dead?

"Gally?"

It was barely a whisper, but it was Ryder's voice, rasping and weak. "I'm dreaming."

"No, no!" Finn assured him. "It's really me, and I'm coming back soon to get you out."

"O' course you are," his brother said, his faint voice dull and lifeless.

"I wanted to come sooner, but we couldn't. Tonight, Ryder, I promise."

There was no answer. Unfortunately, Finn didn't dare linger, so he rose, more determined than ever to get his brother out tonight.

Before it was too late.

PAYING LITTLE HEED to her surroundings except that she was alone, Lizette sank onto the bench in the garden.

So much had changed since she'd left Averette! She'd been excited about attending Marian's wedding and happy to be away from Gillian, with her grave, gray eyes that always seemed to be criticizing her, and Adelaide, with her stern admonitions about how a lady should behave.

It was no great adventure, she'd thought at the time, but it was better than languishing at home.

Then Iain—poor Iain!—had come to take her back to Averette. How annoyed she'd been, how foolishly stubborn, and look what had happened. Good men dead, her own life and Keldra's in jeopardy.

Yet if she hadn't been so loath to return, she would never have met Finn, and if it weren't for Finn, she and

Keldra would be in Wimarc's power, used to bring her brothers-in-law to heel or aid Wimarc's traitorous plans.

If she hadn't met Finn, she wouldn't be here, with proof of Wimarc's treason tucked in her sleeve so no maidservant would find it, and helping Finn rescue his half brother.

If she weren't here now, doing those things, she would be a virgin still, wondering what it would be like to be loved by a wonderful man. Now she knew, and her only regret was that they couldn't stay together.

Unless she ran off with him. Unless she didn't go back to Averette after she'd presented her evidence to the king. Unless she arranged to meet Finn somewhere, and stay with him.

If he were willing.

If he were willing, could she give up her rank, her home, her family, to live in sin with an outlaw?

He didn't have to be an outlaw. He was a clever man, and a good one. As she'd suggested, he could learn a trade, or become a merchant. He'd been tempted by that idea; she'd seen it in his eyes, and heard his dislike of the outlaw's life when he spoke of Ryder.

The answer was clear, and simple, if she listened to her heart.

"What, all alone, my lady?"

She started at the sound of Wimarc's voice and looked up to see him not three feet away.

She had the distinct, and disturbing, feeling he'd been watching her for some time.

"You seem upset," he noted with apparent concern as he, uninvited, sat beside her. "I hope I'm not responsible." He dropped his voice to a low, intimate whisper, and it was like having a snake hiss in her ear. "Perhaps you would have preferred I not send the tub?"

She slid him a glance, and it was no more than that. The lust in his eyes disgusted her too much for her to continue to look at him. "My husband was most grateful."

"But not you?" he pressed.

She didn't answer.

"I thought it best to keep him happy. Men are less suspicious that way, although it disturbs me to think of you with him, especially now that my wife has gone," he murmured, his hand sliding onto her knee.

It was all she could do not to stiffen with revulsion. "I don't think he suspects, my lord."

"Such formality from such lovely lips is dismaying," he said softly, leaning closer, reminding her that this bench was hidden by the trellis.

Ruse or not, with the parchments in her sleeve, she couldn't bear to let him kiss her. She raised her hand to hold him back. "Although we're sheltered, this is still a public place, and after taking so much care to keep my husband happy, it would be too bad if he found out how we felt because we were unable to control ourselves."

Wimarc removed his hand as his brows lowered. "I told you once, my lady, I don't play games. If you're no longer willing, tell me and be done."

And then what? Would he make them leave that very day?

She put her hand on his chest and infused her words with all the conviction she could muster as she lied. "I want to be with you, my lord. I want to enjoy your kisses, your loving, more than I can say. But I fear my husband, too. I can't risk him finding out that I prefer another. Greseld or some other servant might come into the garden and see us."

"Greseld thinks—and I agree—that you would be a better wife for me than Roslynn."

"Wife?" she whispered, her shock genuine.

He took her hand, firmly, and his gaze held hers. "Yes. I can put Roslynn aside—some excuse can always be found to annul a marriage—and you can do the same with Gilbert."

"Giving in to our desire is one thing, my lord, but Gilbert would never agree to an annulment, and the nature of our relationship would be revealed." She vehemently shook her head. "No, my lord, that can *never* be."

His expression didn't change. "If you were free, and I was, would you consider it?"

She rose, agitated and wanting to be away from him. "My lord, please don't ask me!" She had to maintain the ruse. She must maintain this lie a longer. "Don't give me such hopes!"

He reached out and drew her down. "As much as I would have you for my wife, I cannot deny my desire for you. I cannot wait. Come to me tonight, after he's asleep. Come to my bedchamber, and let me love you. Let me show you what marriage to me would be like."

Although she was sure she already knew, she nodded her head. "Very well," she agreed, rising. "I shall come to you tonight after my husband is asleep. Now I dare not linger here with you another moment."

With that, she hurried away, leaving Wimarc in the garden, envisioning what he would do with her and contemplating just what sort of accident should kill Lord Gilbert of Fairbourne. And when.

WRINGING HER HANDS, Lizette paced the floor of the bedchamber, now empty of the tub and linens. Where was Finn? What was he doing? Had he done as he'd said and returned to the dungeon?

Her steps took her once again to the window. This time, though, her vigilance was rewarded by the sight of Finn strolling casually through the courtyard.

She marveled that he could look so calm, while she felt as if every part of her body was tingling with a combination of dread and anticipation, hoping he would come there before the evening meal.

He didn't. Ellie did, to dress her hair and help her into one of Roslynn's remade gowns.

She expected the servant to be as disgruntled as she'd been that morning, but to her surprise, Ellie seemed… smug. Triumphant. As if she'd won a great prize.

Or been with Finn?

"Braids around my head will do," she said, telling herself that was unlikely, especially now that they'd made love. And surely she knew by now that she could trust him. That she could believe him when he said he didn't want to be with Ellie.

"You seem happy," she continued as the maidservant combed her hair, remembering when Finn had done that.

"Do I?" the young woman insolently replied. "Must be the weather."

Lizette didn't believe that for a moment, and never had Lizette wanted a mirror more, so she could see Ellie's face to try to gauge the veracity of her answers.

The ewer would have to do. It made Ellie's face resemble that of a horse—long and narrow—but it was all she had.

"Have you seen my husband recently?"

"Not since this morning."

The answer was calmly, casually given, and there was nothing in Ellie's reflection that caused Lizette to doubt her answer.

It was a relief, even as she silently chastised herself for not having more faith in Finn.

She would ask no more questions, nor did she, and soon enough she was attired in one of Roslynn's gowns.

Ellie went to the door and opened it for her. "The meal should be ready now, my lady."

Since Finn hadn't come and he might be awaiting her in the hall, she followed Ellie out of the chamber.

It was only as she was closing the door behind her that she happened to glance at the wall opposite the bed.

The hole that had been closed was open once again.

How long had it been like that? Had somebody been watching them? What might they have seen? Or heard?

"Something wrong, my lady?" Ellie asked from the head of the stairs.

Lizette finished closing the door and kept her face blank as best she could. "No, nothing," she said before they continued down the stairs and into the hall.

Finn was standing at the high table, with Wimarc beside him. She took her place and tried to act as if nothing was wrong, but all she desperately wanted to do was tell Finn they may have been spied upon.

Yet if Wimarc realized they were impostors, surely he wouldn't still be treating them as honored guests.

With that thought to bolster her courage, she tried to eat. She had some of the lamb stew and nibbled at the greens like a rabbit. She managed to eat more of the chicken cooked with wine in a broth thickened with bread crumbs. She also ate most of a roasted lark, and a bit of salted venison. The bread crusts cooked in sweetened almond milk were the last of it, though. She was nearly overcome by the sight of jellied eels, and made that her excuse for turning down the custard comprised of wine and eggs.

Meanwhile, and as if he really were Lord Gilbert, Finn carried on a conversation with their host about people he must have met at court. It seemed innocuous enough, until she realized Finn was also attempting to discover who else Wimarc might consider his friends.

"Are you well, my lady?" Wimarc asked worriedly when she covered her goblet with her hand to refuse more wine.

"Quite well. It's only that you have such rich food, my lord. And I'm a little tired." She rose, thinking it best if she not stay. Finn could hide his dread, but she was not as experienced as he, and if Wimarc had suspicions, she might give him cause to wonder. "If you'll excuse me, my lords."

"In truth, Wimarc, I'm rather fatigued myself," Finn declared, giving their host a wink as he got to his feet. "What with the wound to my leg and my, ahem, exercise this morning."

"I think an early night will do us both good," she said, smiling at Wimarc. She reached for a flagon of wine. "Perhaps a little wine will help us both sleep better."

Wimarc's lips drew up in a sly, pleased smile as he rose. "Good night, then, my lady and my lord. I hope you both sleep well."

Lizette gave a little bow in response, then led the way across the hall with Finn right behind. Once they were in the stairwell, he asked in a whisper, "What was that all about? Why did Wimarc look at you that way?"

She put her finger to her lips. "Not here." She couldn't be sure somebody wasn't hiding at the top of the steps, listening.

As soon as they reached the bedchamber, she set the flagon on the table and grabbed a square of linen, which she shoved into the reopened hole.

When she turned, Finn looked as aghast as she'd felt upon first realizing it was no longer blocked. "How long has it been open?"

"I don't know. But Wimarc wouldn't be treating us as guests if he knew the truth, would he?"

Finn sat heavily on the end of the bed. "God, I hope he's not toying with us, biding his time before he throws us in his dungeon." He fixed his steadfast gaze on her. "Or waiting until he's bedded you."

She sat beside him. "He's expecting me to come to his bedchamber tonight."

Finn swore softly. "When did you make this arrangement?"

"I was in the garden and he came there. He says he wants to marry me, too."

Finn's scornful sniff told her exactly what he thought of the likelihood of that. "Thank God we're getting out of here tonight. I'll be a happy man when we're well away from here with Ryder—who's still alive. I spoke to him and told him we'd be coming."

"When?" she asked, unable to sit and getting to her feet. "When do we leave?"

When do we part?

"Not till just before the watch changes. They'll be tired and anxious to be done their duty, and less likely to be paying attention."

She nodded. So soon.

He went to her and wrapped his arms around her. "Not long now, Lizette, and then it'll all be over."

One way or the other, she thought, it will all be over. Either they'd succeed and go their separate ways, or fail and die.

She raised her face and looked into his dark, questioning eyes. "Finn, whatever happens tonight, I have to tell you. I love you, Finn or Fingal or Oliver or whatever you call yourself. I love you with all my heart and if we're successful tonight, if we save your brother and escape this terrible place, after I've given the evidence of Wimarc's treachery to my sisters, I'll gladly go with you anywhere."

At first his wistful smile gave her hope, but that hope was dashed when his smile died and he moved away, shaking his head. "It's no good, my lady. We're not meant to be together, you and me." He met her gaze then, steady and sure, yet with a pain that matched her own. "Even if I loved you—and God help me, I do!—

I'm nothing but a thieving, bastard son of a whore, and you're a noble lady."

"I'm a woman who loves you," she said, taking his face between her palms. "Who loves you with all her heart. Who will always love you."

"Don't, Lizette," he murmured, closing his eyes. "Don't say anything more. It can't be. It can't be."

"It *is*," she said. "I love you, and nothing else matters to me—not who your mother was, or what you've done. I'll gladly give up my title and all my inheritance to be with you. We can start a new life together—both of us, somewhere far away where nobody knows who you are."

"You're a ward of the king. You need his permission to marry."

"We could disappear, make a new life far away from the king and his court, or our own pasts. My sisters can tell him I died on the journey home."

"You'd never be able to go home to Averette again."

"My home will be wherever you are, Finn," she said softly. "And we'll find ways to let them know we're alive and well and happy."

He took hold of her shoulders and his intense gaze searched her face. "You mean it, don't you?"

"I've never meant anything more. I would rather be poor with you than rich with anyone else. I want to be with you, Finn, even if we have to live like 'Gyptians traveling from place to place. I feel so free when I'm with you, as I've never been before and never thought I could be."

And then she pulled the final arrow from her quiver. "Besides, the king might try to make me marry somebody like Gilbert or Wimarc. You wouldn't wish that miserable fate upon me, would you?"

"Jaysus," he breathed as he pulled her into his arms, believing her at last, daring to hope for what had seemed so impossible only a short time before. "I'm the most blessed man in England, and from now on, I'll be the most honest, honorable man in England, too."

They kissed, with love and joy and passion, and a dream for the future shining in their hearts.

A SHORT WHILE LATER, dressed expectantly in only his bed robe, Wimarc opened his bedchamber door to find not Helewyse, but Ellie standing on the threshold.

"I didn't summon you," he said, his welcoming smile dying on his lips.

"You're alone, my lord?" she asked, peering past him into the chamber.

Anger smoldered in his eyes as he regarded her with disdain. "How dare you ask such a thing? Go, or by God…" He raised his hand, more than prepared to strike her for her insolence.

To his shock, she had the audacity to grab his arm. "You should be grateful I've come," she declared. "You will be, when you hear what I've got to tell you."

Wimarc studied her face. The wench wasn't lying.

He lowered his arm and stood aside to let her enter. She sauntered past him, as bold and saucy as his first love—and that was no point in Ellie's favor.

"Well? What have you got to tell me that's so important?" he demanded as he strode across the room and poured himself more wine.

"I didn't trust that Lord Gilbert, my lord, so this morning while he and his wife were breaking the fast, I picked out some of the mortar blocking the hole in the wall of your wife's bedchamber. And then I hid inside the secret passage, and I heard some things, my lord. Shocking things. *Valuable* things."

Although his curiosity was piqued, Wimarc didn't reveal his interest. Not when she used "valuable" to describe what she'd heard.

Putting down his wine untouched, he sat in his chair and twisted his ruby ring around his finger. "The value of such things is best left to those most able to judge their worth."

"I've always liked that ring, my lord," the wench noted, sauntering closer, her breasts swaying beneath her bodice.

He laid his hands in his lap. What the devil could she have overheard that would be worth that much? "So have I. I will not part with it easily."

"Does the name Lizette mean anything to you, my lord?"

He stiffened, then wished he hadn't betrayed any reaction at all when he saw the greedy gleam in Ellie's eyes.

"How much would you give to know where she was? A ruby ring maybe?"

CHAPTER TWENTY-TWO

ULDUN WAS THE ONLY GUARD on duty when Lizette and Finn arrived at the entrance to the dungeon just before the changing of the guard. His beady little eyes became mere glints of interest as he grinned and opened the creaking door for them.

"I told you I'd come back," Lizette said, her voice low and full of promise. "My husband wants to see the chains," she added, drawing Finn inside with her.

Finn wasn't surprised the man believed she had unusual tastes. He would believe it, too, when she used that tone and looked that way.

When she made love with him, though, he saw no sly lust, no decadent desire. She loved him as any man would hope a woman would—with trust and joy and pleasure, with honesty and generosity. As if he were the only man in the world she wanted, as if she was the only woman in all the world he would ever love.

He felt that in his heart, in his soul, and knew that in losing her, he would never really be whole again.

Uldun gestured at the wall, his lustful gaze focused on Lizette as he licked his thick lips. "I thought maybe you'd changed yer mind."

"Oh, no," she said, leaning back against the closed door, trying to ignore the stench of the place and the guard's rancid body. "As I said, we like to play with shackles and chains."

Uldun snickered. "We got plenty of them, my lady."

As the guard, practically slavering like a dog, continued to look at Lizette, Finn went around behind him as if to study the iron links. He grabbed one of the battered wooden stools and struck Uldun on the back of the head. The guard's eyes widened for a brief moment before he let out his breath in a sigh and fell to the floor with a thud.

While Lizette grabbed the ring of keys from his belt, he quickly dragged Uldun to the base of the wall and fastened a set of shackles around the guard's ankles.

"I'll meet you and Ryder at the gate," she said, handing him the ring of keys before giving him a quick kiss. Then she slipped out into the dark.

God help him, how he loved her!

Breathing rapidly, he ran down the slick, damp steps lit with the stinking pitch torch he lifted from its sconce.

"Help me!" a voice cried from behind the door of the cell closest to the stairs. "For the love of God, let me out!"

If he let out the other prisoners, they could hardly keep their escape secret, even supposing Lizette was able to create the distraction they had planned, so he continued down the corridor to Ryder's cell.

"I've come to get you out," he called to his brother, trying keys until he found the right one.

When the lock was open, he put the ring over his wrist, put his shoulder to the door and shoved it open.

The stench from inside of the cell nearly knocked him over. His brother—disheveled, filthy, thin beyond belief, his clothes rotting rags—cowered in the corner like a beaten dog.

"Come on," Finn said, hurrying to help him to his feet. "We're getting out of here."

Half stumbling, Ryder touched Finn's face. "Gally, is it really you? I'm not dreaming?"

"No, you're not dreaming. Come! We haven't much time."

Keeping a supporting arm around his brother, Finn helped him from the cell, to be engulfed by a chorus of pleas in a host of voices, an invisible chorus of the damned. "Don't leave me here! For the love of God! Have mercy! Have mercy!"

His mind urged him to hurry and escape with Ryder. Lizette was depending on him, too—Lizette who would risk her life for not only her sisters, but for the king she loathed because of the people who would suffer if there was war and rebellion.

Could he do less? Could he be so callous, so selfish, as to leave these poor wretches here, no matter what they'd done?

He couldn't, not with the image of Lizette's trusting eyes, her generous heart, her belief that he was a good man, to call forth mercy, even if that had rarely been shown to him.

As he fumbled again with the keys, trying to open the next cell as fast he could, Ryder, slumped against the wall, said not a word in protest. Perhaps he was too weak, or maybe he, too, couldn't ignore the pleas. After all, he knew far better than Finn what a torture it was to be locked in this evil place.

Finn got the first cell open, to find the corpse of a poor soul clearly driven to madness as he slowly starved to death. They were too late for him— and it might be too late for them all if he didn't hurry.

Working with frantic haste, Finn opened another door and this time, when the cell door swung inward, a spectral figure rushed forward.

. "Wait for me!" Finn commanded, his voice rough and stern. "We must all go out together or the first will alert the sentries and none of us will escape."

His cadaverous face framed with lank gray hair, the man regarded him with desperate, manic eyes, but he did as he was told. So did all the others, until there was a gang of weak, sick, starving men behind Finn and his brother.

KEEPING TO THE SHADOWS, Lizette crept toward the stable. She had to wait for what seemed an agonizingly long time while two soldiers on the wall walk exchanged greetings and then complaints about their ration of ale.

As soon as they parted, she dashed across the last open space to the eastern wall of the stable and the un-locked door. She cautiously eased it open and held her breath while she listened for any sounds that might indicate people awake in the stable. Fortunately, all she could hear were horses.

Satisfied, she slipped inside and paused, breathing in the scent of hay and horse and leather. Above, two eyes gleamed in the dark. Cat's eyes, and the animal quickly disappeared, drawn by the soft scramble of mice in the straw.

She didn't need to venture far from the door to do what she had to do. First she made a little pile of straw in the center aisle of the stables. Grabbing more straw, she dragged it through the nearest water trough, wetting it and spreading it in a circle around the first pile. She wanted smoke more than flames, to give those in the stable time to flee and free the horses, too.

There was a bridle hanging nearby on a peg, along with other bridles and bits of harness. Biting her lip, she eased it from its place and put it on the small pile of straw in the center of the rough circle. That accomplished, she knelt and struck the flint she'd stolen from the kitchen against the metal bit of the bridle, making a spark. Her hands were shaking, so it took three tries before a flame took hold.

Once it did, the straw burned quickly. Almost immediately, a horse neighed in alarm. She moved toward the side door just as a voice shouted, "Fire!" in the loft above.

More horses started to refoot, neigh, scream and kick at their stall doors as the fire reached the dampened straw and smoke began to fill the stables. Coughing, Lizette opened the door as the alarm spread to the sentries on the wall walk and at the gate, and in the hall and the bedchambers.

She slipped out, planning to go around behind the stables in the shadow of the eaves toward the gate. In the pandemonium, she would grab three horses—one for Finn, one for herself and one for Ryder if he were strong enough to ride by himself. If not, Finn would take

him on his horse. Finn and Ryder would meet her at the
gate, deal with the guards if they were still there and not
gone to fight the fire, then they would open the gate and
ride out. At the outer wall, as Lord Gilbert, Finn would
order the guards to let him pass, and if they hesitated,
he would get them to the shadow of the gate with the
pretext of explaining what was afoot within the castle,
and then do what he must to silence them. By the time
any of the distracted guards on the outer wall realized
anything was amiss, they would have the gate open and
be riding to freedom.

It sounded simple, and yet a hundred things could go
wrong. She knew that, but as she made it to the back of
the stable while servants and soldiers ran toward it, and
coughing grooms and stable boys shouted and led the
panicking horses out, and especially when she realized
there were no guards at the gate, she began to believe
they would succeed.

FINN, RYDER and the other prisoners went up the stairs.
The stronger helped the weaker ones as Finn helped
Ryder, until most had crowded into the guardhouse.
Outside Finn heard what he'd been hoping for: shouts
for water, the frantic neighing of horses and footsteps
running across the cobblestones.

"The stable's been fired to cover our escape," Finn
explained to the released prisoners.

He helped Ryder to sit in one of the guard's chairs,
then addressed the restless group. "You'd all still be imprisoned below but for us," he reminded them. "The fire
may not be enough to enable us all to get out, so I ask

that in gratitude for our help, you give my brother and me, and a noblewoman who's put herself in harm's way to help us, time to escape before you flee from here."

Even as he made the request, he saw the futility of it, for these man had been driven to the brink of desperation and despair. They could think only of themselves.

Almost at once they rushed the door, shoving Finn out of their path—except for the last prisoner, who started to kick Uldun's unconscious body, hurling epithets with what was left of his hoarse voice. And then came other screams.

Before Finn could get Ryder to the door, Draco appeared on the threshold, a bloody sword in his hand and a look of savage glee on his face as he killed the prisoner who had lingered to kick Uldun.

Finn shoved Ryder behind him and grabbed a bucket from the table. He could use it as a shield, or to push back a blade, until more mercenaries came charging in the door, and Finn knew all was lost—for them. His future was finished, but maybe not Lizette's. She could still be free.

Finn threw the bucket at Draco, who lifted his shield to avoid the missile. Backing away, crouching defensively, Finn watched as several men moved to surround him and his brother. He took a swing at the closest and as he did, two more men grabbed Finn's arms from behind and held him. Two more took hold of Ryder, who didn't even try to run for the door.

Still Finn struggled to get free, silently praying that Lizette wouldn't wait, but flee if she had the chance. That she would realize he'd been captured and run.

A drawn sword in his hand, Wimarc strode through the

door, pushing the mercenaries aside. Scowling with scorn, he struck Finn across the face with a backhand blow, cutting his lip. "Thought you could fool me, did you?"

Merciful God, he knew. Somehow or other, he knew Finn wasn't Lord Gilbert. Had he caught Lizette and compelled her to confess?

If Wimarc had Lizette, if he'd hurt her, hell would be too good a place for him to spend eternity, and Finn made another prayer— for a chance to send him there.

Until then, as long as he was alive, he would maintain the deception and hope to save them all...somehow. So he met Wimarc's fierce gaze steadily as he licked the warm blood from his lip.

"This is no way to treat a guest, my lord," he said with the noble accent he'd taken such pains to learn.

Wimarc put the point of his sword at Finn's throat and forced him back against the wall. "Who the devil *are* you?"

"Your wits must be addled. I'm Gilbert of Fairbourne."

Curling his lip, Wimarc took a deep, calming breath. "For a man whose lover is in my power, you are remarkably stupid."

Finn's knees almost buckled, and his throat went dry as a sand dune. Yet even if Wimarc had Lizette, he had to do what he could to protect her still. The first thing was to keep Wimarc here, away from her, for as long as he could. "Ellie's always been in your *power*, as you put it. Wasn't that your plan, to have her seduce me into your rebellion? Or at least be a sort of promise of more rewards to come?"

"You know full well I'm not talking about Ellie. That

insolent wench is lying dead in my bedchamber for daring to try to wring money out of me. I'm speaking of Elizabeth of Averette."

"Who?"

Wimarc raised his sword again, this time putting the tip below Finn's eye. "You know damn well, and now I want to know who you are, and why she was helping you."

"Gracious, my lord, I should think it's obvious. We came to free this poor fellow here—although I have no idea why you think a noblewoman would help me, and why that whore is Lady Elizabeth of Averette."

To Finn's great relief, Wimarc's eyes betrayed doubt. If he could make Wimarc believe Lizette was nothing but some harlot hired to play a part, he might allow her to live, and leave. He would probably rape her, but she would be alive and free.

"She's no harlot," Wimarc growled.

"Oh, I assure you, she is. Peg of the Pig and Whistle Tavern in Fleet Street. Quite renowned in some circles, because she can seem quite the lady if she chooses."

"I don't believe you!"

"Believe me or not as you will. Kill her if you wish, but the only people who'll mourn her passing are the men of the London docks."

Finn spoke with every appearance of calm while also silently hoping that Ryder would realize Wimarc wasn't paying any attention to him. Nor were any of his mercenaries. Ryder might be able to get away.

But to his even greater dismay, his brother was either too weak or too ill to notice.

Wimarc struck him again. "She's Elizabeth of Averette, damn you! Who the devil are *you?*"

Finn spread his hands as if totally baffled. "What proof have you that I'm *not* Lord Gilbert of Fairbourne?"

Again, there was that flash of doubt in Wimarc's eyes, and Finn pressed on. "Since I am Lord Gilbert, I suggest, my lord, you lower your weapon. Otherwise, I shall have to challenge you to single combat on a field of honor—not that you understand the concept of honor, but that is what they call it when nobles come to blows on such matters."

Wimarc clutched Finn's tunic and pulled him forward, so that his blade nicked the side of his neck. "You are *not* Gilbert of Fairbourne and that woman you've been claiming is your wife is Elizabeth of Averette. Now tell me who you really are, and why she came here with you pretending to be your wife, or I'll slit your stinking throat!"

Before Finn could open his mouth to lie again, Ryder sprang to his feet. He grabbed a length of chain hanging on the wall and, in the blink of an eye, had it wrapped around Wimarc's throat and was dragging him away from Finn.

"Back, all of you!" he ordered through clenched teeth, his voice harsh. "Drop your swords! Finn, take Wimarc's blade."

The tendons of Ryder's neck corded and his weak arms shook with the effort of holding their captor. Although determination was giving Ryder strength, it would be only temporary; he was too weak to hold the nobleman that way for long.

Before Finn could take Wimarc's sword, Uldun leapt up from the ground and drew a dagger from his boot. His face and tunic were covered in blood and he bared his broken teeth as he shoved the dagger into Ryder's side. "Let him go, you scum," he ordered through bloody, swollen lips.

The chain fell from Ryder's hand. He looked at his brother with sorrow and then, with a sigh like a tired child, he crumpled to the ground.

STILL UNSURE WHAT TO DO, Lizette waited by the gate and peered through the smoke-filled yard, avoiding the wildly jostling horses as they instinctively tried to escape.

"Open the gates to the outer ward and let the horses out!" a man shouted, just as Finn had hoped.

Footsteps came running, and she quickly slipped into the shadows of the barracks nearby. Two guards lifted the heavy wooden bar from the gate and began to drive the horses through.

The smoke cleared for an instant, and she saw Wimarc, his sword drawn, standing outside the door to the keep, the one that opened into the guardroom and the dungeon.

"Find the woman who calls herself Lady Helewyse!" he shouted at the men in front of him.

Lizette's strength seemed to seep out of her as she leaned against the wall, needing its support.

He knew. God help her, Wimarc knew she wasn't Helewyse—and if he knew that, and Finn and Ryder had not already come, they were either caught, or about to be. They couldn't get out past Wimarc and his men.

They had failed. Despite all their efforts and plans and risk, they had failed.

She stood there stunned and dismayed, until a horse ran close to her, the motion jogging her from her distraught stupor.

She had to get away or she would be captured, too. She must escape. Get help. Come back and rescue them both. Get the evidence of Wimarc's treachery to the king. Save her family.

Save Finn.

A packhorse, old and slow and smaller than the others, came near her. Its ears were back, its eyes wild, yet it still wore a bridle. She managed to grab it. Under cover of the smoke, she ran beside it, using the frightened horse to shield herself from the preoccupied men.

Once in the outer ward, she looked up and saw that there were no sentries on the wall walks. Quickly removing the bridle from the packhorse and speaking softly, she approached a mare nervously pawing the ground by the wall. She managed to quiet it enough to be able to slip the bridle into place. Then, grabbing hold of it, she swung herself onto the mare's back.

She kicked it into a trot and rode toward the barbican. The sentries had been alerted by the shouts and smoke, yet hadn't left their posts. Nevertheless, their attention was not on the gate or the land beyond the castle, but on the courtyard and the smoke rising from it.

Her clothes were stained with smoke, likely her face blackened, too; no doubt she looked little like a lady. Nevertheless, she straightened her shoulders and rode toward the guards. "Open the gates and let me pass!" she called out, as imperious as Adelaide at her most arrogant.

The two men on either side of the gate exchanged surprised and suspicious looks.

"I said, open the gates and let me pass! My husband has been injured in the fire and I require a physician. There's one at the monastery nearby, I understand, and I must fetch him."

"You?" the nearest man asked warily.

"My escort will be here in a moment," she returned. Then she frowned. "I suggest you hurry and get that gate open. Wimarc will not be pleased if an ally of his dies because you moved too slowly, and neither will I."

The men immediately lifted the bar and pushed open the heavy bossed gate.

Before they could change their minds and try to stop her, she dug her heels into the mare's side and galloped down the road.

FINN'S HEAD SNAPPED to the right from the force of the blow from Wimarc's fist. Blood filled his mouth, and pain radiated from his aching jaw. His right eye was swollen shut, and his left cheek bruised and bleeding. He could barely hold up his head from the pain; he was upright only because of the shackles around his wrists that bound him to the wall of the guardroom.

Ryder slumped beside him, likewise chained and unconscious—but at least he was alive, despite his wounds. The other prisoners were either dead, or once more imprisoned in their cells.

"Who sent you here?" Wimarc demanded again,

grabbing Finn's hair to lift his head. "Tell me, and I'll be merciful and kill you quickly."

Finn's only answer was to spit a mouthful of blood onto Wimarc's surcoat.

As long as Wimarc held Lizette, he wasn't going to tell him anything, not even under torture.

Cursing, the nobleman let go. "I should kill you here and now!"

"Without discovering who sent me and what I was really here to do?" Finn scoffed. "Surely you don't think it was merely to rescue some thieving peasant?"

Wimarc's eyes narrowed and he tilted his head to study his prisoner. "So, you admit you had another purpose?"

"I should think that's obvious."

Wimarc twisted the ruby ring around his finger. "Perhaps I haven't used the proper inducement."

He grabbed Ryder's hair and raised his head. "Who's this, then, eh? What's he to you? Obviously someone worth going to a lot of trouble for."

He let go and Ryder's head lolled forward, as loose as a doll made of rags. "I have ways of persuading even the most stubborn fellow to talk, as you'll find out—and perhaps I should start with him."

Finn wasn't about to let Ryder suffer anymore. But he had another lie at the ready, one that ought to spare Ryder for a while. "I wouldn't touch him if I were you. Indeed, I fear you've already done enough to render your life forfeit. That young man is the bastard son of the Earl of Pembroke."

Wimarc stared with disbelief. "You're lying!"

"What, you don't believe a man of the earl's vigor

has sired children out of wedlock? He most certainly has, and he intends to use this one to enrich his family and create an alliance by marriage, the way John's natural daughter has helped him ally with Llywelyn of Wales."

"I would have heard of such a plan!"

"You're such good friends with the earl that he would confide all his infidelities and future plans to you?"

He had him, Finn thought as he saw the look in Wimarc's eyes. Wimarc believed him—or was at least uncertain enough that Ryder should be safe for now.

"Suppose I believe you, why didn't he tell me who he was? And what was he doing traveling with only two companions?"

"You *are* slow, aren't you? Discretion, of course. The earl cares for his wife, and for her sake, doesn't parade his bastards before her as some men do. I suspect he also sought to keep the young fellow safe, not counting on the lad's natural pride that prompted him to attack some louts at an inn."

"Then why not send an envoy to me?"

"And tell you who you had in your keeping so you could demand a ransom?"

"Why was the lady Elizabeth with you?"

"Oh, God spare me! How many times must I tell you?" Finn retorted. "I don't know this Lady Elizabeth you keep going on about. That woman is a whore hired to play my wife. I wasn't about to bring my own wife here. Everybody at court knows your reputation, Wimarc, and that no beautiful woman is safe from your lust. I thought it best to keep Helewyse away from you."

"Then why did you call her Lizette? Ellie heard you."

"I didn't. Ellie didn't hear properly, wherever she was hiding. I said *coquette*."

"I don't believe you!"

"If you don't believe me, who does the harlot say she is? Or have you terrified her so much, she'll say anything?"

With a curse, Wimarc struck Finn again, so hard, his head hit the stone wall and he slumped forward, unconscious.

CHAPTER TWENTY-THREE

As THE FIRST LIGHT OF DAWN broke in the east, Keldra watched Garreth shimmy down the tall oak to the ground. "It's smoke, isn't it?" she asked. "Near or far?"

Garreth landed with a light thud and brushed some of the bits of leaf and twig from his tunic as he answered. "Something's burning, all right. Something big."

Keldra turned pale and her lips thinned with tension. "I told you it was the smell of smoke that woke me. Is it the village or…?" She couldn't bring herself to whisper the rest of her question.

Garreth tried to look confident and not sick with dread. "I can't be sure. It *could* be the castle. It's the right direction anyway—but even if it is, that doesn't mean—what are you doing?"

Keldra had abruptly wheeled around and started along the path that led in the general direction of Castle de Werre.

"We've got to go. They may be in trouble and need our help."

Garreth grabbed her arm to halt her. "I'll go."

Her hands on her hips, Keldra regarded him sternly. "I'm not going to wait here like some…some child!"

"What if they've rescued Ryder and escaped?" Garreth countered. "That smoke could mean a distraction—

Finn likes to do that sort of thing. Saves having to hurt people, he says. What if they're on their way and they get here and we're both gone—and Lord Gilbert and Lady Helewyse, too?"

Keldra chewed her lip. "Does he really do that—make distractions? You aren't just saying that so I won't worry."

"No," Garreth replied. "He really does."

"Then you think we should both stay here?"

"Not both of us," he replied as he strode to the lean-to and got his bow and quiver. "I'll head for the castle and see what I can find out."

"What, stay here by myself?"

"Are you afraid?"

"No," she lied, lifting her trembling chin.

Garreth's expression softened, despite his efforts to be stern. "I won't be gone more than half a day. You can hide in the trees if somebody comes. I'll whistle when I return, so you'll know it's me." He straightened his shoulders and cleared his throat. "You're my responsibility, so don't take any foolish chances while I'm gone."

"When have I ever taken a foolish chance?" she retorted, sounding angry.

"Well, don't start now," he shot back.

"Don't you do anything stupid, either."

"I won't."

They looked at each other and then she reached up to caress his cheek. "Be careful, Garreth."

He was about to answer when they heard the soft thuds of hoofbeats nearby. His cheek still tingling from the touch of her fingers, Garreth shoved her behind him. "Go to the hut."

Instead of obeying, she gave a cry and started running toward the horse and rider. "It's my lady! Hurry! I think she's hurt!"

Lizette raised her head and silently thanked God for guiding her here. She'd ridden there in the dark, hoping she was going the right way.

As Lizette slipped exhausted from the back of the horse, Keldra put her arm under her to help her, running an anxious gaze over Lizette's smoke-ruined clothes and dirty face. "Oh, my lady, are you hurt?"

She shook her head.

Garreth grabbed the mare's bridle. "Where's Finn? Where's Ryder?"

"Still at the castle," she croaked, her voice raspy from thirst, fatigue and the smoke. "We were trying to escape in the commotion of the fire, but they were taken."

Keldra helped her down onto a log, then pressed a water skin into her hands. "Drink, my lady."

She did, gratefully and deeply. Garreth stood by the fire biting his fingernail, while Keldra sat beside her, leaning forward to catch every word.

"We got into the dungeon and knocked out the guard," she told them, feeling better for the water, and her voice was stronger, too. "I left Finn there and went to set fire to the stables to distract the guards and sentries. I was waiting for Finn and Ryder to come from the dungeons when I heard Wimarc order his men to look for me. When I realized he knew I wasn't Helewyse, I didn't dare wait. I got that horse and came here."

She shook her head. "I don't know how Wimarc discovered the truth, but he did."

Garreth's expression was coldly grim. "Once Lord Wimarc realizes you're not in the castle, he'll send his men searching for you."

"Yes," she wearily agreed. "Even if he doesn't yet realize I'm Elizabeth of Averette, he'll try to find me."

She blinked back her tears, for they would avail her nothing. She must believe Finn and Ryder were alive. Wimarc would surely enjoy making them suffer, so he would not kill them quickly.

She glanced at the hut. There was no stick barring the door.

Staring with dismay at Garreth and Keldra, she got to her feet. "Lord Gilbert and his wife escaped? They must have gone to Wimarc and—"

"No," Keldra interrupted.

"They tried to escape, but we caught them," Garreth supplied.

"Then where are they?" she demanded. "Why is that door not barred?"

"We let them go," Keldra said.

"Lord Gilbert's no rebel, or like to be," Garreth hastened to add. "He was on his way to Castle de Werre at the request of the Earl of Pembroke to learn what Wimarc was up to."

Lizette was not comforted. "You took him at his word?"

"Not at first," Garreth defensively declared, crossing his arms and glancing at Keldra as if for her support. "It took some convincing, but we both came to believe him, so we let them go. He said he'd go to the king and bring back a force to take Castle de Werre."

If Gilbert could be trusted.

Whatever Gilbert was doing—or not—they had to rescue Finn and Ryder.

"I've got a plan—" she began, and then she fell silent, her stomach churning at the sound of more horses coming closer.

Garreth swiftly nocked an arrow. "Into the hut," he ordered. "If it's Wimarc's men, I'll hold 'em off. If I look to be losing, crawl out the back through the hole Lord Gilbert dug and run away."

"Oh, Garreth!" Keldra cried.

"Go!" he ordered, as imperious and determined as a man twice his age.

Keldra and Lizette hesitated no more. They hurried toward the hut, until Lizette saw a rider through the trees—a rider she recognized from the set of his shoulders alone. "Iain?" she whispered incredulously.

The head crowned with gray-and-black hair turned as if he'd heard her and when she saw the even more familiar face, Lizette shouted with joy, relief and hope. "Iain!"

Renewed vigor surged through her as she ran toward the garrison commander of Averette, who wasn't dead. Oh, thank God, he wasn't dead after all!

Nor was he alone, but she paid little heed to his companions as he dismounted and jogged toward her. He went to go down on one knee to salute, but before he could, she'd thrown her arms around him and hugged him with all her might.

"I thought you were dead!" she cried, laughing and crying at the same time.

"I feared you were, too, or taken," he said, pulling back to smile at her.

Then he frowned. "What the devil have you been doing, my lady?" he asked as he studied her smoke-blackened face.

Before she answered, she was distracted by a movement behind him. She looked over his shoulder to see what must be a noblewoman dismounting.

"Where have *you* been?" she queried, wondering who this woman was and if the soldiers with him belonged to her.

"I think we both have a tale to tell," Iain said. "You first, my lady. You look like you've been working in a smithy."

"That would have been more pleasant," she grimly replied.

"AND SO WE'VE GOT TO rescue them both," Lizette concluded a short while later. She had briefly described her recent activities and Iain had told her about being found and helped by Lady Jane.

"I really had no choice," Lizette repeated. "Wimarc is an evil man, and he *must* be stopped."

Iain turned to Lady Jane, who was perched on the fallen log. "Didn't I tell you she might get up to anything?"

Jane's sweet smile was nearly as welcome as Adelaide's would have been. "You didn't go so far as to say she would try to save the king."

Her thoughts never far from Finn and the danger he was in, Lizette jumped to her feet. "We must rescue Finn and his brother, and quickly. Iain, you take Keldra and go back to Averette. Explain what's happened to Gillian and tell her that I need as many of her men as she can spare. They should go to the castle of Lord

Bernard de Valiese, about thirty miles north of here. I'll meet you there."

"Nay, my lady. You'll come home with me," Iain declared with that stubborn glint in his eyes.

"No, I can't. Not yet. Garreth and I must go to Lord Bernard without delay."

"Why?" Lady Jane asked quietly. "What has he to do with this?"

"I think we'll find an ally there, and maybe more than one."

"I'm not leaving you again, my lady," Iain sternly declared. "Once was enough."

"I can go to Averette with Garreth and Keldra and half of my men," Jane offered. "Iain and the rest of my men can escort you to Lord Bernard's castle."

Lizette and Iain looked at each other, then nodded their agreement, although Iain with considerably less enthusiasm.

THREE DAYS LATER, Wimarc stared into the cup of wine he was nursing as he sat by the glowing brazier in his bedchamber.

Three days since that damned Irishman had opened the cells of his dungeon. Three days and three nights during which the blackguard had been beaten and starved and promised more pain to come if he didn't reveal who he was and why Elizabeth of Averette had come here and where she'd gone.

The man still insisted he was Lord Gilbert of Fairbourne and the woman a whore.

Was that young man he'd tried to rescue really the

bastard son of the Earl of Pembroke? What a pawn he would be if he was—and in case he was, Wimarc had had him moved to a larger cell, his wound tended to, and given plenty of food and water.

Not Gilbert, or whoever he was, though. He was in the smallest cell and hadn't been given either food or water since he'd been caught.

Where was the woman? Three days, and his men hadn't found her yet. They were all as useless as that lout Lindall. By the saints, he thought as he twisted the ring that had once belonged to his weak, detestable father, he was surrounded by knaves and imbeciles.

Somebody scratched like a mouse at the closed door. "My lord?"

Recognizing Greseld's trembling voice, he shouted, "What?"

"My lord, there's a messenger waiting for you in the hall."

Wimarc set down his goblet and heaved himself to his feet. Maybe his men had finally found something— or someone. Maybe it was news from one of his allies at court, or the men he'd sent to Fairbourne.

He unbolted the door and threw it open. "Messenger from whom?"

"Y-your wife, my lord," Greseld stammered, spittle at the corners of her lips. "About Lady Elizabeth of Averette."

A coarse epithet burst from his lips. What in God's name did Roslynn have to do with Lady Elizabeth of Averette…unless she, too, had gone to Lord Bernard's for sanctuary. That was possible, considering the way that strumpet had taken Roslynn's part against him.

By God, he should have thought of that and sent one of his men to Lord Bernard's castle, or even gone himself. Scowling, Wimarc pushed past Greseld and charged down the steps.

But it was no soldier or servant standing on the dais in his hall. It was Roslynn herself, surrounded by soldiers wearing Lord Bernard's colors. "What are you doing here?"

She winced, but didn't look away. "I should think you would be glad to see me. I have news of Lady Elizabeth of Averette."

Wimarc gritted his teeth and his hands balled into fists at his sides. "Well?"

"You knew her as Lady Helewyse, your recent guest."

Damn that lying blackguard! He'd rip out his tongue for this! Then he'd kill him slowly and enjoy every single moment of it.

Roslynn clasped her hands before her and her bottom lip quivered a little as she spoke. "She came to Lord Bernard's and told us many interesting things about you, my lord. Serious, disturbing things."

He fought to contain his building rage and focus on Roslynn, who once would have done anything he asked of her. "Then she admitted that she's a duplicitous impostor who came here pretending to be someone else for some nefarious purpose. Obviously you can't believe a word she says."

"But I do, and you've put me at grave risk with your schemes. Fortunately, I'm innocent of any wrongdoing, so after Lizette told me of your treason, she offered me

the protection of her family if I help her—which I fully
intend to accept."

"What schemes?" he charged. "Even if I were up to
something, how would she know about it? Damn it,
Roslynn, if I never confided such things to you, why
would I tell a stranger?"

"I never said you told her anything. She found
evidence on her own. Between that, and certain things
I myself had noticed, I believe you *are* a traitor."

He'd always assumed Roslynn was too stupid and
ignorant to gather the significance of the friends he
courted, or the letters he wrote.

Nevertheless, he wasn't going to admit to any wrongdoing, and certainly not to her. "How do you know she's
really Lady Elizabeth? Her companion claims she's a
whore from London."

"He must have his reasons," Roslynn replied, showing more backbone than he ever would have guessed she
possessed. "And you're forgetting that I've been to
Averette with my brother and met the ladies there. It was
long ago, but once she told me who she was, I realized
that's why she seemed familiar. I also put the evidence
Lady Elizabeth provided before Lord Bernard, and he
found it very interesting. Very interesting indeed."

Her words struck Wimarc to the heart and he had
to struggle not to reveal his dismay as a shiver of
dread went down his spine. "Evidence?" he scoffed.
"What evidence?"

"Correspondence between you and your fellow conspirators. It was in a secret compartment in a small chest
in your solar. Lady Elizabeth and her companion stole it."

Fear rushed through Wimarc's body. He kept the most damning letters there, letters he also planned to use to ensure his fellow conspirators didn't betray him to the king for hope of reward.

If they were in his enemies' hands, if Bernard had seen them, he was indeed in grave danger. Bernard was rich and important and many barons would listen to him—and so would the king.

Something of his fear must have shown on his face, for Roslynn seemed more confident when she spoke again. "Do you think Lizette herself is without resources? Are you forgetting the men her sisters have married? Don't you realize she'd sent word to them about what you've done and plan to do? Fortunately for you, you have something Lizette wants very much, so we propose a trade. You give the prisoners in your dungeon—all of them who still live—to her and she'll give you the letters. And you may leave England with what wealth you have here, on pain of death if you return."

Surrender to a woman? Let a woman tell him what to do? "I have friends, too," he countered, "who will stand by me and deny these allegations, no matter what scraps of parchment she produces."

"Of course you may try your luck and hope that you'll overcome the king's justice despite the evidence."

She walked up to him, regarding him with scorn in her sky-blue eyes. "However, Lady Elizabeth assures me that if you don't agree, or if the Irishman and his half brother are already dead, she won't rest until you're executed, even if she has to hunt you down all over Europe to do it."

Half brother? God's blood, was that lying Irish scoundrel a bastard of the Earl of Pembroke's, too? Surely he was too old....

And then Wimarc realized he'd been played for an even greater fool. That younger man was no bastard of the earl's.

Rage roared through him, hot and strong and more powerful than anything he'd felt before. He would never let them win! He would find a way to defeat those lying, scheming scoundrels.

Masking his anger as he had so many times in his life, whether at his useless father or pathetic mother, he said, "And all Lady Elizabeth offers *you* for this assistance is some promise of friendship? John's more fickle than a woman. Today the de Boisbastons are in favor. Tomorrow, they may just as well be out. How much good will their support do you then?"

With perception honed by years of sly skulduggery, he saw a flicker of doubt in Roslynn's blue eyes and pressed on. "What can they do for you then—you, who aren't even related to them?

"I'm not the only one dissatisfied with John," he continued as she silently regarded him. "There are many eager to join my cause—so many that even if I'm imprisoned and executed, the rebellion will surely happen regardless. If you throw your lot in with the de Boisbastons, what will happen to you then?"

More doubt bloomed, and he inched toward her, mustering every ounce of persuasive charm he possessed. "I know I haven't treated you as you deserve, and for that, I am truly sorry. I beg your forgiveness and another chance. You are the only woman I've ever loved, Roslynn."

The certainty seemed to drain from her with every word he said. "You're still my wife, Roslynn, and if the rebellion succeeds—as it surely will—I shall be richly rewarded by Eleanor, the true heir to the throne, when we set her upon it."

"Eleanor?"

"Yes. As Geoffrey's child, she has a better claim to the throne than John. Why else does John keep her imprisoned?"

Roslynn's gaze searched his face. "And you seek the throne for Eleanor, not yourself?"

"Of course! I have no right to rule, nor would I wish the responsibility. I seek only to right a grievous wrong, and save our country from a greedy, lascivious usurper.

"So you have a choice, beloved—join with people who are no relation to you and claim to be your friends, or stand by a husband who's on the brink of righting a serious wrong and earning a rich reward."

He dropped his voice and used his most seductive tones, the way he'd spoken when he'd convinced her that he loved her, and wooed so many other women to his bed. "Please, Roslynn, don't abandon me, for we *will* defeat the king, my love. He has most foully stolen the throne and has too many enemies who wish him dead. And on that day, I shall be more powerful than even the Earl of Pembroke—and so will my wife, a wife I've most foolishly dismissed as too young and ignorant to be worthy of sharing my plans.

"I see my error now, Roslynn, and I shall beg your

forgiveness every day of my life if you'll stay with me. I understand now you deserve all the wealth and power I can bestow upon you."

He caressed her cheek, and she didn't turn away. Her face colored with a blush as her lashes fanned upon them.

He sidled nearer, angling his body close to hers. "If we're to rid this country of that leech of a ruler, I will need your help, and those letters back in my possession."

She closed her eyes and leaned her cheek against his palm as he brushed the pad of his thumb over her lips. "It was jealousy that made me berate you," he murmured in her ear. "I care for you so much, and when I thought that impostor was taking you from me...when I believed he was trying to seduce you..."

He gasped as if the thought had just occurred to him, as indeed it had. "Perhaps seducing you was part of their plans!"

Roslynn's eyes snapped open. "Oh, do you think so?"

He must tread carefully here. Her pride must not be too wounded, just pricked enough that she would be vulnerable to his apologies and promises. "Perhaps. Whatever his motives, I should never have hit you, and I never will again."

"Do I have your word on that?"

She was nearly there. Now to bring her fully back to him.

"You have my word," he promised, pulling her into his arms and kissing her with every appearance of passion. "Send word to Lizette that I agree to her terms. Tell her to come here and that I will turn the Irishman, his brother and all the prisoners over to her. Tell her I'll leave England, never to return."

"And when she comes?"

"You'll see how clever your husband is."

CHAPTER TWENTY-FOUR

HIS ARMS AROUND HIS WIFE, Gilbert guided the horse through the stone fence surrounding the inn's yard. The sign hanging over the door depicting a goblet, as well as the soldiers sitting on the bench outside and grooms leading horses toward a stable, declared it to be such an establishment.

Gilbert slipped off the horse's back and helped his tired wife to the ground. Taking her hand, he led the horse toward one of the grooms. "See that it's fed and watered and brushed down," he ordered, his thoughts more on Helewyse than the animal.

"Show me your purse and I will," the groom replied, running a skeptical gaze over Gilbert's stained and muddy clothing, then Helewyse, whose clothes were equally filthy and torn.

Gilbert's expression hardened. "I'm—"

"Gilbert? Sweet heavens, is that you?"

He and Helewyse both turned to look at the woman standing in the inn's door. "Adelaide!" he cried, grabbing Helewyse's slender hand.

He paused a moment and glanced back at the groom. "I'm Lord Gilbert of Fairbourne. Take care of my horse."

Flushing scarlet, the groom tugged his forelock, and Gilbert went toward Adelaide, who was regarding him with concern. "Were you attacked?"

"Something like that. I have news of your sister Elizabeth," he replied as they followed her inside.

The taproom's low ceiling was held in place by smoke-stained, aged oak beams. A central hearth provided heat, light and not a little smoke, which escaped through the windows, the shutters open wide. Despite that, it was still dark and murky inside, and Gilbert instinctively put his hand on the hilt of his sword, while Helewyse shrank closer to him.

"Who's this?" a tall, dark-haired man dressed in mail and surcoat demanded as he rose from where he'd been seated on a bench at a table in the corner, his helmet at his elbow and a sword belt around his waist.

"Who are you?" Gilbert warily replied.

"This is my husband, Lord Armand de Boisbaston," Adelaide supplied, worry etched on her lovely face.

As his eyes grew accustomed to the dimmer light, Gilbert realized there was another mail-clad man in the room, standing on the other side of the hearth. Beside him was a woman he also recognized—Gillian of Averette, although she was looking rather less stern than he recalled.

"I'm Bayard de Boisbaston," the second man announced as he pushed off from the hearth and approached him. "What do you know about Lizette?"

"She's in danger, and so is the king. I'll explain everything while you get my wife some food and ale."

"WHERE ARE THEY TAKING US, Finn?" Ryder rasped as they stumbled across the courtyard in the dim light of dawn, his voice weak and hoarse, his hand against his injured side.

They're taking us to our deaths, Finn thought as he, Ryder and the other prisoners from Wimarc's dungeon shuffled toward the gate. Their wrists were shackled and bound by chains, and he'd not been given food or water in days, although he wasn't sure exactly how much time had passed in that cell, or while he was being beaten.

Nevertheless, he tried to have hope, to believe that somehow, they would be saved. "If they were just going to kill us, they could do it in the cells or the yard."

Or so he told himself as he watched the backs of Lord Wimarc and his wife as they rode ahead of them into the outer ward. He'd been shocked to see Roslynn again and even more shocked that she seemed to be content riding beside her husband.

Who really knew a woman's mind? Or what love might make them do, both good and bad?

Perhaps Roslynn had something to do with what was happening. Maybe she had interceded for them, although that didn't seem likely.

He tried not to trip and fall as the slow-moving group made their way through the barbican and outer gates into a meadow. The gash in his leg ached, and the chains were nearly as heavy as his despair, until he saw a large group of armed soldiers waiting, dressed in unfamiliar colors, with a woman at their head.

Lizette! Oh, sweet merciful God, she was alive, and not Wimarc's prisoner after all. That lying bastard—but she was safe and she had come back with a small army to support her.

"Who's that woman?" Ryder asked softly.

"Lady Elizabeth of Averette."

Before Ryder had been taken elsewhere, Finn had told his brother all about Lizette, although not how much he loved her. He didn't want Ryder to feel guilty that he had lost a lover trying to help him.

Not surprisingly, Lizette looked anxious and as if she hadn't slept in the time they'd been apart.

He tore his gaze from her, dressed in a blue woolen gown and fur-lined cloak, with a hood over her head, to look at the soldiers behind her. There were at least fifty, well armed, wearing mail and helmets, carrying shields bearing a device he didn't recognize.

There was one man he did recognize—the Scot they thought was dead. By some miracle he had survived and found Lizette. Perhaps with another miracle, he could help them now.

"My lady," Lord Wimarc announced, "as you can see, I've done as you've asked. Here are the prisoners, including your erstwhile husband and his outlaw brother."

He'd obviously realized the Earl of Pembroke wasn't Ryder's father.

Lizette—beautiful, bold, brave Lizette—nudged her horse closer and held out something in her hand. "Here are your letters as promised. Release Finn and the others from their chains, and the letters will be yours."

She was trading the evidence of Wimarc's treachery and the possible safety of the realm for him, his brother and these other poor wretches?

She must not! She could not!

He opened his mouth, ready to call out to her to stop, when she glanced his way. And then he knew. How exactly he couldn't say—whether it was something in her eyes, or the tilt of the corners of her lips, or some other subtle thing he'd learned about her during their time together—but he knew that this bargain would not be to Wimarc's benefit.

"Yes, your lover lives," Wimarc said, his eyes on the parchments clutched in her gloved hand. "A little filthier than the last time you saw him, but alive."

He barked an order and two of his men started to remove the chains and shackles from the prisoners, beginning with Finn, who rubbed his aching, bruised wrists while keeping his wary gaze on the nobleman.

"Be ready," Finn said under his breath to his brother.

"For what?" Ryder muttered.

"Anything."

When all the men were unchained, Lizette said, "Let them come to us and then we shall make this trade."

"How do I know you will, or that the letters are real?" Wimarc demanded.

"Because I have given my word," she replied with scornful hauteur, as if she were a queen.

With a brusque gesture, Wimarc signaled Finn and the prisoners to move toward Lizette and the soldiers with her.

She watched them come, a smile on her lovely lips, and his heart filled with fear and longing, dread and hope.

"You look like you could use a bath," she said as he drew near her horse.

Even now, even in the midst of his dread, she made

his heart light. "Tempting notion," he replied as he made a formal bow. "My lady, may I present my half brother, Ryder. Ryder, this is Lady Elizabeth of Averette."

"My lady," Ryder mumbled as Lizette nodded a greeting.

"Are you going to give me those letters or not?" Wimarc demanded.

"Of course. I've given my word," Lizette repeated, her expression resolute as she rode toward Wimarc and his wife, although she didn't so much as glance at Roslynn.

When she put the parchments into their enemy's hands, Wimarc studied the documents carefully before raising his eyes to her. "A wise decision to return these, my lady, or I would have had you killed where you sit."

"You made a wise decision to free these men, or I would have brought the wrath of my family and the king down upon your head," Lizette returned. "Will you likewise take my advice and flee England?"

"You think I'm afraid of John and fools like your brothers-in-law who remain loyal to him? That I have so few allies, or that we aren't powerful enough to overthrow the king right now? You're the fool if you do, and you were a greater fool to think you could defeat me."

He glanced back over his shoulders. "Draco!" he shouted.

Heavily armed mercenaries ran out of the gates. Wimarc's men must have gathered in the outer ward after the prisoners had been marched out.

"Lizette!" Finn cried as she wheeled her horse so

hard, it sat back on its haunches. Meanwhile, Iain rode forward, angling his horse between her and their opponents to protect her.

The rest of the soldiers in her party drew their swords and moved forward to meet their attackers. Volleys of arrows flew from the castle battlements, striking men who fell to the ground either dead or wounded. Blade clashed on blade, men shouted and screamed and moaned. The prisoners, caught between the opposing forces, scrambled to get out of the way. Some succeeded, running down the road; others, too weak or frightened to move, died where they stood.

Finn ran toward one of the downed soldiers and grabbed the sword from his limp, dead hand. "Run into the trees," he ordered his brother. "You're too weak to fight."

"No, Finn, I—"

"Do it!" Finn roared, and this time, unlike the fateful night in the tavern, Ryder did as he was told.

Determined to save Lizette, Finn whirled around and watched, stunned, as Lady Roslynn broke from her husband's party and rode toward Lizette's. She looked back over her shoulder to shout, "Traitor!"

Then Lizette and her horse were beside him. "Take my hand!"

"Ryder first," he replied, pointing at his fleeing brother with his blade. "I don't want him to die now."

"Finn!"

He smacked her horse hard on the rump to send it galloping toward Ryder. "Come back when you've got Ryder out of harm's way!" he called out.

Lizette pulled her horse to a halt and looked back, but as he hoped, she then punched the mare in the sides with her heels and headed for the fleeing Ryder.

While Finn turned on his heel and went to kill Wimarc.

A LITTLE WHILE LATER, Lizette drew her horse to a halt some distance down the road.

"Get down and hide in the trees," she said to Ryder, who was mounted behind her, his hands clasped firmly around her waist. "I've got to go back for Finn."

"I thought he was going to come with us—that you must have a horse for him nearby, or I wouldn't have got on this one," Ryder replied, his voice weak and full of anguish and frustration. "I don't want him to die. I would rather he left me to starve in that dungeon than risk his life for me."

"He couldn't," she said with sympathy, but resolve, too. "He loves you. If you were to die now, after all the trouble he took for you, what kind of repayment would that be for all his efforts prompted by that love? Please, Ryder, do as I ask. You're too weak to be of any use and time is short. Get down and hide in those woods. Stay there until we come for you, or if we don't by dark, or you see any of Wimarc's men instead, hide and flee in the morning."

Mercifully, he made no further protest.

Her heart softened as she prepared to leave him there alone. "I'll do my very best to save your brother," she promised, looking down into his eyes that were very like Finn's. I give you my word. And I love him."

"As do I, my lady," Ryder said, his voice catching. "So go with God and save him."

SILENTLY CURSING the weakness in his limbs, Finn had
no strength to waste fighting other men, or defending
himself from them. Instead he ducked and wove around
the other combatants and made his way toward Wimarc
with grim purpose.

However weak he was and whatever else he did this
day, he was going to ensure that Lizette and her family
need never fear Wimarc de Werre again and that no
other men would suffer in his dungeon. Not even the
sight of Wimarc mowing down hapless soldiers from the
back of his horse could stop him. "Wimarc!"

Slashing at the soldier trying to drag him from his
horse, Wimarc looked up to see who had called his
name. The moment's distraction was enough to enable
the soldier to get a better grip on Wimarc's leg and with
a mighty effort, he pulled Wimarc from the saddle.

Unfortunately, in his zeal, the man had miscalculated and Wimarc fell atop him, crushing him with his
body, heavy armor and shield. The soldier flailed his
arms and legs like a turtle on its back, helpless, the
sword knocked from his hand, until Wimarc rolled with
more speed and agility than Finn would have expected
and, getting to his feet, drove his sword into the neck of
his assailant. Meanwhile, his horse trotted away from
the fighting, snorting and tossing its huge head.

As Wimarc killed his attacker, his back was to
Finn—his armored, helmeted back, and although Finn
wasn't trained as a knight, he knew that the man's
mail, helmet and coif that guarded the back of his neck
made it nearly impossible for him to be killed from

behind. Not with a sword, and especially not one wielded by a weakened man.

"Wimarc!" he shouted again, so that his enemy would turn around and come to him.

The nobleman pulled his sword from the dead soldier's neck and with his blade covered in blood, did what Finn wanted. Finn couldn't see his face, for it was hidden by his helmet, but arrogant confidence fairly oozed from the man.

Why not? He was well trained, well armed, well fed and well rested, and his mercenaries were making short work of the soldiers Lizette had brought. Not Iain Mac Kendren, though. This time, he'd been prepared for the attack and despite the serious wound he must have suffered, was fighting like a man possessed.

Wimarc paid no attention to Mac Kendren or anyone else, focusing only on Finn, who held his sword so low that the tip nearly touched the ground to conserve what vitality he had left.

"So the starving impostor seeks to kill me," Wimarc scoffed as he lifted his shield and strode toward Finn. "You're welcome to try, and as you die, you can think about the pleasure I'm going to have when Lady Elizabeth is in power, for she will be, my friend, she will be."

"No, she won't," was all Finn said in reply.

He didn't want to waste his vigor responding to taunts, and although he was regrettably ignorant of the finer points of fighting with sword and shield, he did know enough to keep his eye on his enemy and never, ever let down his guard.

"I should, perhaps, reward you with a swift death," Wimarc said, stepping over a body that blocked his path. "It's not many men who can trick me as you did. But I have been duly warned, and will take more care with the next man who seeks to be my ally."

"There won't be another time," Finn said, panting a little as he waited, studying the man's armor, wondering where it might be weak, knowing he might only have one chance to strike a lethal blow. "This is the last day of your life."

Wimarc threw back his head as if he were laughing in that noiseless way he had while Finn took another step closer and raised his sword with both hands, more to defend himself than strike a blow. He had yet to see a weakness.

Wimarc likewise raised his sword and swung hard. His blade struck Finn's with such force, Finn went down on his knee, his arms shaking as he kept his sword high and tried to push back.

Wimarc thrust Finn's blade downward, then stepped on it, snapping it in two. With that same foot, he kicked Finn in the jaw. The pain nearly blinding, Finn fell back. He managed to scramble upright as Wimarc raised the visor of his helmet, exposing his sweat-streaked face.

"It's over, you lout," Wimarc crowed. "You're going to die—but not today, and not quick. You're going to starve to death in a cage hanging from my castle walls."

Wimarc had forgotten his opponent was no knight trained in honorable combat and used to fine weapons; that Finn had learned to fight in the streets and alleys and gutters of various towns and villages, that to him, honor was something he couldn't afford, and a weapon anything that came to hand.

Including a broken sword.

Finn raised his arm behind his head and threw the broken sword as Jacapo would a knife, sending it flying through the air.

Right into Wimarc's left eye.

Screaming, Wimarc dropped his sword. His shield slipped from his arm as he fell to his knees. He grabbed the hilt of the broken weapon and with another scream, pulled it out and threw it aside. He covered the wound with his gloved hands, the blood pouring through his fingers.

Finn, too, fell to his knees, panting and exhausted. Now he could die in peace, knowing he had saved Lizette and her sisters.

Then a battle cry rent the air.

In the moment of stunned silence that followed, broken only by Wimarc's moans as he staggered to his feet, two mounted knights clad in full and shining armor burst out of the wood on the other side of the road. Behind them came a host of soldiers, while archers took their places on the verge.

Who they were or where they were from, he neither knew nor cared, as long as they had come to fight Wimarc and his men. An arrow landed near his foot and he looked around to see Garreth running toward him, his bow in his hands. "I'm coming, Finn!" he shouted.

Whether he was with these new allies or not didn't matter. Finn was glad to see him and happy for his help, especially when Wimarc's men started rushing back into the castle.

As Garreth lent Finn his support and led him from the battle, the newly arrived archers sent volley after volley of arrows into the ranks of the mercenaries. Several fell, but some made it to the gates that began to close.

Not Wimarc. Stumbling and nearly tripping over dead men and fallen weapons, Wimarc was too late. By the time he reached the gates, they were closed, and no one within would open them. Wimarc screamed and shouted, but the gates remained closed.

Finn heard another voice calling his name. A lovely, familiar, beloved female voice. He turned, to see Lizette waiting for him a short distance down the road.

As Finn started toward her, an arrow from the battlements flew directly across her horse's path. The animal neighed and reared back, and Finn watched in horror as Lizette tumbled to the ground.

CHAPTER TWENTY-FIVE

HIS WEAKNESS FORGOTTEN, Finn pulled away from Garreth and ran toward Lizette like a man pursued by fifty wild boars.

"Lizette! Oh, God, Lizette!" he cried as he threw himself on his knees beside her. If she was dead, if they'd killed her...

Then, to his relief, she blinked and smiled up at him like an angel beholding visions. "Finn?"

Alive! Thank God, alive! "Are you hurt?"

She shook her head. "I'll be bruised, but I've never been happier in my life!"

Laughing while tears of relief and exhaustion ran unheeded down his cheeks, he gathered her into his arms and captured her mouth with a fiercely passionate kiss.

"I hate to disturb what seems to be a most delightful reunion. Unfortunately, I believe a battleground is not the best place for such expressions of affection," a deep voice said from somewhere above them.

A familiar voice.

Finn drew back and now recognized the device on the shield of the knight looming over them. It belonged to the de Boisbastons.

This was Armand de Boisbaston, in the flesh—
Armand de Boisbaston, to whom he'd told a monstrous
lie, and now Lizette would hear it, too.

But when the knight removed his helmet and tucked
it under his arm, revealing very handsome features, dark
brows and dark hair that waved nearly to his shoulders,
it wasn't Armand.

Finn felt a brief respite, until the man addressed them
both. "I am Sir Bayard de Boisbaston and I've been sent
to find my sister-in-law, Lady Elizabeth. Unless I'm
much mistaken, you must be she. I, and my brother
Armand, are at your service—although you seem to
have found a worthy champion on your own."

As Bayard de Boisbaston spoke, Finn's experience
urged him to keep his secret and not reveal the truth, even
to Lizette. But he didn't want to lie to Lizette. He loved
her, and she deserved to know the truth—about everything.

Determined to confess all without further delay, he
got to his feet and held out a hand to help Lizette stand,
although he himself was none too steady. His head
began to throb and his leg that had been wounded by the
boar felt as if it were on fire.

"I *am* Lady Elizabeth," she said before Finn could
speak. "I'm very glad you and your men arrived when
they did, or it might have gone badly for us. How did
you get here from Averette so quickly?"

"Ah, now that's a very interesting story," Sir Bayard
replied as Finn struggled to ignore the pain. "We met a
lord and lady at an inn a short distance from here who
suggested we come here without delay. We did, and on
the way, we met a young man who was extremely

insolent but also insistent we come to your aid at once. The young woman with him was most annoyed by his tone, but we realized it was his sense of urgency that compelled him to be impertinent."

The insolent young man could only be Garreth, and the young woman had to be Keldra; the lord and lady must have been Gilbert and Helewyse.

Although Bayard resembled Armand, and their voices were similar, there were obviously differences, too. Armand had never sounded so merry when they were at court…and he had told his monstrous lie.

While Finn was happy to hear everyone was safe, and very pleased Bayard and his men had come, his need to tell Lizette the truth before she heard it from another made everything else less important, although the fatigue seemed to be rolling over him like waves upon the shore. "Lizette, there's something—"

"You're exhausted," she declared as she anxiously studied his face. "You must rest at once!"

She turned to Bayard as she put her arm around Finn's waist. "There's an inn nearby, you said?"

"Yes, and your sisters are waiting for us there."

"My sisters?" she gasped. "They're with you?"

If her sisters were here, Finn realized as he tried to ignore his pounding head, maybe he should wait to make his confession at the inn. That way he could get it all over with at once. Hopefully Lizette's sisters would understand, as Lizette would. She must.

He winced as Lizette shifted. He didn't think he'd ever been this tired in his life. Or thirsty.

And then Armand de Boisbaston appeared in front of

them, staring at Finn as if he were seeing a ghost. "God's blood—Oliver? What the devil are you doing here?"

"You know him?" Bayard demanded, his voice sounding as if it were coming from far away.

"Yes. He's the fellow who was pretending to be Sir Oliver de Leslille."

"He's also been saving the kingdom from rebellion and disaster," Lizette answered.

He had to tell her. Right now. But his head hurt so much...

"I take it you're Lizette," Armand said. "Adelaide thought you'd be in the thick of things, although I don't think she meant a battle."

"I had to find out why Wimarc wanted to abduct me, and then to get evidence of his treachery to take to the king if I could." She reached into her bodice and pulled out some parchments. "And I did."

Wait. That wasn't...how could she still have them?

"You gave the letters to Wimarc," Finn muttered, trying to concentrate despite his pain.

"Copies," she returned with immense satisfaction. "Roslynn and I made copies. She's been of great service. We must do all we can to see that John knows that, and that she's innocent of treason."

There was something else important...the lie he'd told. He opened his mouth to tell her...

His eyes rolled back in his head, and he went as limp as damp linen.

"Finn!" Lizette cried as she staggered beneath the sudden weight of his inert body. "Finn!"

Both the de Boisbastons rushed to her aid and helped

lower him to the ground. Lizette knelt beside him, anxiously searching for any wounds.

Thankfully she could find none, although fresh blood was seeping through the bandage on his calf, the linen filthy and caked with old, dried blood.

"We must get him to Gillian," she said, looking up at the two men. "She'll know what to do."

THE INN WAS NOT MANY MILES down the road, but they didn't dare ride quickly. Finn was on Bayard's horse, still unconscious and held by his strong arm, while Lizette rode beside them, her gaze far more often on Finn than on the road.

Bayard tried to keep up her spirits, telling her what Armand had said about Finn's time at court, asking her if Finn had told her much about his adventure there. She wordlessly shook her head, her attention on Finn as she silently prayed that he would recover.

At last, though, they reached the inn and as soon as their party was seen, several people rushed out to meet them. First was Keldra, then Lady Jane and then—

Lizette rose in her saddle and waved frantically. "Adelaide! Gillian!"

"Lizette, Lizette!" Adelaide cried, running toward them, the silent, but widely smiling Gillian following. Lady Jane hurried to Iain's side, while Keldra looked anxiously at the others arriving behind them.

"Garreth's gone to find Ryder," Lizette explained as she jumped from the back of her horse.

"We feared we'd never see you again!" the normally reserved Gillian sobbed, holding her tight.

Fervently, gratefully, she embraced her sisters, and she suddenly realized Adelaide must be with child. How wonderful for her—and if someday, she should be so blessed… But now was not the time for such speculation.

"Gillian, Finn needs your help," she said as two grooms helped lift him from Bayard's horse.

"Sweet savior!" Adelaide gasped, staring at him as if she couldn't believe her eyes. "It's—"

"I know he claimed to be Sir Oliver de Leslille and he's not, but he's a good and honorable man, Adelaide. He saved my life, and Keldra's, too, and helped save the kingdom, as well. I'll explain all that later. Right now he needs Gillian's expert care."

"Of course," Gillian replied with a brisk nod, and with no further ado, she and Lizette hurried after the men carrying Finn into the inn.

A worried expression on her beautiful face, looking from one dark-haired, brown-eyed man to the other, Adelaide addressed her husband and his brother as they joined her. "She doesn't know yet, does she?"

"No, I don't believe she does," Armand gravely answered.

WHEN FINN OPENED HIS EYES, the first thing he saw was Lizette smiling down at him, her eyes shining with happiness as she held his hand. Behind her were wattle-and-daub walls, and a small window and open shutter through which he could see the sunset.

Lizette squeezed his hand. "We're in the upper room of an inn not far from Castle de Werre and Ryder's safe below, with Gillian watching over him like an anxious hen.

"Garreth and Keldra are here, too, as well as my sisters and their husbands. As for Wimarc, he's imprisoned in his own dungeon to await the king's judgment."

Finn struggled to sit up. Blessedly his head didn't throb, and although his leg still hurt, it was bearable. Meanwhile, Lizette removed the linen covering from a small platter on the table beside the bed, revealing fresh bread, thick cheese and an apple. "Gillian says you should eat sparingly for now, until your stomach is used to food again."

"Has Adelaide seen me, too?"

"Aye, as you would say. Everyone was quite interested to learn your true name."

No doubt they would be. "Lizette, there's something—"

"He's awake, is he?"

Adelaide and Gillian stood at the door, their husbands behind them.

Seeing that he was, the two couples didn't wait for either Lizette or Finn to answer. Instead they crowded into the small room, Armand and Bayard bending down slightly so they wouldn't bump their heads on the slanted ceiling.

Even though Finn was grateful for their help, he wished they'd left him alone with Lizette a little longer. But if he must confess to an audience, he would; besides, his lie involved Armand and Bayard's family, so perhaps this more public humiliation was just.

Armand and Bayard were both studying him intensely—looking for the family resemblance, no doubt, which also spurred him on.

But it was at Lizette he looked, and to Lizette he spoke

when he confessed. "Lizette, I've told a lot o' lies in my life. I'm not ashamed of most of them, since I lied to live, but there's one I *am* ashamed of—so ashamed, I didn't want to tell you. But I don't want any lies between us."

He looked into her questioning, trusting, loving eyes. "I told Armand and your sister that I'm Armand and Bayard's bastard brother, and I'm not. I'm no relation to them at all."

Armand straightened and, forgetting the low ceiling, bumped his head with a thud. "That was a *lie?*"

"Aye, it was," Finn readily admitted, relieved that the worst was over, and most relieved of all that Lizette was still holding his hand and looking at him with love in her lovely eyes.

"I'm sure you had a good reason to say so," she said.

He blushed and shook his head with regret. "No, I did it out of spite."

"Then that wasn't your mother who came to our castle and told my father the boy with her was his son?" Armand demanded.

"That *was* my mother and I was the boy," Finn replied, "but she was lying, trying to get money from your father because they'd been together and we were starving.

"I don't know who my father was, and neither did she, but I'm sure it wasn't Raymond de Boisbaston. I was born a full year before she met your father, who's not Ryder's sire, either. He was born the year after their liaison. My mother lied about my age, too, you see."

"But the likeness..." Adelaide murmured wonderingly.

"My mother said it was a lucky chance, that's all. There are many men with dark hair and brown eyes."

"Yet you do look alike," Gillian noted. "I find it hard to believe that's a mere accident."

Finn shrugged. "Perhaps if we could ask my grandmother or her mother, there might be some explanation—a liaison or adultery kept secret out of shame. I know nothing of that. All I *do* know is that I'm not Raymond de Boisbaston's son, and I was angry and bitter to think you had so much and I so little.

"When I met you at court, Armand, that feeling came back as strong as if I'd been at Boisbaston Castle the day before. I wanted to shock you, to hurt you, to make you feel as bad as I had. So I lied, telling the tale my mother had spun for gain, and for that, Armand and Bayard, I'm truly sorry."

After he fell silent, Lizette squeezed his hand and as he'd hoped, spoke to him not with disappointment, but with understanding and sympathy. "I know what it is to envy someone, Finn. I know how tempting it can be to tell a lie. I've done it myself, and men have died for it, as Iain nearly did."

Forgetting they weren't alone, he pulled her close and whispered, "What happened on that road wasn't your fault, Lizette. It was Wimarc's. Never yours."

He kissed her tenderly, adoring her, amazed that of all the women in the world, he would find one who could truly empathize with him, and his history.

"Well, thank *God* that was a lie!" Bayard declared, his voice loud in the silence. "It makes things a lot easier."

"What things?" Lizette asked, her pretty brow furrowed with puzzlement.

Finn knew, but it was Adelaide who answered first.

"Marriage. Since Armand and I are married, if Finn were really his brother, the church would consider you blood relations. Marriage would be forbidden."

"You do *want* to marry?" Gillian asked, although there was the definite implication that they should.

"Nothing would make me happier," Finn answered truthfully, again reaching out for Lizette's hand. "If she'll have me."

"I most certainly will, and it would take more than that foolish restriction to stop us even if he was a de Boisbaston," Lizette declared with the boldness he admired.

"It wouldn't have been a hopeless situation," Bayard remarked. "Not for such an accomplished liar as yourself. We would simply keep it a secret between the six of us."

Bayard de Boisbaston had confessed to being a changeling child, no true brother to Armand, and now he was married to Gillian. Was that the truth, or a tale told to get around canon law?

Finn was rather sure he knew the answer to that, and that he, and Lizette, weren't the only accomplished liars in the room.

But all was not well yet, it seemed. "Lizette's the king's ward, so there's still the matter of his permission," Armand grimly noted.

"You can tell him I died," Lizette suggested, "of a contagious illness, so I had to be buried with haste and in private."

"Or we could bribe the king," Bayard proposed. "Tell him Finn's a rich merchant and willing to pay well for the privilege of marrying Lady Elizabeth."

"John can have my dower lands if he lets me marry Finn," Lizette said. "He can have my whole inheritance."

"And what will you live on, then?" the ever-practical Gillian inquired. "How does this man intend to earn his living after you're wed? You can't be an outlaw's wife."

"I'm not going to be a thief anymore," Finn replied at once. "I'll find a way to make an honest living."

"My lords? My ladies?"

They all turned to see Iain and Lady Jane standing on the threshold. "If I might have a word?" the Scot asked.

Lizette moved closer to the head of the bed, while the ladies and the two knights moved toward the window.

"It's good to see you again, Sir Ol…Finn," Jane said with her gentle smile.

Iain nodded a greeting and gruffly addressed Finn. "Quite a throw of that broken blade. I've always said to my men, in a fight of life and death, use what you can when you can. Never seen that done better than today. It's too bad you didn't kill the rogue."

"I'm glad I didn't," Finn said. "I'm sure there's plenty he can tell us about his fellow conspirators."

"Aye, there is that," Iain agreed.

Lady Jane nudged him.

"Oh, aye, well," he said, giving her a sheepish look before regarding the others in the room. "We thought to tell you while you're all together. Jane and I are going to be married."

"Married?" Adelaide gasped as if such a thing were not possible.

"Married?" Gillian repeated as if she'd never heard the word before.

"Married!" Lizette cried happily, rushing around the bed to embrace him.

Blushing like a lad caught kissing the milkmaid, Iain patted her awkwardly on the back while Jane fairly beamed with pride and happiness.

Adelaide soon took Lizette's place hugging the veteran guardian of her home, and then Gillian, who held him tightest and longest.

When she moved back, Gillian said, "I'm glad for your sake, Iain, although I suppose that means you won't be staying at Averette?"

"No, nor at Lady Jane's estate, except for a yearly visit to collect the tithes, I suppose."

He reached into his belt and pulled out a parchment, then regarded them all with a surprisingly bashful grin. "It seems, my ladies and gentlemen, that I'm a lord myself."

He unrolled the parchment and Lizette remembered him looking at such a document on the road before Lindall attacked them. "Apparently I'm the last of the Mac Kendrens, which I never thought I'd be, so that makes me the laird." He reached out for Jane's hand. "I suppose I'll have to give the king a rich gift to get his consent for our marriage, but I'd give him everything I own as long as he gives me Jane.

"And we've been thinking, Jane and me, that we could use a clever fellow to help run my estates. We're of the opinion that this Irishman is just the sort of fellow we need. I can command a garrison, God knows, but against a tricky merchant or trader, I'm likely to be as helpless as the babe newborn. What do you say, Irishman? Care to try your hand at an honest living as my steward?"

It was a tempting offer, but Finn admitted, "I can add up to the hundreds in my head, but I can neither read nor write."

"I can teach you," Lizette said with a smile that warmed him and sent his thoughts far from numbers and Scotland. "It's a wonderful offer, Iain, especially after I almost got you killed with my selfish dawdling."

"Aye, but if you hadn't dawdled and pretended to be sick, I'd never have met Jane, so dwell no more on that, my lady."

Tears came to Lizette's eyes, and Iain's were suspiciously moist, too, as he gruffly cleared his throat. "No need to get sentimental. I need a man like him, and you need a home. Besides, this way, your sisters will know there's somebody making sure you don't get into any mischief."

"I should think that would be a husband's job," Finn said, his expression grave but his heart as light as heart could be, and a joy such as he'd never felt filling him. Now, as never before, his future looked bright and wonderful and full of promise, with Lizette by his side.

"I think it'll take you both," Adelaide declared.

"*I* think it's hopeless," Gillian remarked.

"I don't think I need *anybody* keeping me out of mischief," Lizette protested. She sat beside Finn and gave him a merry smile, while her eyes smoldered with quite a different emotion. "I believe I'll be too busy with my household."

"Thank God!" Armand de Boisbaston declared with heartfelt relief.

LATER THAT NIGHT, Lizette nestled beside Finn as they lay in the bed in the upper room of the inn. Adelaide and Gillian had gone with their husbands and the majority of their men to Castle de Werre, to hold it for the king who would likely, upon Wimarc's condemnation as a traitor, give it to one his friends. They were all hopeful that while John would also probably claim any property Roslynn had brought to the marriage, they would be able to persuade him to let her keep her movable goods. After all, she was still a young noblewoman who could hope to marry again and she would need a dowry.

They also hoped that, whatever Wimarc and men of his ambitious ilk thought, the worst of John's excesses and greed could be curbed by men like the Earl of Pembroke.

Finn lifted a lock of her hair and kissed it. There had been some protests from Gillian that he should sleep alone in order to rest, but that had fallen on deaf ears. After all they'd been through, Lizette wasn't about to spend any more time away from Finn.

"To think we should owe our future happiness to Iain," she said with a rueful sigh. "I was so terrible to him! I used to complain he treated me like a child, but I didn't realize that I acted like one. And then to discover he's a nobleman—and in love! He's so gentle and considerate with Jane, it's hard to believe he's the same man."

"I doubt he is," Finn said softly, caressing her cheek. "Love changes a man. Look how it's making an honest and honorable fellow out of me."

"You've always been honorable," she replied, "but

you had to survive, too. Now you can be the honest, upstanding man you were meant to be.

"Love has changed me, too," she added. "I might have continued to be selfish and spoiled if I hadn't met you."

He heard the regret in her voice and sought to tease her out of guilt and remorse. "What, you don't think I spoil you? I most certainly do. I give in to you far too often."

"Only because you know I'm right," she answered, rewarding him with a pert little smile and a bold caress.

"Since I don't want to quarrel with a naked woman who's doing such interesting things with her fingers, I'll not argue—and that's spoiling you, too," he finished with a kiss on the tip of her nose.

Then he sighed with melodramatic woe and a twinkle in his eye. "Once my leg is healed and we're married, I'll have to be more strict with you."

"Do you think so?"

"Well, I hope you'll let me assert my manly authority from time to time, my lady, or how will the people respect the steward?"

"I wish you wouldn't call me 'my lady' anymore," she said with a pout as she toyed with one of his curls. "It sounds so formal." She stopped pouting and moved her hand to caress him again. "I don't want to be formal."

"Lizette, my love, my darling. My wife-to-be?" he suggested.

"Much better," she agreed, her lips trailing down his jaw.

"I'm almost afraid to believe my good fortune," Finn murmured as he made a few bold caresses of his own.

"A wife to love, a place as steward in the north, my brother alive and safe, Wimarc in a cell."

Lizette traced the edge of his nipple with her fingertip. "A wife who loves you, who would live with you anywhere, her sisters and the kingdom saved from the machinations of a vile man who'll pay for his crimes. We *have* been blessed, Finn. And I'm so pleased Garreth and Keldra are coming with us, too."

"Although I suppose we'll have to listen to them bickering for the rest of our lives."

Lizette laughed softly. "They were very cozy in a corner when I left them earlier. I wouldn't be surprised if they want to marry someday, too."

She grew serious and her hand stilled. "What of Ryder? Could you convince him to come north with us?"

"No," Finn replied with regret. "He says he wants to go somewhere where it's always warm and dry, and I can't say I blame him."

She heard the disappointment in his voice and sought to comfort him. "I know how much you love and care for your brother, but he should follow his own desires and seek his own happiness. After all, I did, and look where it led me—to you."

She slid her hand below Finn's navel. "Are your desires leading you anywhere right now?"

He closed his eyes and leaned back. "Indeed, my love, they are. Shall I take you with me?"

"Please," she whispered. "You know I'll gladly go with you anywhere."

"And I with you, forever and always," he promised before he sealed that vow with a kiss.

AUTHOR'S NOTE

THANKS TO THE STORIES of Robin Hood, most people know that John succeeded his brother, Richard the Lionheart, as king of England.

What is less commonly known, perhaps, is that Richard and John weren't the only two sons of Henry II and Eleanor of Aquitaine. If you've seen *The Lion in Winter*, you'll know there was another son, Geoffrey. However, Henry and Eleanor actually had five sons: William, who died in infancy, Henry, known as The Young King although he never ruled, Richard, Geoffrey and John.

Young King Henry died in 1188 without a legitimate son.

Richard was next in line and despite rebelling against his father, succeeded to the throne in 1189.

Geoffrey, the third brother, was trampled to death by a horse in 1186 after having three children: Eleanor; Maud, who died in childhood; and Arthur.

Upon Richard's death in 1199, John took the throne—and "took" was considered by many to be exactly what he did. Arthur, as the son of John's older brother, had a legitimate claim to the throne, and should have been king.

Supported by Philip of France after declaring himself a vassal of the French king, Arthur tried to assert that claim. He was captured in 1202 and disappeared in 1203. Rumors circulated that John himself, in a drunken rage, had murdered the boy; others claimed he hadn't died at all, but gone into hiding. Whatever happened, Arthur was out of the picture. His sister Eleanor, however, remained.

Because she was her father and brother's heir, Eleanor—or her husband, if she married—might have tried to claim the throne. To prevent that, John, and later his son, Henry III, kept her imprisoned, and unwed, for the rest of her life. She died in 1241.